Satan's Angel

'I'm a generous woman, Collin. A woman who understands a man's needs and isn't embarrassed by them. After all, do you think there'll be a privy every few miles between here and the Klondike?' I asked. 'Chances are good you'll see my bare backside when I need to pee, and you'll flash your pecker to relieve yourself. Might as well get that bashfulness behind us.'

'Well, you've got a point there.'

'No, *you've* got the point, sweetheart. And it's Rosie DuBris who wants to show you how much she appreciates your faith in her.' I leanded against the back of the tub, placing an arm behind my head which raised my breasts out of the water so he could watch the droplets flow down their rounded sides. 'Take down your pants, Collin. Straddle the tub and let me bring off your first bonanza before we even start out for the gold fields.'

Other books by the author:

Devil's Fire
Demon's Dare

Readers may contact the author at
melissa_macneal@hotmail.com
or visit her website at www.melissamacneal.com

Satan's Angel
Melissa MacNeal

BLACK LACE

Black Lace books contain sexual fantasies.
In real life, always practise safe sex.

First published in 2002 by
Black Lace
Thames Wharf Studios
Rainville Road
London W6 9HA

Copyright © Melissa MacNeal, 2002

The right of Melissa MacNeal to be identified as the Author of
the Work has been asserted by her in accordance with the Copyright,
Designs and Patents Act 1988.

Design by Smith & Gilmour, London
Printed and bound by Mackays of Chatham PLC

ISBN 0 352 33726 5

Contents

1 A Letter from Satan

July 1897

Most days I didn't mind living in this one-whore town called Oblivion, Oregon, and most days I didn't mind being the woman who gave it that distinction. We didn't have any celebrities like Butch Cassidy shooting us up, nor had Carrie Nation ever axed our bar. About the closest we came to having a real character here was Dynamite Dick – who thought he had one, but didn't. Far as I could tell, Dick was a feisty little guy living out his legend as a blaster in the Cripple Creek gold mines rather than his reputation with the ladies. No doubt in my mind he knew just where to put a stick of dynamite.

But on this particular summer day, when I'd lost count of how many rounds I'd cheated at solitaire while Jimmy Crystal polished a spotless bar, I began to hope Dick would come in. Jawing with him about why he didn't deserve his fucks for free sounded like better entertainment than shuffling my yellowed deck of cards again.

When Jimmy opened here, the Well-Come Inn caught the booze and floozy business from the lumber camps, as well as pulling in a tidy profit from my homemade pies. But once the trees were all cut and the timber business moved on, Jimmy didn't. Other enterprising barkeeps and madams had packed up months ago, following those burly, beer-swilling boys farther into the forests, but staying in Oblivion was Jim's way of settling down. Putting down roots, he called it. Damn nice fellow, Crystal was, but you couldn't fault him for being fast.

Although I'd stayed with him out of loyalty – appreciation for nearly ten years of treating me decent – I was beginning to feel like a charity case. He was a quiet sort, not prone to prattle even when he'd been hitting the whisky, and I'd never seen him drunk. Held his liquor the way he held his cards and his pistol, with a firm grip and a steady eye. But his days as a hired gun were over. Legend said Jimmy Crystal had brought down many a big-time outlaw with a single shot, yet he'd hung up his holster after a bullet killed the wrong man's woman. He didn't talk about that, and I didn't ask.

I watched the dark blond hair fall boyishly over his forehead, shading chocolate eyes that hid secrets nobody could guess, and succumbed to habit: I flicked down the strap of my red lace camisole and unfastened my skirt, willing him to look my way. I knew he'd respond – knew exactly the words he'd say and the moves he'd make, like most wives complained about their predictable husbands. But today it seemed like the compassionate thing to do, seducing Jimmy. It got both our minds off the way nobody was in here spending their money.

I stood, stretching like a lazy cat, letting my flouncy skirt slither down my legs as I stared straight at him. The muscles of his upper arms bunched. Those long, strong fingers clenched around his rag. Then he looked at me, his moustache flickering with his grin as those two dark eyes peered from beneath his hair.

'Hot in here,' I murmured, fanning my face with my hand, ready to recite along with him: *The heat in this room comes from between your legs, Rosie-girl.*

Jimmy grinned, getting into the game. 'The heat in this room comes from between your legs, Rosie-girl ...

those long silky legs I wish I had wrapped around me about now.'

'What's stopping you?'

'Why would I want to start something somebody might walk in on?'

'Because you want it. Because you love the way my hot, wet pussy sucks your cock so deep you get lost and can't find your way out.'

I was swaying towards him as I said this, leaving my skirt on the floor and untying the string of my silk drawers with a purposeful look that always widened those brown eyes. The tip of Jimmy's tongue brushed his lower lip. He was about to tell me how wicked I was.

'You're a wicked thing, Miss Rosie. Why not let me make you an honest woman?'

'You just answered yourself, Mr Crystal. I'm brazen. Don't want to play by anybody else's rules, and you can't *make* me.'

'I can make you –'

He lunged, playfully catching my wrist to twirl me into his embrace, with my bare backside against the bulge in his fly. It was prodding me though his pants, that erection, and it was the most aggressive thing about him when he let it out to play. 'I can make you scream for it, missy. I can make you holler so loud the boys in the next county'll come to see what's gotten into you. And it'll be me.'

'Tell them to bring their money! I'll take them all on at once,' I rasped, gripping the rim of the walnut bar. I leaned forward, wiggling my butt against him, making him grunt and fumble with his fly as he splayed his other hand over my bared belly. 'The town pump needs to be primed every now and again, you know.'

'And I'm just the man to do it.' He pressed his naked thighs to the backs of mine, parting my knees to let that pecker slip up against my dewy slit. 'I know all

3

your secrets, Rosie. I can make you slither like a snake and cackle like a jackal – know where all your sweet spots are –'

'So quit yapping and prove it,' I challenged. My last words came out with a grunt, because when Crystal took me from behind, the fireworks started in a hurry.

With one plunge he filled me, diving inside while he held me back against himself. His pants rustled around his ankles, and the empty saloon echoed with a wet slapping sound that drove us on, into that mindless place of pleasure we could find nowhere else. His hands, hooked around my hip bones, branded me with their heat as they inched forward. I felt full and hot and urgent, lunging back against the cock I knew so well, feeling its ridged head stretching me, up and then back . . . up and then back. Waiting for his fingers to meet in the middle, to lift the lips of my pussy and expose the clit that ached for his attention.

'Come on, touch it!' I rasped, grasping the bar so hard my knuckles went white. 'You know I've boarded the train and I'm chugging down the tracks . . . can't make it to the station without you playing with me . . . kneading my clit against that root you're ramming into me. Oh, Jimmy . . .'

My muscles went tight inside. I panted his name while my hips danced uncontrollably.

'I'm gonna squirt you full of it, Rosie,' he muttered, running feisty little nips down my neck. 'I'm gonna shoot such a wad you'll end up in kingdom come – and then what'll I do?'

'You'll come again, most likely. Because you'll come looking for *me*.'

'Damn right I will. You might be too stubborn to marry me, but you'll never stop spreading your legs for Jimmy Crystal, *will* you, Rosie?'

'Nope,' I grunted, guiding his fingers in their wanton

massage. 'Got this aching, gaping hole and it takes a helluva cock to handle it. It never gets enough.'

'Better open up,' he rasped. 'I'm gonna let fly. I'm gonna thrust so deep the cream's likely to shoot out through your mouth.'

'Take it,' I begged. 'Take it until I collapse – until I can't stand any more. Shoot me, Crystal – come on, now, make me scream, make me –'

He stiffened, and with a wheeze he shoved his shaft so deep I felt his balls rustling my own wiry curls. Our bodies convulsed, bumping against the bar as our impassioned cries rang out. I was vaguely aware that out on the street a stagecoach raced past and raised up enough dust to choke us, but it didn't really matter. For those few blessed moments I forgot how bored I was, and how dreadfully dull our days had become ... could lay aside those dreams every woman hides in the deep recesses of her heart, loving them even though she doubts they'll ever come true.

When the convulsions racked me, I gave myself over to them. What else was there on a sultry day in a nowhere town, where Rosie DuBris passed her time as a sporting woman sorely in need of sport?

'God almighty,' Jimmy groaned, leaning against my back to catch his breath. It didn't seem to matter that we'd followed the same script as yesterday, and the day before that. He kissed the hollow between my shoulder and neck, tickling me with his thick moustache as he reached into my camisole to squeeze my breasts.

I swallowed my laughter, my head snapping up at the creak of the batwing doors. Here I stood, falling out of my underthings at the end of the bar, while my boss fondled me, still buried to the root.

Jimmy straightened, politely covering my bare bosoms with his broad hands. 'Afternoon there, Dick. What can I get you?'

'A piece of that pussy-cream pie you're making, and then a piece of Rosie's chocolate, if you've got it.' Dynamite Dick smoothed his shock of silvery hair back, drinking in the sight of us in profile, naked from the waist down and joined at the hip. 'Got a letter here for the lady, but I can see she's busy. I'll just mosey along –'

'You'll do no such thing!' I wriggled free of Jimmy's prick. My pulse raced, and I ignored the wet *smack* that sent honey gushing from me. 'You give me that –'

'– across the way, where a man can get a drink without having to watch such –'

'– letter!' I reached around his retreating form to pluck it from his pudgy fingers. Who on earth could it be from? I couldn't recall the last mail I'd received, as my family died in a cabin fire years ago – and they would've written me off rather than writing to me, if they knew what I'd become.

'It's from Satan, up in the Klondike,' Dick announced, as much for Jimmy's benefit as mine. 'What the hell kind of a name is that for a town? Who do you know up there?'

'Guess that's *my* business, isn't it?' I retorted, although I didn't really have an answer for him. The envelope felt fat and heavy. The way it was shaking in my hands, I was afraid I'd tear the letter inside, trying to open it.

'That's the thanks I get for coming all the way down the street to –'

'Whisky's on me, Dick. Let the lady read her mail.'

The empty saloon rang with the finality of Jim's low command. I stood for a moment, still flummoxed, very aware that this plucky little blaster wanted to follow me upstairs to collect on his favour.

'Thank you,' I murmured, tugging my camisole strap back on to my shoulder. And before Dick got any ideas about sloppy seconds, I scampered across the plank floor with a grateful grin for the man at the bar. Bless his heart, Jimmy was just as curious as Dynamite about who my letter came from, but he knew I'd fritter and fret until I had the chance to read it.

My bare feet beat a quick rhythm on the wooden stairs and I slammed the door behind me. On to the rumpled bed I sprang, giggling with the sheer delight of receiving *mail*, and wanting to make this moment – the suspense of it – last as long as possible. There was no one's name in the return address, simply the location Dick had read aloud, which I'd never even heard of.

And once I tore open the envelope, I couldn't believe my eyes. Five hundred dollars fell out, in crisp new bills. I swallowed hard. It was more money than I'd ever seen at one time, and I still had no idea who'd sent it.

My dearest Rosie, the letter began in a bold, flowing script. *It's been so many years, I hope you'll remember me, Angel-Face ... remember the way we used to play naked behind my daddy's barn and skinny dip in Cherry Creek?*

I sucked air. There was only one boy who could've written such things. Sure enough, when I flipped the page, Grant Galloway's signature marched across the bottom with all the cocksureness he'd shown when he plucked my cherry. Lord, that was ... fourteen summers ago. Half a lifetime, and water under a lot of bridges.

How had he found me? And why would that brash young man from Colorado contact me now? His daddy's money and his mama's ambitions for him had taken him far from Denver – away from the skinny girl with the birthmark, whose early development branded her a floozy long before she fell into the trade by default. Grant had sworn he loved me each time he reached into my drawers – and he probably did, the way he saw it – but I'd set aside my girlish longing for him years ago. Only a naive little fool would cling to such promises.

I swore I'd send for you someday, Rosie – when the time was right and I could give you the fine life you deserved. I hope my letter doesn't arrive to find you already married. I've never stopped wanting you, Angel-Face. Never stopped believing we'd be together someday.

A woman like me heard that often enough to brush such sentiments aside, like flies that buzzed in the summer. But this was different. This was coming from the first boy I'd ever kissed, the handsome Grant Galloway I'd given myself to because I believed I loved him, and that he'd marry me. My throat tightened. I gripped the vellum pages and read on.

This money's for your passage to Satan, up in the Klondike Territory, because it's a rip-roaring town poised on the brink of a gold rush! Last summer they found gold in Rabbit Creek, and two ships carrying those first prospectors will soon dock in San Francisco and Seattle, with more money in nuggets than they'll be able to spend in a lifetime. I'm here, Rosie – right in the thick of it. And I want you to join me!

My breath left me. My heart was pounding so hard I wondered if it might crack a rib. Here in Oblivion, we'd had no word about the discovery of any gold – and the Klondike seemed almost as remote as heaven. The country, overall, was in the grip of hard times that had set all but the wealthiest families back on their heels. So how had Grant managed to position himself so well?

I'm the Mayor of Satan, right-hand man to Dr Devlin Meeh, who established his town over vast veins of salt to become the world's largest producer of that all-important mineral. Satan is much more than salt mines, however. Our hotels and opera houses rival those in Europe, and Meeh imports the finest wines and food and clothing for us.

Since most of our population is male, a girl like you could do well here, Rosie –

So he knew what I'd become. I nipped my lip but kept reading, simply because the town Grant described sounded like a never-ending party compared to where I was living now.

– and a woman of your independent spirit will survive the cold, dark winters and prosper during these summer days when the sun doesn't set. It's a fantasy up here. Dr Meeh – a man of vision and ambition – has positioned us to take best advantage of the mining claims, to provide food, lodging and entertainment for the rush of prospectors we expect in the next few months.

So get yourself outfitted and come north! You and I can cash in on this opportunity and live beyond our wildest dreams. What have you got to lose?

As I glanced around a room barely bigger than my bed, and at the single armoire that held all my worldly possessions, the answer to that question seemed very clear. Why, in a place like Satan, I'd have men lining up at my door. Not that Grant Galloway would want me to ply my trade any longer.

And if it came to that, I reasoned, I'd be a damn sight farther ahead than if I stayed here in the backwoods of Oregon. I stood up to pace, clutching the money as I considered a decision that, deep down, I'd already made. Grant had always insisted on the best, so I had no doubt that Satan was everything he claimed. And if he could afford to send me five hundred dollars – could afford to lose that money if I ignored his invitation – he was a man of standing in a thriving town. A glance outside, where Mack MacIntire wove his way back to his mercantile from the tavern, past boarded-up storefronts, provided a striking contrast to the picture Grant painted.

I leaned against the window, clasping the letter to

my heart. The brash young man I remembered wore the face of success even then – had a strong, squared chin and chiseled features set off by deep, vertical dimples and chestnut hair. His pale green eyes glinted silver and made a girl's heart wobble when he gave her that look. He'd been as sleek as a mountain lion and a man of the world, to this little bumpkin who'd come in from the range once a month to shop with her family.

Yet he'd singled me out from the others. Hadn't just said, 'I want you, Rosie,' but rather, 'I want *you*, Rosie.' He thought the unsightly mark on my left cheek resembled an angel with her wings spread. A girl never forgot that.

And now his letter had travelled across the miles and years that separated us. He'd singled me out again – for, Lord knows, Grant Galloway could've chosen any woman from his constant flock of admirers.

A jolt of white-hot electricity surged through my body, the same molten heat I'd felt at his first forbidden touch through the slit of my drawers, behind his daddy's dry goods store. I relived his kiss, the lips that opened mine so his tongue could probe my innocent mouth ... so I couldn't cry out when his finger slipped into my puss and made it purr for more. He'd branded me then, as plainly as Daddy branded his cattle. Even now, the steam rose from the places he'd fondled.

Quivering, I tossed the letter on to my bed. I placed a foot on the window sill as one hand dipped into my camisole and the other parted the still-sticky lips that now needed more attention. And in my vivid imagination, I was fourteen again ...

2 **Like a Thief in the Night**

'You're leaving me.'

I froze, so caught up in my desire I hadn't heard Jimmy open my door. I had nothing to hide from this man – and nothing to prove – after all these years of working in his upstairs rooms and warming his own bed. Yet my cheeks prickled. I loved him, after a fashion, and hurting him was the furthest thing from my mind.

But he knew.

So now I had to face him, and suffer his questions like a tin can taking target practice. And I had to make my goodbye sound like it was the best thing, the only practical way for both of us to get on with our lives. I couldn't look at him, so I gripped the window frame and lowered my leg. 'Letter's on the bed. Read it, if you want.'

'Don't have to. Somebody's reeling you in like a fish. Calling in an old marker, I'd guess.'

'A girl never forgets her first love, Jimmy.'

'If he loved you so much, where's he been all these years? Why'd he leave you in the first place?'

His voice was soft and low, trying to reason with a woman's heart that was beyond rational thought. I could deal with Crystal's anger or accusations, but it wasn't in him to rail at me. He stood at my door unruffled, awaiting my answers. The silence bespoke his sorrow and disappointment more eloquently than any words, filling my little room with their weight.

'His family sent him back east to school, so he could manage their stores and properties. Acquire even more of them,' I explained in a thin voice.

'And did he?'

A frustrated sigh escaped me. 'I – I don't – why are you asking me all these questions? I don't answer to you!'

Again his silence pointed to the way I'd just hurt him.

'True enough,' he finally said. 'But people change, Rosie. This fellow's not the same boy you fell for back then, just like you're not the same starry-eyed innocent who let him have you. I hate to see you rush into a situation that might not be all you want it to be.'

I hugged myself, still not looking over my shoulder at him; furious for the calm control he tried to impose on my galloping imagination. If he was such a master at providing a woman with the life she wanted, why were we still here in Oblivion, while the world passed us by? Behind me, water splashed into my bowl and he wrung out a wash cloth, lathered it with the lavender-scented soap he special-ordered from Mack at the mercantile.

Jimmy slowly approached me. The first touch of the warm, wet cloth against my bare backside made me shiver, but with yearning rather than dread. Slowly he circled my sensitive flesh, lathering the rounded halves with an affection that made me nip my lip. The freshness of the lavender mingled with the pungency of my sex, and when he slipped the cloth down my crack, my legs parted of their own accord.

'Why are you being so nice to me? Not making it any easier, you know,' I muttered.

He chuckled, his breath fluttering the fly-away wisps of hair that had escaped my upsweep. 'If you're bound for the Klondike, who knows when you'll get to bathe again? And, frankly, I'm sorry about the way you got caught with your drawers down, and the way Dick made light of it.'

My heart constricted at this simple statement of kindness. 'I'm a whore, Jimmy. Takes a lot more than that to embarrass me.'

'You're a woman, Rose. You have feelings, and you deserve better treatment.'

I sighed as he refreshed the rag and wiped the lather from my behind. When he soaped it again, that secretive rubbing sound made me tingle in the places I hoped he'd wash next. When the damp warmth caressed my inner thighs, I felt as languid as a cat ... stretched my arms, and then lifted off my camisole. No sense in denying Jimmy, if he wanted to touch me one last time. He'd provided me with bed and board for years, after all, and kept the drunks from roughing me up.

'You have glorious skin, Rosie. Soft and smooth, like the petals of a daisy.'

This from a barkeep who'd once been a bounty hunter. A moan escaped me as the wash rag found my nipple and rubbed it into a prominent nub that ached for more. Around and around he circled, watching over my shoulder as my breast swayed and conformed to the shape of his cloth-covered palm. He loved my breasts and could watch endlessly as he fondled them to make the dark, pebbly nipples ride like rafts on the plump, pale waves of my flesh. When he grazed my neck with a kiss, my head fell back against him.

'You're trying to shame me into staying.'

'If that's what it takes then yes, ma'am, I'll do it,' he breathed, making goose flesh cascade down the front of me. 'But if you leave, I want you to remember Jimmy Crystal at his best. I strive to make a lasting impression on the ladies, you know.'

I giggled, for the poor man had so few of them to choose from here – although he only needed his quiet smile to attract more females than he could handle. His other hand closed around me then, and both breasts moved in a slow, tantalising rhythm as he gently squeezed them and tested their weight.

'How could I forget you?' I replied – but even to me, it sounded lame. Truth be told, my eyes were closed and I was seeing Grant Galloway, letting him drive me into this fine frenzy as I yielded to his touch again. He'd been clumsier and more eager than this, but certainly sincere, and his technique had improved with age and experience, no doubt.

Jimmy rinsed the rag, wiped off the lather, and again kicked up the heady warmth of the scented soap. This time his hands landed lower, following the shape of my ribcage, rubbing slowly over the concave of my belly with a deliberation that always made me want him. My slit was overflowing, and my hips thrust forward to encourage his intimate touch.

He took his own sweet time, however, rubbing my backside against his cotton shirt and denim pants while his hands took a sinuous trail towards my mound. My body swayed with his, rocking in the easy rhythm of lovers who know each other well. Too well, perhaps? Exasperated, I grabbed his hands and coaxed them lower, until the rag rustled against my coarse curls.

Jimmy was stronger, however, and held steady, grasping the flesh of my lower belly in a firm caress. He dragged the rag in a slow, damp circle around my abdomen, his other hand poised with the fingers splayed over my mound. I was breathing through my mouth in quick, shallow bursts, willing those fingers to plunge inside me and relieve the ache that grew more insistent with each second.

He lifted the fleshy pad, exposing my folds. Then he got lost in kissing my neck and shoulders, gentle flick-erings of his soft, full lips accentuated by the brush of his moustache and the rasp of his shaved chin. Jimmy smelled of lemon wax from polishing the bar, and clothes that could use a washing, and that heavier male musk from pulling up his pants after I'd pulled away from him downstairs.

'Take off your clothes,' I whispered, wiggling suggestively against his bulging fly.

'Not yet. This is about you, Rosie-girl, about the way your body responds to me. About the times you've had to take whatever the boys dish out, without seeing to your own pleasure.'

My eyes teared up. When had this man ever waxed so eloquent? If this was his going-away present, he was making it extremely difficult to leave. But we both knew I had to go, if I intended to make something of myself before I got old and worn down. I resolutely called up the images of Grant Galloway leaning me against the back of the mercantile in Denver, pawing at me and making me feel so heavenly even as I knew I was headed straight to hell for it.

Jimmy's fingers speared into my bush, tugging on the curls and slipping into my dew. He spread my honey along the length of my folds, dipping that finger now and again, circling the rim of my hole with a teasing wiggle. I bucked against him. 'More! Harder – please!' I rasped.

His chuckle rumbled against my back. 'So impatient, and making such demands!' he teased against the hollow of my neck. 'You'll get it when I say you'll get it, Rosie-girl. The longer I keep you wanting it, the longer you'll be mine.'

Shameless, we were, playing on each other this way. Yet he'd made no move toward his buttons, to release the rock-hard erection now rubbing at the crack in my backside. Again his fingers dipped – two of them this time, and deeper, testing the wet flesh inside me as his palm pressed against my clit. I thrust against him –

couldn't stand this much longer! My puss was wet, and the pressure was in all the right places. I suddenly needed that inner explosion more than the musky air we breathed.

Yet again Jimmy pulled out. He swallowed my protest with a kiss that eased over my mouth and controlled me, that provocative caress of soft lips and furtive, purposeful tongue. I had no choice but to share his every breath, and receive the heat of his advances, for, wrapped in his arms this way and pressed against his strong, swaying body, I was his.

Such a thought spurred me to contradict it. I called Grant to mind again, his demanding kisses and the way he'd pinned me against the building with his undulating body. Every nuance came back to me in a rush, embellished by the schoolgirlish perceptions so fresh and dangerously daring at that time, and undimmed despite the years that had carried us in separate directions. Grant was a man, after all – and I was a woman with dozens of tricks and techniques. He knew what I'd become and still wanted me ... probably more now than back then, because my guilt and innocence and uncertainty would no longer come between us.

Jim's fingers delved inside me again, with a squelching sound that drove me higher, into that final phase of excitement. I could no longer be denied. I captured his hand, pressing his knuckles to force the fingertips deeper, against that sweet spot high up inside my passage that made me writhe beyond control. I gasped into his open mouth, my lips still its prisoner. My pussy pulsed until I began to thrust hard and mindlessly against his bulging crotch and his persistent palm.

On and on I convulsed, gushing honey and having it rubbed against my engorged folds by fingers that knew my every crevice and craving. I collapsed against him, sending us backwards on to the mattress with a loud creak of its ropes.

Still Jimmy held me, shifting me to his side so I faced him. He continued his kiss, his long lashes fluttering against his cheeks as he poured his affection into me. Not missing a beat, he reached overhead to rinse out the rag, and then brought it out of the bowl sopping wet, to squeeze out the warm water over the length of my bared side. I gasped, slapping at him, but he held me fast.

He wiped me then, broad firm strokes that cleared the lavender's lather and our earlier come from my thighs. Upwards he moved, thoroughly removing my fresh honey from every petal and fold, playfully rasping the rag's texture against my still-throbbing clit until I surged again.

This was madness! This man had no right to detain me this way, shamelessly using my own wanton desires against me. When I could breathe again, I realised the crackling stiffness beneath me was Grant's letter. My hands scrambled to free the papers, fearing they'd be ruined by the wet rag or my own copious juice. Jim let me sit up long enough to slide them on to my night stand, his eyes glimmering in the dusk.

Then he was on me again, rolling me on to my back. Like a panther he poised above me, parting my legs to kneel between them. I'd seen this move dozens of times – he was now going to pay me lip service, tonguing me senseless until my legs flailed around his head and I yelped his name in helpless abandon.

He grinned, his teeth flashing as he read my thoughts. 'Yes, I'm stalling you,' he admitted, his fingers finding the springy hair around my slit. 'If you honestly believe this other fellow can pleasure you better than I can – if you think the promises he's dangled in front of you are a better bet than what you've got with me, then go with my blessing, Rosie. Never let it be said that Jim Crystal kept a woman from what she really wanted.'

I could've cussed him, except he ducked his head between my legs and made me squeal with the sudden plunging of his tongue. He was far too good at this! Way too proficient at licking every inch of my inflamed flesh and kicking up another round of honey and musk.

Spearing my fingers into his thick, warm hair, I guided him in and out at a quickening pace, clenching my eyes in ecstasy. In and out he drove, his tongue solid at the root and a quivering point at the tip. He circled my helpless little hole, and then flicked my clit and sucked it between his teeth. I had no choice but to thrust and writhe and surrender to yet another onslaught of inner frenzy.

I clawed at his clothes, but he shook away my hands. Relentlessly he sucked and lapped, cushioning his teeth against me, until I saw dazzling fireworks behind my eyelids. I screamed his name until it filled the little room – until I blacked out from the force of yet another orgasm he'd brought on.

I came around, panting, foggy along the edges. Jim had removed his clothes and was curling himself around me, to settle in for the night. Except then he began to kiss me again, very softly, holding me so my bare breasts bristled in the down on his chest and our stomachs rubbed ... and I couldn't ignore the shaft pressing against my cleft. My uppermost thigh slid on top of his and he entered me gently, sweetly, pausing between slow thrusts so I could draw his cock deeper. Moaning low, he rocked with minimal effort, letting the bed sway to his advantage, keeping the pace so slow it felt like he intended to take an eternity to satisfy himself.

With some men, I couldn't wait for it to be over. With Jim, this night, I had only enough energy left to accept him again, filling and refilling with his sweet, solid girth as he held my hips. He stiffened, approaching the point of no return. He grimaced, gritting his teeth against the urge to drive himself harder. Air hissed as he inhaled, still moving at that hypnotic beat to keep us both hovering on the edge of an ecstasy we sensed would be our last. I arched backwards and squeezed, until his heartbeat matched mine in our pressed-together bellies and I could feel his sac quivering against my sensitive lips.

He let go then, with surges that expanded into magnificent, soul-shattering spasms. His seed filled me, hot and thick, until each thrust made a sucking sound that drew our juices out in a torrent of warmth. For several minutes we lay there, catching each other's breath, awed by the force of the love we'd made.

'Don't leave, Rosie,' he murmured. 'Tomorrow we'll make our plans and move on. I promise you won't be sorry.'

But in my heart, I was already Grant's. And I was already gone. When he was snoring softly, I left Jimmy Crystal and his saloon. Stole out into the night with only the letter, the money and the clothes on my back. I was bound for a glorious adventure like Rosie DuBris could only dream of before this – was on my way to becoming *somebody*. And nobody was going to stop me!

3 My Ship Comes In

On the train from Portland to Seattle, I read the rest of Grant's letter. Instructions on the best route to take, mostly, with a long list of supplies for the trek north to the Klondike. Hundreds of pounds of flour and bacon and beans; bags of coffee and evaporated apples and potatoes; eating utensils and a tent and – the enormity of this undertaking overwhelmed me, so I quickly returned to the body of his letter.

Buy sturdy shoes, Rosie, and a warm coat, with heavy gloves. And a hat that won't blow off in the Arctic wind.

Hard to believe such advice as I wiped the sweat from my brow on this sultry July day. But Grant had made the trip and he would know; the gallant Grant Galloway wouldn't lead me astray. He even suggested stores in Seattle, near the piers, where I could find these supplies. But it was the last few lines of his letter I read again and again, revelling in the way they made my heart speed up:

Come to Satan and be my angel again, Rosie. Spread your pretty wings, and we'll fly like before – but we'll soar so much higher than we did as kids.

It felt like a dream come true, having a man send for me just when I thought I couldn't endure another day in the cut-over Oregon forest. And he'd sent *money*!

As we approached the next train station, I fingered the crisp bills, still amazed at the solid sense of purpose they gave me – the euphoria, knowing I wouldn't have to turn tricks along the way. Why, if I bought a couple new dresses, who would have to know I was a whore?

Who could tell, if I were all bundled into that heavy coat and boots? I would arrive at Satan in style, passing for a lady!

Then I paused, counting again, thinking my ciphering skills had gone to mush after Jimmy's lovemaking. Eight hundred dollars. And I was positive Grant had only sent me five.

I choked on a knot of resentment. Somehow Crystal had slipped me another chunk of money he could little afford to part with. For a moment I went soft inside, thinking I should board the next train back to Portland, and the man who'd let me go without belittling my dreams or finding other ways to make me stay.

But I hardened myself against such sentiment. Plenty of opportunity he'd had, to move elsewhere and find us a livelihood again. If anything, this money made me feel more like a whore than ever, because we'd agreed that Jimmy would never pay for my services. I gave them in appreciation for his protection, and because we truly enjoyed each other in bed.

The iron wheels squealed and the train steamed to a halt in front of a small station's platform. I quickly tucked the money and letter into my bodice. The last thing I needed was for nosey passengers to read over my shoulder, or catch a glimpse of my cash. I was a woman alone, travelling like few ladies dared, vulnerable to whoever challenged me. Keeping my own counsel was best – and it was a relief when the two boarding couples eyed my shabby dress and proceeded down the aisle as though I were an urchin dirtied with something contagious.

The appearance of poverty had its advantages. I arrived in Seattle tired but none the worse for rubbing thighs with gentlemen who boarded at various stops, and who tried to engage me in conversation. When I disembarked, I went directly to Cooper and Levy, an outfitter Grant had mentioned, which had a reasonably priced hotel upstairs. The streets teemed with people, a mass of humanity like I hadn't seen since I'd lived in Denver, multiplied a dozenfold.

The tang of the pickle barrel and earthier scents of garden seeds tickled my nose as I wove between the customers in the front of the large, two-level store. First thing, I spied some ready-made dresses and chose two fashioned of a lightweight wool. As I held them against myself, facing a mirror in the back corner, I felt someone staring at me. He was much younger than I – but old enough to know what to do with that knot in the front of his trousers. Tall and broad of shoulder, he was. Clean, and wet enough behind the ears that I could lead him around by his cock without even touching it.

'I realise you're nearly ready to close for the day,' I began in my coyest voice, 'but I'll take these dresses, and I'm hoping you can have the rest of my supplies ready by tomorrow morning.'

I fumbled the supply list from my bosom, with enough sway to make his eyes wander.

'Yes, ma'am, I'll see to it personally.' He stepped forward with his hand extended, fingers curving as though to fondle my assets. His raven hair and olive complexion gave him a rakish air, compounded by eyes the colour of cornflowers. 'Of course, if you need it sooner, I could stay late to –'

'No need for that, thanks. You see, I'm headed for the Klondike, because there's a gold strike the likes of which we've never seen! I'm travelling with the first wave of prospectors, so I'd appreciate your … prompt, personal attention.'

His Adam's apple bobbed with a hard swallow. His fingertips grazed mine as he glanced at Grant's list. 'Ma'am, this is enough rations for –'

'It's a long journey. Your store comes highly recommended by the same reliable source who tipped me about the gold.'

His eyes widened at the second mention of that gilded word. Even here in Seattle, folks were feeling the pinch of hard times, and this fellow looked ripe for an adventure – or that's what I was counting on, anyway. He appeared sturdy enough to earn his keep, too. An important consideration for a woman like me.

But my salesman's forehead furrowed, and he cast another dubious glance at my clothes. 'How're you intending to pay for all this, ma'am? If I go to the trouble of – of . . .'

My hand was steadying the side of one breast as I fished for my wad of bills, taking my time about it. 'If you're smart, you won't judge this book by its cover,' I replied in a low voice. 'You a betting man? I'll wager that within the week, your store won't be able to match the demand for these rations and supplies! Folks'll be outfitting themselves in droves, stampeding to the gold fields! What a shame, if you missed out on this chance of a lifetime.'

He read my list again, his colour deepening. Then he stepped closer, to speak in confidence. 'What's the bet? You don't look crazy enough to set out for the Klondike alone, so you must know –'

'Oh, I know,' I assured him with a wink and the lightest caress of his cheek. 'So I'll float the price of *your* supplies as well, if you'll provide a way to haul them overland and up the Chilkoot Trail.'

'You've got a map?'

'Do I look stupid enough to start such an adventure without one?'

He grinned, his face lighting with a conspiratorial air I found extremely appealing. 'But what if you're wrong? What if your source has bamboozled you?'

I leaned forward until our noses nearly touched. 'If

my prediction doesn't come true then the bet's off and you're out nothing. Just another chat with a chit who doesn't know her place, nor have sense enough to stay there. Put these dresses on my tab. I'm getting a room upstairs and I'll be down first thing tomorrow for my supplies.'

I grinned, liking the way his eyes sparkled directly into mine as he took the two dresses. He'd do nicely, if nobody convinced him I was full of hot air – and I sensed he'd know better than to tell anyone of this opportunity, anyway. 'Whom do I ask for, when I come to settle up?'

'Collin Cooper, Miss –'

'The proprietor's son?' I arched a brow over our clasped hands. 'What'll your father say if you abandon him, when the rush for supplies catches him short-handed?'

'Do I look stupid enough to ask his permission?' Collin quipped. 'Or to stay behind clerking, when there's a fortune to be had? I'll wrap these for you and be right back.'

I turned on my heel to hide my glee. Hook, line and sinker I'd reeled him in, with a smile and a wad of bills I hadn't even unfolded! Not that I'd told him any more of a story than I believed myself. If I were to navigate icy waters and negotiate the miles and mountains ahead, I'd need a convincing companion to keep me out of the compromising positions a woman alone often found herself in. Collin Cooper would fill the bill nicely.

He returned shortly with a paper packet tied in string. 'Thank you again, and I'll see you in the morning, Miss –?'

'You won't be sorry, Collin.' I turned, tossing him a final smile over my shoulder as I made my way through the last-minute crowd at the dry goods counter.

* * *

A few hours later, I heard the thump of boots on the hotel stairway, quick footsteps approaching my room, then slowly walking past ... then returning. I smiled, blowing at the filmy bubbles floating in my small copper bathtub. It had taken Collin longer than I'd expected to get here, but I'd left the door unlocked and was ready for his knock. Two hesitant taps – and when I didn't answer immediately, three urgent rappings.

'Yes? Who is it, please?' I called out, grinning as my nipples extended like tiny periscopes above the water.

'It's Collin from the store. I have a question about your order.'

Of course you do, I mused, leaving him to stand there a few more moments. 'Do come in then. It's open.'

He stepped inside as though not wanting anyone in the hallway to know his mission – and then gaped at me. I sat near the fireplace in my tub, my arms and legs extended over its low sides, and the rest of my body submerged in soapy water. 'What kind of lady asks a man into her room when she's – *bathing*?' he demanded, colour creeping up his cheeks.

'What kind of man finds a lady's room, pretending to ask about a perfectly plain supply order?' I countered. 'Would you rather wait outside while I dry and dress?'

'No! I –' His blue eyes flashed, but then he grinned. 'I have news, actually! Dad's received a telegram from his cousin in San Francisco. Seems a ship has docked there, and prospectors from the Klondike have arrived with hundreds of thousands in gold! And they say a similar ship, the *Portland*, will dock here tomorrow or the next day!'

My heart fluttered wildly. So Grant wasn't just telling a story! And just as importantly, Collin Cooper was gazing at me as though I possessed wondrous powers of prediction. He stepped closer, trying not to stare at what bobbed on the surface of my bath water.

'So your father's preparing for a rush?' I asked demurely.

'Of course he is. Contacting his warehouses from all over –'

'Does this mean our deal is off?' I demanded, raising up as though to confront him.

Collin got a good eyeful of my wet breasts and stomach, but managed to answer. 'Not a chance. I've already set aside the provisions on your list, and the same amount for myself. I'll haul our load to the pier when the *Portland* docks. If you'll see to our tickets north, I'll repay you – and we're Klondike bound!'

I grinned at his enthusiasm. He was a handsome thing, when his blue eyes sparkled in his dark face. And he was standing right beside my tub, looking down at me. I'd lowered myself back into my soapsuds, noting the bulge that now throbbed at his crotch. 'So what's your question about my list?'

Collin cleared his throat, his fingers curling as though they wanted to handle what he saw. 'You didn't mention any tools for prospecting. We'll need shovels and picks and –'

'*You'll* need them, yes,' I replied, thinking quickly to stay ahead of him. I couldn't have him thinking I was an unscrupulous sharper, only wanting his ... physical abilities. 'My source has already staked a claim, you see. He didn't want me hauling equipment – extra weight – I have no need of, since I'll probably keep house for him while he mines the gold.'

Collin thrust his hands into his pockets, as though his itch there really needed scratching. 'So we'll just be partners along the way? No strings or ... romantic attachments, just because we happen to be a man and a woman?'

'Yes, there's a man at the end of the trail for me – a man I've known since I was a girl,' I replied matter-of-factly. 'But we should see ... what comes up, before we deny the possibility for ... closer companionship. We'll be traveling hundreds of miles, through all manner of conditions, after all. It means a great deal to me not to negotiate the trail alone.'

'I see.' Collin glanced nervously about as his fingers toyed with the lump in his pants. 'So why'd you pick me? If my brother Stan had waited on you, would you have made him the same offer?'

'I guess we'll never know, will we?' I dipped my hands into the water between my legs, my gaze steady. 'I appreciated the way you assisted me when I wasn't dressed very well. Why'd you accept my bet?'

He coughed, his eyes following the swirl of soapsuds that revealed my thatch beneath the water, where my fingers played in the dark hair. 'You had a certain way about you. And – if you don't mind my saying so – I saw that mark on your face and thought it must be a good omen.'

'Do you want me to suck your cock, Collin?'

His hands sprang from his pockets. 'I don't even know your name. I –'

'It's Rosie, partner. Do you want to feel my lips sliding up and down your shaft? I bet it's a nice big one. Probably poke my eye out, if you're not careful when you turn him loose.'

'I – what kind of a lady – ?'

'How old are you, Collin?'

'Twenty-two!'

'*How* old?'

He shifted, watching my fingers part my folds to slip into my slit. 'All right, I'm nineteen. But I'm old enough to go on this trip, and I'll – I'll take good care of you while we – why are you doing this, Rosie?'

I had to smile. For a looker his size, he was a little behind in the skirt-lifting department, yet I found that as endearing as his loyalty. Like a puppy he'd be ... a pup with a big tail to wag, unless I missed my guess. Young men never forget their first time with an experienced woman, and this would be one of the many bonds we forged to survive the long trek ahead of us. I licked my lips, looking blatantly at his bulge; watching it twitch as he shifted again.

'I'm a generous woman, Collin. A woman who understands a man's needs and isn't embarrassed by them. After all, do you think there'll be a privy every few miles between here and the Klondike?' I asked. 'Chances are good you'll see my bare backside when I need to pee, and you'll flash your pecker to relieve yourself. Might as well get that bashfulness behind us.'

'Well, you've got a point there.'

'No, *you've* got the point, sweetheart. And it's Rosie DuBris who wants to show you how much she appreciates your faith in her.' I leaned against the back of the tub, placing an arm behind my head, which raised my breasts out of the water so he could watch the droplets flow down their rounded sides. 'Take down your pants, Collin. Straddle the tub and let me bring off your first bonanza, before we even start out for the gold fields.'

Feverishly he unfastened his fly, watching me undulate under the water. With my knees hooked over the edges of the tub, I raised and lowered myself suggestively, sending the soapsuds running off my stomach and into my thatch, letting the rivulets dribble toward my slit.

'Miss Rose, I still don't understand why you're doing this.' His boots hit the floor. When he lowered his pants his erection sprang free, jutting proudly from a thick coil of dark hair and two plump, rosy testicles. Lord, but he was a sight like I hadn't seen for awhile! I couldn't help licking my lips in anticipation.

'Are you telling me you weren't hoping for this – just a bit – when you came up here?' I arched my brow, like a teacher quizzing her student.

Collin shoved his pants past his feet, a becoming flush colouring his cheeks. Why some young lady hadn't initiated him was beyond me ... perhaps something we could discuss when we were better acquainted. 'I had no idea you were a – what I mean is – you didn't come across as a –'

'Thank you,' I murmured. 'Maybe I'm just a lady who enjoys making a man feel good. Any harm in that?'

'Lord, no! From what I hear, most women get disgusted or fearful about such things.'

'That's not my style, Collin. Straddle this tub and and let me suck that gorgeous cock. I can't wait to taste you.'

His awkwardness fell away then. It was a joy to watch the ripple of his muscles, the sway of that impressive erection as he swung a leg over my tub. His body was firm and fit, narrowing from burly shoulders to lean hips and sturdy thighs ... a body that would perform well on the long journey, in ways that had nothing to do with packing provisions. I wiggled my tongue at his tip, noting the droplet of cream coming at its eye and its reddish-purple shine. He pulsed visibly, still standing an inch or two shy of making contact.

'Hold on, big fella,' I murmured, 'it's going to be a helluva ride.'

I licked my lips, continuing that motion midair until I touched his inflamed head. Collin moaned and surged forward, filling my mouth with his hot length, sheathing himself as though he'd waited half a lifetime for this experience. He smelled pleasantly of sweat and maleness, and his skin felt like warm velvet as I ran my fingertips over it to hold his shirt-tails out of my face.

Cushioning my teeth with my lips, I slid up and down his shaft, feeling the vein that pulsed on its underside, and the heat that increased with each slow stroke.

It wouldn't be long. Collin, bless his heart, was too engrossed in the sensations racking his body to show any control. He began to thrust, tentatively, as though afraid he'd hurt me. With a low growl, I gobbled him, opening my throat to ease him further down, until he was buried inside me and his wiry hairs tickled my nose.

'God – oh my God, Rosie, I –' Collin grimaced, gripping the high back of the tub on either side of my head for balance, hunching himself in and out of my mouth.'I'm gonna – it's getting –'

I wrapped my thumb and forefinger around the base of his cock, holding him back. He was panting now, all but thrashing as I guided him in and out of my wetted lips, teasing the length of him with my tongue. With his head thrown back and his eyes closed, groaning with the pleasure-pain that preceded his climax, Collin Cooper was a magnificent sight ... a study in male perfection I'd never forget. He towered above me, bucking, his skin slick with sweat. An alluring pattern of black down funnelled up his stomach, over the broad, muscled chest that strained against the buttons of his white shirt.

I felt the first spasms, felt his balls tighten as his breath came in gasps. He braced himself, and then shot a torrent of hot cream down my throat. For several moments he thrust, each spurt accompanied by a little cry. Finally he opened his eyes, gracing me with a smile like I'd only seen on the faces of angels in religious paintings.

'Holy mackerel,' he panted. 'Now why'd you go and do such a thing, Rosie? I intended –'

'I did it because I wanted to. That's the only reason I

do *anything*, young man.' I ran a teasing finger down the still-stiff length of him. 'Next time it'll be my turn. And I believe in coming right out and asking for what I want. Do we understand each other, Collin?'

He ran his long fingers through that midnight hair as he looked down at me in the bath water. 'Yes, ma'am. And you can bet I'll be holding up my end of this bargain.'

'I thought you'd see it that way.' I grinned at him, wiping my mouth with the back of my hand. 'Get your rest, and I'll meet you bright and early tomorrow. We've got a long way to go.'

When the *Portland* docked the next day, the seventeenth of July, it looked like the entire city came to the piers to greet it. Newsboys were crying out about gold in the Klondike, waving papers that passers-by snatched to read all the details, igniting imaginations with a wildfire of gold fever.

When I went into the store to settle up, the aisles were already filling with curious shoppers who chattered about provisions that might be needed for such a trip. On a hunch, I gathered a basketful of kitchen utensils, a stack of pie plates, a large tin of cocoa powder and an entire case of chocolate bars. Collin met me at the cash register with a secretive wink, handing me back Grant's list before totalling my tab.

I was wearing my new blue dress, with my hair arranged in a neat knot and a touch of rouge on my lips and cheeks – feeling more the lady than I had in ages, yet with a devilish glee pulsing in my veins. The store was arranged on two levels, so I skipped to the centre of the stairs.

'Gentlemen! Ladies!' I called out over the crowd. 'I have here a list of the very provisions you'll require for the Klondike – direct from a friend who's sent for me to join him, and who's already staked his claim! How much am I bid for this invaluable information?'

After a stunned silence, a man in a derby raised his hand. 'Two dollars!'

'Make it five!' another one crowed, and the auction was on. Collin shot me an astounded grin, but I was too busy following the bids to glance his way again until one old coot chomping a cigar shut them all up.

'Three hundred dollars,' he intoned, waving his cash above his head.

Another stunned silence quivered in the air. I gave him my biggest grin. 'Thank you, sir. My best to you as you seek your fortune.'

With that I paid my bill, whispered to Collin that I'd meet him pierside and proceeded down the bustling street to buy our tickets. No doubt in my mind that this was all meant to be! Grant had provided me the opportunity of a lifetime, and far more than gold awaited me at the end of the trail.

4 My Ace in the Hole

It dampened my excitement to discover I was prone to sea sickness, and to learn we had a voyage of more than a thousand watery miles up the wind-tossed Inside Passage to reach Skagway, Alaska, and then our destination of Dyea. Grant's instructions gave no indication of days required or the precise length of the trip, so I spent most of my time in our airless little cabin with my head over a basin. Collin made a patient nurse: he encouraged me to walk outside and cling to the railing for fresh air each day, and spoon-fed me from his own bowls of soup.

'Don't give up, Rosie,' he coaxed. 'Once we've got solid land underfoot, the trip will get easier. You'll see.'

His childlike enthusiasm kept me going – although the prospect of returning to Portland, thus prolonging my malady, was incentive enough to forge ahead. 'I'm no quitter,' I assured my roommate with a wan smile. 'Takes more than choppy waters to keep Rosie DuBris away from the Klondike!'

I couldn't wait to get off that damn ship – until I saw Dyea. If this isolated spot, dotted with a few ramshackle cabins, passed for a town in Alaska, how could Satan be the hotbed of activity Grant had promised? I felt so pathetic and pale, Collin made the dozens of ship-to-shore trips with our provisions, leaving me encamped beside our stockpile. The rest of the passengers, all but a few of them men, swarmed ashore and proceeded towards the Chilkoot Trail, propelled anew by their gold fever.

Grant's letter suggested I hire Chilkat Indian guides to help haul our supplies, so while my partner made the final trips off the ship, I procured this help. The two men I approached, so stocky and stoic, with skin the color of bricks, gave each other a look that didn't need a translation: they had me figured for a goner; were perhaps discussing how they'd divide my provisions after I keeled over on the trail. Thoughts of being buried in a snowy grave while the others marched over the top of me bolstered my resolve, however. I wrapped my coat resolutely around me, arranged my precious cooking utensils and chocolate in a back pack, and trudged along beside Collin.

Again I wondered why I was here, and wondered how strong my feelings for Grant Galloway – or any man – could be. Then I saw the line of insignificant-looking humanity already snaking up the treacherous, snow-packed section of the trail called the Golden Stairs – steps literally carved into the icy mountainside by the parade of Klondike prospectors. The elevation was so steep, and the loads of provisions so large, each party would make several trips up to that summit, which was often obscured by blowing snow.

Word spread quickly that losing our spot in line meant going to its rear again. As I contemplated how many trips it would take us, even with our pair of well-paid Chilkats, I didn't want to calculate how many miles we'd actually pack our provisions before we finished with this thirty-three mile stretch of the trek.

Step by step we rose up that frozen mountainside, staring at the backside of the person before us and hearing the wheeze of the one who stared at our own butts. My mind slipped numbly out of gear. I shut out the grim reality I'd gotten myself into – and had coaxed Collin to join me in. By the time I reached the summit with my little pack of last-minute luxuries, I barely noticed my frozen hands and feet. I could've curled up in the snow for a nap, not caring whether I ever awoke. A sad state of affairs for a woman of my ilk!

'We need you to keep watch over our pile, Rosie,' Collin gasped when we finally topped the trail that first time. With his heavily gloved hands, he signalled for the two Indians to stack our provisions so I could sit inside a barricade built against the stinging wind. Grant had insisted we take this route rather than the White Pass because it remained open year-round, but he'd said nothing about the blizzard conditions we would encounter this early in autumn!

Once the three men slid down the mountainside to fetch another load, however, my curiosity kicked in. I observed the other prospectors; overheard rumours of how rich the gold fields were, and how finding this El Dorado would rescue their families back home from poverty and despair.

Their hope buoyed my spirits. I wasn't going for the gold, but a woman would have to be blind and deaf not to notice the *opportunity* this gold rush provided: here were hundreds of men, away from home and seeking their fortunes. Even if I never set foot near a gold field ... even if this rendezvous with Grant Galloway didn't pan out ... I could get rich beyond my wildest dreams just being myself! I was a woman, warm and so very willing to give these men what they'd left behind – or never had – with their wives and sweethearts. Unconditional, unfettered sex. Any way they wanted it.

I sat straighter, knowing I'd overcome the illness that made the steamer trip a weak-kneed blur. I breathed deeply, and then – my God, there were men circulating among the prospectors, collecting tariffs. Men in natty red jackets with dimple-crowned hats – the living legends idolised in dime novels and newspaper accounts!

'Mounties,' I breathed, watching them with an

interest as piqued as my nipples. I hadn't considered that we'd be crossing into Canadian territory – indeed, all accounts I'd read placed the Klondike in Alaska. But these uniformed troopers spoke in crisp British tones, tallying up taxes and requiring all prospectors to stock up on provisions before continuing to the next Mountie outpost and the gold fields beyond.

Every fibre of my body stood at attention, alert to their muscled forms as they bent over stacks of supplies. How many layers of longjohns did they wear beneath their distinctive red jackets to stay warm in this beastly weather? Probably too many to make a quick proposition worth my time, but the thought got my blood pumping. And then I heard a rustling behind my barricade and a bold, moustachioed face peered into my little shelter.

'I say there, are you alone, madam?' the man in the crimson coat intoned.

I shook my head briskly, my heart pounding so hard I couldn't breathe. Lord, but he was a looker: dark curls – just long enough to defy regulations – escaping the sides of his hat, and that waxed handlebar moustache giving a devilish lift to his upper lip. His skin was ruddy from the wind. His brown eyes bored into mine as he awaited my reply.

'Are you all right, darling?' he asked more subtly.

My slit went wet for the first time since I'd set sail. *Dahling*, he'd called me! I'd always detested that endearment, but coming from this gorgeous man's mouth it sounded like he was addressing Herself the Queen.

'Feeling *so* much better now,' I breathed, and then felt immediately foolish. 'Thank you for asking. My – my partner and our two Indian packers have gone for another load, while I rest.'

'You look pale. Are you quite well?'

His concern touched me – and then *he* did, brushing back my hood for a better look at my face. I wanted to climax then and there, but I managed to answer, 'I *have* been ill, actually – aboard the ship – but I'm recovering,' I admitted. 'Damn shame to be a working girl plunked down in this oasis of opportunity and not have the strength to drop my knickers!'

Dammit, I'd done it again – betrayed myself, when I'd thought to take on a fresh start. Would he chastise me, or announce an added tax upon my professional activities?

But he stood up, his laughter ringing around the stacks of provisions, bouncing off the barracks lined alongside this snow-covered checkpoint.

Then the noble, red-coated lawman leaned down for another look. 'I hope you weren't foolish enough to attempt this journey without adequate provisions, love. We're requiring a ton of food and supplies – enough for a year – for each person crossing into the Klondike Territory.'

'Enough for a *year*?'

'Because the Yukon River will soon freeze over,' he explained, pushing his hat back to reveal more of his smooth forehead and alluring dark eyebrows. 'Most of these stampeders have *no* idea of the hardships they'll encounter in this unforgiving terrain; nor do they plan on camping beside Lake Bennett for several months, once the river's impassible. Wouldn't want all these men to start . . . eating each other, you know.'

Something about his words made me snicker in a most unladylike way. Something about his dimpled grin suggested that beneath his starched, by-the-book demeanour, this handsome Mountie loved to play as much as I did. The very thought made the hero of the dime novels I'd read spring to a new dimension of life, and I caught myself gawking at him shamelessly.

'So tell me, sir, do you Mounties always get your man, as your motto proclaims?'

'Never met a man I didn't like,' he quipped. But then he resumed a more proper formality, extending his hand. 'Broderick Manley – but I go by Ace – at your service, Miss –?'

'DuBris. Rosie DuBris, from Oblivion, Oregon,' I replied, sorry we wore gloves as I briskly returned his handshake. 'And frankly, I never met a man I didn't like, either. I *do* have the required amount of provisions along, as does my partner, because we received a complete list from my – my friend, in Satan. That's where I'm headed, rather than to the gold fields.'

He raised an eyebrow, but apparently thought better of commenting. Instead, he stood straighter to scrutinise whoever was approaching my shelter. The crates around me shuddered as though an earthquake had struck, and I sprang from the dimness into the bright snow-shine of afternoon. It was Collin and our two packers, of course, adding another load of our supplies, but it made my heart flutter to see Ace Manley stepping between me and the three other men.

'Do you know these fellows, Miss DuBris?' he asked in a voice that brooked no argument – a low voice that rang with *authority*, on my behalf. The British timbre of it made my slit quiver deliciously as I studied the powerful shoulder muscles straining the seams of his uniform.

I squinted beneath the hand I'd raised to my brow. 'This is Collin Cooper, my partner. And Collin, this kind gentleman in red ... Mr Manley here – uh ...'

The two of them were clasping hands as though reuniting after years apart. This thought passed, however, as I realised I'd jumped too quickly from my little cave, after being so deathly ill. The Mountie assessed the man who'd just added several more bulging cloth sacks to our stockpile, with a glance towards the two Chilkats.

'Glad to hear you came adequately prepared, Cooper,' he said in a businesslike voice, 'and ever so pleased that you're allowing Miss DuBris to rest after a treacherous climb.'

'Ordinarily I'm as hale as the next fellow,' I chirped, which brought forth Ace's grin like sunshine after a storm.

'And ordinarily I maintain a professional distance from this madding throng of prospectors,' he said with a slight bow. 'But I'd be pleased if you and Collin would put up in my quarters tonight. You'll do much better after a good rest, Miss DuBris. I can assist you with information about the journey to Lake Bennett and beyond. And about Satan, as well.'

I almost protested his hospitality, because I didn't want to put him out – or to lose precious hours, while the other prospectors would be hiking ahead of us. Something in his tone struck me, however. A warning, perhaps. Or did I dare interpret it as an invitation to more than a night's bed and board?

'I'd gladly accept your offer,' I hedged, 'but I hesitate to break any barracks rules or – or inconvenience you in any –'

'I'm commander of this post, Rosie,' he replied slyly. 'Out here in the hinterlands, who's to defy Captain Manley? I'd love some company for a night. Perhaps some . . . do you cook, Rosie?'

'Will the devil roast my chestnuts over his fire?' I shot back with an impish grin. 'Matter of fact, my specialty is a chocolate pie that tastes even better than I do.'

'A pie? Of chocolate?'

I smiled, for most people ate their chocolate as candy or drank it for breakfast, rather than placing it in pastry.

'Sweet, creamy chocolate filling, with a froth of meringue on top. Better than the best sex you've ever had, Captain Manley. I guarantee it.'

He gave me another debonair bow, looking and sounding so charmingly English I again flashed hot between the legs. What was it about a man in uniform? Especially a scarlet uniform moulded to those broad shoulders and hugging a firm, well-regulated waist.

'I'd be less than an honourable man to refuse such an offer. Come with me, Miss DuBris,' he said, his voice becoming official-sounding again as he looked at the crowd around us. 'It's my sworn duty to protect and defend all guests entering our territory, and I'd be remiss, allowing you to sleep out in the elements tonight. In your condition.'

I strapped on my bundle of utensils and the chocolate, and then we strolled towards a row of wood-shingled buildings. 'And what condition is that?'

Captain Manley chortled, looking me directly in the eye with those huge brown peepers. 'A state of arousal so heightened you'll have these miners rutting like elk, if they catch a whiff of you, Rosie. I'm not sure your young-buck partner understands the crisis this could create, if left ... unchecked.'

I swallowed, my body thrumming with lust. 'Check anything you like, Captain,' I breathed. 'It's your sworn duty, after all.'

'It'll be my pleasure, darling.'

As he opened the door to the largest cabin in the row, his hand found my back and then roamed lower, to the curve of my backside. Even from beneath my heavy cloak I felt his suggestive, teasing fingers as I looked up into a smile made delightfully wicked by his handlebar moustache. Ace helped me out of my heavy wrap, and then devoured me with a gaze I thought might smoke the dress right off me. But then he bowed.

'You'll find fresh water,' he said, pointing to the bucket beside the wood-burning stove, 'and other necessities on those shelves, and a few eggs and such in this hidey-hole beneath the floor. All very mundane, compared to what I'll find in *your* cave, no doubt. I'll be back in a few hours, whetted and ready for a sampling.'

Captain Manley turned smartly on his heel, leaving me to gaze longingly after his jaunty red jacket. He stopped at the door, however, wearing a purposeful expression. 'What are you leaving behind in Oblivion, Oregon, that makes Satan so appealing, dear heart?'

He knew things he wouldn't share about my destination. But I saw no harm in an honest reply. My mind was made up about going, and even a handsome rake like Ace couldn't change it.

'I worked from the room above Jimmy Crystal's bar far longer than I should've,' I responded matter-of-factly. 'The letter I received from an old flame in Satan seemed the perfect opportunity to move on, to bigger and better things.'

Surprise sparkled in his dark eyes. 'You know Jim Crystal? The gunslinger who cleaned up Cripple Creek and those other wild mining towns?'

'*Former* gunslinger,' I amended. 'And now that the lumberjacks have abandoned their camp near Oblivion, he doesn't sling much whisky, either. You've met him, I take it?'

'Only through the newspapers, and the passing along of legends and lies we lawmen love to indulge in.' His gaze turned speculative, as though he wondered what sort of woman left such an upstanding man behind. But he was polite to a fault. Not the sort who'd question my decision any more than he had my profession.

'Just curious,' he added, adjusting his hat to go back outside. 'I've heard all manner of answers, mostly from those who've leapt before they looked. I predict more prospectors will find disappointment and heartache than the fortunes they seek, and I hope you're not among them, dear Rosie.'

With that, he returned to his post, leaving me to stare after him with my fingertips at my lips. Never had I met a man like Broderick Manley, and thoughts of what he intended to do with me later made me forget how tired and weak I felt. I focused instead on his home – Spartan by all accounts, but a damn sight better than that rocking, rolling steamship and a relief from the biting wind outside. It was a one-room dwelling with a bunk in the corner, pegs on the wall for his clothing, two stiff chairs near the Franklin stove, a kitchen table and a dry sink. A few rays of sunlight struggled through the window, despite the clock saying it was nearly eight in the evening. At home, it would've been pitch dark.

At home, Jim's sitting in his empty saloon. Or in my room, looking down on the empty street.

I forced this sentiment out of my head: the pang I felt after leaving Crystal without a word or a kiss was something I'd have to live with. A necessary chapter about my past.

For the next hour I mixed flour and lard for my pie crust, and melted two of my chocolate bars to prepare the delicacy which had bought me a night's reprieve from the Chilkoot Trail. It wouldn't be the masterpiece I whipped up in my own familiar kitchen, but it would do – as would the stew I concocted from some cooked venison and a few carrots and potatoes I found in the little cave beneath Ace's floor. I was arranging biscuits on this bubbling pot when Captain Manley and Collin came in, with a gust of chilly wind.

'Smells like heaven in here!' the Mountie remarked as he removed his hat. 'How lovely, to return with dinner nearly ready, and company to share it. No doubt Collin's worked up an appetite, as well.'

Again I caught a glimmer of electricity between them, and again dismissed it as my imagination. Manley set out plates and forks, while my young partner looked around the cabin – and then at me – with an appreciation that made me tingle.

'Somehow I knew you could cook, Rosie,' he remarked with a wink. 'And your pie isn't all we've been anticipating, is it, Ace?'

'By no means,' the Mountie agreed with a chuckle. 'But we'll sample the lady's culinary offerings before we indulge in her . . . dessert.'

What a treat, to eat with two admiring men, sharing my first decent meal in weeks. Now that both fellows sat hatless, in shirtsleeves, I was astounded at how alike they looked – Collin with his dark hair longer and a clean-shaven face, and Ace with his tousled raven waves and rakish waxed moustache. Two sets of eyes lingered on the lift of my bosom as I breathed, and then watched my mouth as I talked.

Ace cleared his throat, as though attending to business before pleasure. 'I've explained to Collin about getting to Lake Bennett within the next few days, before it freezes, and about the treacherous rapids on the Yukon,' he began. 'I've also spoken with your guides, who have been paid to take you to that point. You'll be needing a boat to float the river.'

'A boat?' I glanced at Collin, my heart fluttering. 'Grant – my source in Satan – said nothing about needing a –'

'Never fear, love,' Manley murmured, reaching for my hand. 'Most will have to build boats for themselves because they came unprepared – and several will lose their provisions, and perhaps their lives, once they hit the Squaw and Whitehorse rapids. But I have a vessel for you. And I've instructed Collin on the best way to negotiate that five-mile stretch of the river, while you, my dear, walk along the shore. The five hundred remaining miles to Dawson City – the gateway to the Klondike – are relatively tame.'

I swallowed hard, from the perilous details I envisioned as well as the heat of the Mountie's firm grip. His large, weathered fingers dwarfed mine, yet I sensed I'd been taken care of even before I knew I'd be in danger. 'I can't expect you to just – please let me pay you for your boat and –'

'We've already worked it out, man-to-man,' he replied softly. 'Collin says his part of your bargain was safely hauling your provisions – and you. So I feel confident he'll carry through like the fine gentleman he is.'

I was about to protest, but Collin took my other hand. 'Nothing you can do, Rosie. I owe you this, for getting me in on the first wave of the gold rush. Now dish up that pie, woman, before I get distracted by other . . . sweets.'

Collin sounded much bolder than he had in my hotel room; wore a ruddy, rugged look of anticipation the man across from him shared. It was sheer joy to watch them take their first bites of chocolate pie, holding the firm, sweet pudding in their mouths as they closed their eyes, moving it slowly over their tongues, like they'd died and gone to heaven.

Ace sighed languidly. 'Had I not tasted it myself, I wouldn't believe such fabulous fare could be concocted in my primitive kitchen. Rosie, my love, you're a wonder!'

I giggled as he kissed the back of my hand. Collin, too, seemed transported beyond the candy and eggs and crust he was eating, which was all the praise I needed. The filling was thicker than I preferred it – almost like soft fudge – yet after the beans and hard tack we'd eaten for the past several days, the pie seemed like fine cuisine even to me.

When we finished eating, Ace hurried our tin dishes to the dry sink while Collin added logs to the stove. The shimmers of heat radiating from its cast-iron surface were pale imitations of the fire overtaking my own body. We three had implicitly agreed to a pleasure we had no need to name – and having two such handsome men take charge of it was a thrill a lady like me seldom got to enjoy.

'Shall we lose these clothes, Rosie?' Ace murmured as he knelt at my feet. With purposeful hands he removed my sturdy shoes and stockings, stroking my legs as though he'd never felt a finer silk. 'I hope you don't mind that Collin and I flipped a coin, and I won.'

'And what does that mean?' I breathed. He was backing me against the table's edge, anticipation shining in eyes that steamed like coffee.

'I get your pussy first.'

He urged me backwards with a kiss that sucked the breath from my lungs, a kiss that cast aside what little resolve I had left. His hand, meanwhile, had snaked up my thigh to fondle my flesh with a passion that ran contagious. When his fingers found the slit in my drawers, I gasped inside his mouth.

Two long digits delved into my wetness, making us both groan. He started gently, circling as he slipped in and out, pressing his palm against my mound with each upward stroke. Lord, but this one knew what he was doing!

With a devilish grin, Ace then ducked beneath my skirts, playfully pushing me back into Collin's waiting arms. My partner had fumbled my buttons from their holes and was reaching into the back of my dress to shove it down my shoulders, baring me to the waist. As he claimed my breasts with his hands, Ace stuck his tongue up me and I bucked with the sudden, reeling sensations.

'I want to lick your tits, Rosie,' Collin whispered against my ear. 'Travelled all this way with a bulge in my pants, just thinking about it.' His hot breath sent a shivery parade of goose flesh down my spine. 'After the way you sucked me in your room, I want to feel that friction again ... want to take you into my mouth and return the favour, every place I can.'

It was a dream I desperately wanted to come true. Collin's swarthy face made a fine contrast against my paleness as he approached my breast, stuck out his tongue and wiggled it against my nipple, which jumped to attention like a soldier on guard duty, or a Mountie in his red finery. Not to be outdone, Ace yanked down my drawers and inhaled deeply of my essence, remaining beneath my skirts.

When he curled his tongue and slowly circled my clit, the little bud sprang from its bush like an excited rabbit. Ace's chuckle rumbled against my thighs as he settled his head against one to continue his game, chasing and then eluding my throbbing little nob; instinctively knowing when he'd pushed me to a limit, before making me moan when he stopped.

'Dammit, Ace, give it to me,' I grunted, my legs flailing around his head. He put that to a stop, grabbed my thighs, and then forced them apart with his unyielding grip, while his tongue resumed its relentless assault.

The waves washed me higher then, coaxing me into a foam as Collin laved my nipple. When he saw I was watching, he sucked the entire lobe of flesh into his mouth, holding my gaze with blue eyes that sparkled like a lake dancing with sun diamonds. I stared back, spellbound, as my handsome young lover cupped my breasts up from the sides, into pale, quivering mounds.

I arched, on the brink of a wild climax – but my two men had other ideas. As though they'd arranged it beforehand, Collin came around behind my head to lift me from the table top, just high enough that as Ace tongued me with increasing vigour, he also pulled down my clothes. The moment he raised his head, to disrobe me completely, was incredible agony.

I was so lost in this pleasure that I reached back to grab Collin around the neck while my legs pleaded with Ace to finish me. Neither man humoured me, however. The Mountie unbuttoned his scarlet jacket with crisp movements, watching me writhe as though he enjoyed doling out such extreme punishment. His trousers fell to reveal a union suit stretched to perfection over a muscled body that made me convulse at the mere sight of it. Broad and strong his chest was, patterned with wiry black hair that rustled as the knit slithered down past his navel. When his cock sprang up to greet me, Collin sucked in his breath.

Suspended between their heated gazes, like a girl in a hammock, I began to rock with my wanting. The Mountie stood magnificently naked, facing us – daring us to take what his body offered. I began to pant, unable to hold still as Collin gently let me go to relieve himself of his own clothing. Ace took up then, running his arms alongside my body – and then deftly flipping me on to my stomach.

'Cooper says you've got a suck like nobody's business,' he murmured, running his warm hands along my sides and the rounds of my hips. 'I want to watch ... as much as he wants to. Want to see his shaft ramming in and out of your mouth like he wants to watch me fuck you. We didn't think you'd mind a little three-way gratification, love.'

Mind? My Lord, most men would've bolted from my room, perceiving another lover as competition. It was one thing for a man to watch two women tangling, but few fellows would tolerate another male ... unless ...

It came to me then, why these two had become such fast friends in the twinkling of an eye, in a way I hadn't before perceived. They gave me no chance to be repelled: Collin, now proud and nude and rampant, stood with his monstrous cock jutting just inches from my lips. I reached for him and he moaned, closing his eyes as I slipped my wetted lips firmly down the length of him.

Ace let out his breath behind me, his fingers slipping into my pussy to spread my wetness. The head of his dick probed between legs I spread eagerly; slick and sure it was, as he lifted my hips so I could receive him. I groaned around the cock I was sucking, amazed at the sensation of being filled so completely, both openings stretched to accept erections that surged within me. I gripped Collin's hips, driving my lips up and down his hardness, flickering my tongue along the vein, and then fondling the crimson sac cradling his root. He thrust in time with me ... in time with his cohort at my other end.

And Ace knew all the angles! Deep and slow he drove, urging my inner muscles to wrap tightly and hang on to every pulse of his shaft. When I moaned around my mouthful and flexed, he knew he'd found a sweet spot. He proceeded to rub it until I thought I might die – and I couldn't cry out, because Collin was thrusting down my throat. My own spasms began in earnest then, my body writhing and pulsing beyond my control, which brought on the most intense surge of desire I'd ever felt. Somehow I knew the two men were engrossed in each other's gazes above me, and that only drove me into a deeper heat.

Without warning, I convulsed. Ace thrust himself as far as he could go, rutting rapidly as his sac slapped my wet, spread pussy. Collin, too, surged forward and I could feel the come racing up from his root with each quivering of his prick. Totally trapped, I was – unable to scream with my own release, unable to escape the rockings from either end as my lovers went beyond control as well.

I thought I might pass out, smothered by thrusting, musky maleness, and then a torrent of cream shot down my throat. Collin's cry echoed in the small cabin and inspired Ace to answer him. On and on the one in front pumped, and then the Mountie gushed, his come splattering out of me with his rapid ramming. Caught between them, I became a mindless, quivering mass, swallowing and gasping, clenching and spending, until I realised I wouldn't suffocate: I would drown from both ends at once.

Collin caressed my head, making satisfied little noises as he eased himself from between my lips. Ace collapsed on my back, catching his weight on the table with his elbows. For a moment the room reverberated with our breathing. None of us knew what to say.

Then the Mountie sprinkled kisses across my shoulders. 'Are you all right, love?' he whispered. 'We quite forgot ourselves, I'm afraid.'

I turned, my mouth still full of Collin's come – and damned if that Mountie didn't swivel my head to suck the buttery stuff into his kiss! I relaxed beneath the warm weight of him, suddenly exhausted. Bless them, they made short work of wiping me down with a warm, wet cloth and tucking me into the bed. They were far from finished with each other, but I fell into such a rock-bottom sleep I didn't care.

5 Satan Welcomes Me

'Be very careful around Devlin Meeh and his paramour, Venus. They aren't what they seem.'

All along the five hundred miles between Lake Bennett and Dawson City, Ace Manley's words rang like a siren. I helped Collin navigate the Yukon River, once we passed the rapids at Whitehorse, but during those long hours afloat, my mind returned to the Mountie's rather ominous remark. His glowing words about Jimmy Crystal haunted me, too. But I was running from Oblivion to Satan, too far along to turn back. Too far along to consider the consequences of responding to Grant Galloway's letter.

While the voyage between the Mountie's outpost and the gold fields went as well as we could hope, the shorter, colder days and the open boat took their toll. I'd thought our steamer ride from Portland pretty damn precarious, yet this vessel was barely big enough to hold us – and most of our supplies bobbed along behind us on a raft Collin fashioned the day before we left. More than once we feared we'd lose everything to the white-capped waves.

Collin, bless him, kept us from crashing into the lesser vessels of the other prospectors who'd escaped the lake just before it froze over. Frigid winds rocked us and chapped our poor faces, numbing us through. The sunlight grew scarcer by the day, and when I realised the Land of the Midnight Sun was about to enter several weeks of perpetual winter darkness, I began to doubt my decision. Even if Satan was the rollicking town

Grant claimed, I'd heard rumours that one could go insane from the total lack of sunlight, up near the North Pole.

So I spent the next several days and miles huddling in my cloak with my numb hands tucked against my body, willing myself not to be sick ... willing myself to eat and sleep when we camped along the shore each night ... willing myself to endure this unthinkable madness as the price I was paying for a more exciting, satisfying life.

By the time we landed at Dawson City, Collin and I were exhausted. I'd insisted all along the river trip that he should take our remaining provisions to the gold fields – and he promised to stop through Satan sometime, to tell me of his adventures and the fortune he'd found. His youthful exuberance warmed me, just as his fine body occasionally kicked up that wicked heat I'd come to love. For the most part, however, we conserved our energy for each day's leg of the journey. My partner didn't want the other travellers overhearing my outbursts and getting ideas about sharing my favours, anyway. Collin had lost his initial shyness, but he'd become as possessive as he was protective.

When we finally hauled the boat and our supplies on to the frozen shoreline, however, it was time to go our separate ways. Collin offered to escort me to Satan before he continued to the Klondike, but I thought he should get to the gold fields in front of this pack of prospectors – and I wasn't sure Grant would like my arriving with a man whose perpetual erection testified to his feelings for me. We got a room in a makeshift inn – for Dawson wasn't much of a town yet – and spent our last night together making lusty love that kept everyone but the most seriously exhausted guests awake. Much better than a tearful goodbye, since we agreed to meet again someday.

Come morning, the disgruntled innkeeper was happy to point me towards my destination.

'Satan, ya say?' His gaze suggested I'd be going to hell because I'd interrupted his sleep without satisfying his needs. He pointed to the horizon, dusky even at this hour of the morning. 'Head east towards that reddish glow. Can't miss it. You'll think you're walking into the sunrise, but it's really the devil's furnace.'

He looked me over – I was decked out in the new dress I'd kept clean for my arrival – licking his lips with a speculative glint in his eye. 'Gal like you could do well staying here in Dawson, dancing with the miners.'

I declined politely. After all these weeks and miles, my destination was finally in sight. I didn't ask why the distant sky had such an eerie glow, nor did I worry about what I'd find when I got there. Satan was now more than my goal and ambition: Satan – and Grant Galloway – would soon be my dream come true!

I set off pulling a small sled with my meagre clothing and about three days' provisions, my burden feeling as light as my heart. The wind still whipped at my cloak, viciously at times, and the glazed snow challenged the worn soles of my shoes. But I forged ahead, alone.

Collin and the other prospectors remained visible, if tiny, in the distance, so I felt secure while savouring some time by myself. Time to consider what lay ahead of me; time to marvel over the miracle that I'd survived a trek like I couldn't possibly have anticipated and – thanks to Ace Manley – that I hadn't been stuck at Lake Bennett until the spring thaw. Destiny was prodding me onward, towards my rightful, exciting life, now only a day away!

With just a few flakes' warning, however, I found myself enveloped in a blizzard that blew in on a monstrous gust, surrounding me with a swirling whiteness so opaque I couldn't go forward or backwards – couldn't determine which was which, anyway. For several minutes I stood in heart-pounding terror, fearing I'd travelled more than fifteen hundred miles in vain, and that I'd never be seen or heard from again. The driving snow was so thick I could barely see the sled tether in my gloved hand. No sign whatsoever of the supplies behind me.

Was this how it all ended? I sensed it would be more dangerous to trudge on, perhaps to tumble over the side of a ravine or back down the treacherous trail, than to stand still and wait for the air to clear. Yet being buried alive held no merit, either. I stepped slowly along, if only to allay the sensation of the snow piling up around my feet, and to keep my provisions from being buried on the sled. Inching forward, I squeezed my eyes shut against the driving snow – for I could see nothing, even if I squinted to ascertain the trail. The world was cushioned by an icy silence, and my body was going numb from the cold, and the only thing that felt alive was my terrified heart, pounding frantically in my chest.

Little wonder that when a carriage approached, I nearly walked head-on into the team of horses pulling it. Four ebony Percherons suddenly towered above me, tossing their majestic heads and snorting vapour as they halted with a jingle of harness bells.

I thought I was dreaming. I thought I'd died and passed into some swirling white Other Side, and that whoever was in charge had sent this conveyance to fetch me. Seemed a bad omen that the carriage and horses were a funereal black, yet I had no choice but to step inside when a door swung open. It was either that or freeze in my tracks.

A gust of wind shut the door behind me. Through my frozen-shut eyelids, the dimness felt warm, after trudging for minutes that passed as hours in blinding white. I sensed a presence on the seat before me, yet no one spoke. It was as though we were both waiting for me to thaw before any introductions could be made, and as warmth and feeling returned to my limbs, I dared believe Grant had come for me. He'd braved the blizzard to guide me the rest of the way in the comfort of his fine carriage – for I had no doubt I was surrounded by sleek leather and opulent upholstery, standing before a man who exuded an extremely sensual power without saying or doing a thing. I gave myself a few moments before opening my eyes, wanting my first gaze, my first words, to rise to the occasion of our long-awaited reunion.

I wiped the melted ice from my eyelids. I took a deep, steadying breath. I opened my eyes, smiling warmly – only to squeak, 'You're not Grant!'

Laughter lit the golden features of the little man lounging on the carriage seat. His strawberry-blond hair fell softly to one side, over an impish face that would've looked childlike except for the twinkling of a monocle at his right eye. He had the most flawless skin I'd ever seen and, as he leaned forward to grace me with a smile, I saw freckles sprinkled across his nose. His cape was made of ermine as dazzling as the snow outside, and the suit beneath it shimmered from purple to red as he shifted. The delicate hand he extended bore a gold ring with a ruby that could've choked a horse.

'We meet at last, Miss DuBris,' he said elegantly, his grip filling me with a startling awareness ... an energy that shot through me like white-hot lust. 'After hearing Grant describe you, I wanted to greet you myself, to welcome you to Satan. Take off those wet clothes, my love. Let me warm away those goose bumps covering your tender flesh. Let me make your nipples stiff with need rather than cold.'

I could only stare. This chubby cherub seated before

me knew who I was but hadn't mentioned his own name – and he wanted me naked, while a blizzard raged outside! I jerked my hand from his disquieting grip to clutch my cloak, feeling compromised even with my clothes on. He stroked his chin, making that ruby shimmer in the dimness. My inhibitions melted like the ice on my boots.

'Who are you?' I breathed, for again I sensed a mystical power wrapping itself around me, leaving me helpless except to do this man's bidding. He looked almost angelic, yet something in me didn't trust him.

'Dr Devlin Meeh at your service, dear heart,' he crooned, gazing at me with the leisurely air of a cat who's cornered a plump mouse. 'You've no need to fear me, Miss Rose. We're going to become fast friends.'

Why did that sound more like a threat than a come-on? I fought the desire that danced inside me, yet I was too exhausted – or just too weak – to resist his request. As a last resort I looked away from him, studying instead the rich midnight upholstery that lined his coach and filled it with the musky scent of leather.

Dr Meeh chuckled, and when I glanced at him again, his monocle flashed a reflection from the nearest candle ensconced on the wall. Jimmy Crystal gazed back at me in the little lens.

My heart stopped. I was more than two thousand miles from Oblivion and Jimmy, standing before a man I'd never met. So it was utterly impossible to have such a vision ... an illusion that shook me to the core, even as my defences slithered down around me like my clothes soon would.

Had I been bewitched? My hand began to unfasten my cloak ... the buttons down the front of my dress ... the ribbon that held my drawers at my waist. As these garments fell to the floor of the carriage, I became aware we were moving – aware that my few provisions were still outside in the snow, just as I soon realised it didn't really matter because now such things were beyond my control. Now, Devlin Meeh was directing everything. Even my every breath.

As he sat back to peruse my bare body, his feet didn't quite reach the floor. A laugh bubbled up inside me, which I quickly swallowed. Wouldn't do, to make light of a man who'd spirited my clothes off me. Especially since his tawny-eyed gaze gave the impression that he could read my deepest thoughts. For a woman who was used to controlling men by anticipating everything they wanted or would try, this was an unsettling idea.

'You're as lovely as I'd hoped,' he breathed, although he made no effort to touch me. 'Take down your hair. I want to watch you move.'

Nothing makes a woman more skittish than knowing she's being scrutinised, naked, by a man who has a stake in her future. Slowly I raised my arms, feeling my breasts press together as they bulged toward him, in an invitation I hadn't knowingly extended. My belly tightened as I pulled the pins from an upsweep crushed by my hood and in need of a washing. To brace myself against the sway of the carriage I spread my legs, and as Meeh's gaze lowered to observe this, the first trickle of honey buttered my thighs.

He extended his hand with maddening slowness. My inner muscles clenched in anticipation, while my pussy quivered beneath my thatch. The coarse curls whispered to his fingertip, and I sucked in sharply at the first contact of his skin on mine. My hips thrust forward, shameless and without my permission.

Meeh slipped two long fingers inside me and then pressed his thumb into my mound, his hold on me gentle yet like a vice. My hair fell in a rumpled curtain, I was so surprised. And when I stared from between the wayward, dark tresses, he smiled beneficently.

'Never forget who holds you, Rose,' the elf in ermine murmured. His voice filled the carriage, low and flowing, like I'd imagined God spoke.

But this man was far from holy. He pressed the crotch of his thumb and forefinger against my clit with a purposeful, knowing boldness until I had to suck air, had to squirm with the intense heat building inside me. My cunt quivered around his hand, despite my efforts to retain a shred of decency, of dignity, before this total stranger. And with my next breath, I had to cry out with a climax that struck like a storm, making me gush as I thrust against him, with my breasts slapping wildly against my chest. My knees went weak with a surge of pure electricity, and had he not caught me I'd have fallen to the floor.

'Did you like that, Rose?'

I'd landed awkwardly, with my knees against the edge of his seat, straddling his lap. He smelled clean and sweet, and as I clutched his shoulders for balance the ermine stole tickled the tips of my breasts.

'I don't know. What're you trying to prove by –?'

'Did you like that, Rose?' he repeated, more softly this time.

I nodded emphatically, clenching my eyes shut against acute embarrassment. It was my experience that men came to *me* – and usually came all over me because they'd lost control. Scary, to think Dr Devlin Meeh had humbled me to such a shaky state with two fingers and a thumb, and without preamble or even showing desire on his part. Still he sat there, bearing my naked weight, pressing against my pussy, awaiting my acknowledgement of his power and control.

'H-how did you do that?' I whimpered.

'I have a way with women.'

A simple statement; yet again I heard an omen in his controlled tone. And again I felt the urge to convulse with intense pleasure, when this childlike man wiggled his two fingers against the sensitive pad of flesh deep within my passageway. I held out as best I could, willing myself to stay sane while he moved nothing but those two fingertips, watching me with a catlike smile.

My cry filled the carriage, and my juice spewed all over his hand again, to run down my naked legs. I was reduced to a quivering mass of mindless need, straddling a razor's edge of desire that refused to ebb.

'Please. Enough!' I pleaded, gripping his cloaked shoulders to retain my hold on reality.

'I don't suppose you've ever begged anyone to stop,' he remarked, leaning back against the seat to better observe my desperation. He clearly enjoyed holding me hostage this way, with just two fingers and a thumb that could send me into spasms again at his bidding.

'Can't say that I have. I – I didn't realise my endurance had limits.'

The angel-faced Meeh grinned then, and removed his dripping fingers from between my legs. 'In Satan, there *are* no limits, my sweet,' he said softly. 'We are there to live out our fondest fantasies – to indulge every whim without counting the cost. And it is I who allows it to be so.'

While he was lording it over me, as sure as I was dripping all over him, Devlin Meeh remained the image of understatement; the king of all he surveyed, demanding due homage.

I took a breath to collect myself, and then stood upright to remove my bosom from his face. 'Grant has told me wonderful things about your city. It seemed an invitation I couldn't refuse, at a time I needed it most.'

'That's what all our residents say. The pursuit of happiness is our only business, Rose, and we're so pleased you chose to join us. Nothing will ever be ordinary or mundane again, my love. I can promise you that!'

My heart sped into a girlish, gleeful beat, as though he'd just handed me the keys to his kingdom. The gruelling miles and weeks of my journey fell away, and for the first time since I could recall, I felt light-hearted. Excited about life!

And as my escort parted the curtains, I saw the gates of a magnificent city just ahead – a large archway that glowed crimson, as though the words WELCOME TO SATAN radiated with an infernal glow of their own. Beyond this grand entryway, the streets teemed with cavorting people, lifting glasses in a mass toast and dancing – some of them naked. Yet here it was November, in the Klondike! As we rolled past an opulent opera house, two saloons and a paradise of fine shops, I couldn't hold back an excited sigh.

'Everyone seems to be celebrating,' I remarked, unable to tear myself from the window. The women I saw were beautiful, arrayed in jewel-toned gowns of the finest fabrics, while the men all seemed extremely wealthy and debonair.

'Yes, I'm afraid we've just lost Pearly Gates. She was the madam of Satan's most exclusive parlour house, Le Coq D'Or.'

'Lost? As in ... passed away?' Then why were these people dancing in the streets? And why would a brothel have a door coated with sooty old coke?

'Precisely. The dear lady was challenged to bed every man in Satan, nonstop, and she died trying,' he explained. 'But Pearly went out happy, and she'll be forever immortalised as a saint who gave her all for the cause. I daresay ladies have died for lesser objectives.'

The raucous beat of a stage band sped my heartbeat up again as I considered this. Something seemed amiss, yet who was I to be the naysayer among so many revellers? I glanced at the man on the seat beside me, once again caught in the quick glimmer of his monocle ... this time seeing myself reflected there, dressed in finery beyond my wildest imaginings.

I blinked, and words tumbled out before I realised I was thinking them. 'And who will take the reins of the – what did you call it?'

'Le Coq D'Or – which means the Golden Cock.' Dr Meeh assessed me, his tawny gaze following the curve of my waist and hips along the length of my thighs. 'I'll be conducting auditions at the opera house, starting tomorrow. While the final decision will be mine, the audience will be cheering its favourites – and the candidates will play to a packed house.'

Visions of such public acclaim spurred my thoughts, and again I saw myself as I'd been reflected in Meeh's monocle for that brief, shining moment: resplendent in satins, bejewelled and beloved by all, as Pearly obviously was. What a contrast to my life in Oblivion, or to anywhere I'd ever lived for that matter!

Again I glanced out the window, caught up in the celebration of those who now waved and called out to us as the fine carriage made its way through the throng. So far, Satan was everything Grant Galloway had promised me – a hotbed of opportunity not to be missed!

It occurred to me then that my old flame had similar ambitions for me when he'd invited me to join him ... to be his angel again, in this oasis of delight that glowed like a hot coal in the wintry wilds of the Klondike.

'I want to audition for Pearly's place,' I stated, a brazen glee making me grin at my escort.

'And so you shall, my dear Miss DuBris. I thought you'd see it that way.'

6 **My Debut as an Angel**

As I watched the revellers from my hotel room, I had a hard time believing what I saw. On this November afternoon the sky was inky black, yet the scene below was clearly visible, lit by the crimson glow of street lamps with ruby glass domes. Hellish it looked, yet I couldn't take my eyes from the merrymakers dancing with such wild abandon. I'd heard Mardi Gras in New Orleans was a public orgy, and this couldn't be much different – except no one had a mask. Those who wore any clothes were dressed strictly for the provocative nature of them.

Wine and whisky flowed freely from nearby saloons, and across from my window Le Coq D'Or blazed with festive lanterns draped across its facade. Raucous laughter rose above the music of numerous stage bands and barroom pianos. People strolled the sidewalks in chummy clusters, glasses sloshing over, talking and laughing as though it were New Year's Eve rather than a wake for Pearly Gates.

I had a lot to live up to, if the madam had inspired this much celebration by dying at what she did best.

As I leaned against the window sill, my thoughts swirled through my tired mind. Where was Grant Galloway? How had Dr Meeh known when and where to find me? Had I really dropped my drawers in that carriage, for that odd little man who commanded it?

Ace Manley's warning about Meeh came back to me as I recalled the ermine cloak that shimmered like shifting snow, and the suit of clothes that changed colour when he moved. He looked all of fourteen, with that baby face – no sign of any facial hair, now that I thought about it. Yet the monocle and that voice bespoke a man much older than myself … a man who had things his way. When Devlin Meeh wasn't happy, *no one* was happy!

Yet he was a most accommodating host: he'd escorted me to this finely appointed room to get my rest. He'd invited me to the auditions for Pearly's replacement, so I could observe my competition. He would schedule me last, he said, since all the other candidates – madams from the other houses and a few girls wanting to better themselves in a big way – were familiar with how things happened in Satan.

'It's about playing out your fantasies,' he'd repeated as he left my room. 'Make a spectacle of yourself, Rose. Make those men in the audience jump from their seats and fuck you right there on the stage. The final decision's mine, but I must be sure the new madam will please everyone who sees her, as well.'

That was a whore's job, after all – pleasing. I was no stranger to the tricks of my trade, for before Jimmy's business left with the lumberjacks, I'd earned far more than any other local sporting girl. Probably because I refused to feel ashamed for a profession I was really good at, and because I wasn't afraid to flaunt myself. To hell with those goody-goodies who thought prostitution should be abolished! Those were the women who didn't – or wouldn't – give their men the satisfaction they sneaked into the brothels for.

I shut the window, crumpling with exhaustion. More than two thousand miles I'd travelled these past four months, and now that I'd arrived in Satan, I could get on with my new life. But first I planned to sleep like a hibernating bear, so I'd be at my best when I stepped onstage.

Meeh entered my room without knocking. He was lighting the candle on the night stand when I sat up in the canopied bed, clutching the satin sheet around my bare body, my eyes and mind still heavy with sleep. This time, my host was arrayed in royal blue: a suit cut to show his short, stubby body to best advantage, a blinding-white shirt and a cravat and matching pocket handkerchief in a print of mustard and red. He lifted the dome from his tray with a flourish, revealing a platter of spicy sausages, coddled eggs with cream sauce, generous slices of hot, fresh bread and a compote of fresh berries.

'Strawberries! And blueberries!' I exclaimed, eagerly settling the tray across my lap. 'How'd you find such fancy fruit – and so large – this time of year?'

Meeh smiled, hefting himself to sit on the edge of the bed. 'I thought you'd enjoy something special for your breakfast, after your long journey. Did you rest well, Rose?'

'Yes, thanks,' I replied between mouthfuls of the heavenly breakfast. 'First real bed I've slept in for awhile, so –'

'Audition well, and you'll claim a bed fit for a queen.'

He reached towards my plate with those pale hands, setting that huge ruby on fire when he plucked two large red raspberries from my bowl. I could only stare, speechless, as he lifted my bare breasts from the white satin sheets and deftly positioned one of the berries over each of my nipples.

'My breakfast,' he murmured, and then leaned forward to eat the nearest berry.

Once again his touch went through me like a jolt of

lightning. He'd made no sexual overtures, nor did I find him particularly attractive, yet Devlin Meeh's gentle chewing motion, as his lips lingered on the peak of my breast, made my nipples stick out so far the other berry dangled loosely.

He chuckled. 'Very sensitive to this, I see,' he said, stroking around the dark circle of my breast with the lightest touch of his fingertip.

I jumped, giggling nervously. 'You have a provocative touch,' came out before I knew I was saying so.

Devlin grinned again, his monocle glimmering in the candlelight. This time I caught the image of Grant Galloway flickering there – or was it my imagination? I hadn't seen him since we were young, yet I recognised the mature man immediately ... and had to wonder how such phenomena took place in Meeh's mysterious eyepiece.

I couldn't ask, however: the blond was shifting my tray to the bedside table, a purposeful expression on his face. Then he dipped towards me again, to swirl his tongue around my other breast before mashing the raspberry against my nipple with a forceful kiss. I gasped, writhing with the sudden hunger that made my cunt clench. He then suckled more urgently, his breath falling warm upon my skin as he covered my breast with hot, wet kisses and a suction designed to drive me out of my mind.

I fell back against the pillows and he followed, never releasing his insistent lips, yanking back the sheets to bare me completely. His hand wandered the hollows of my belly, kicking up a keen anticipation for where it would eventually land. And when my legs spread for him, of their own wanton accord, he slipped first one finger, and then two ... and then three inside me, gliding in and out with the slickness of my honey.

How many men had teased me this way? I couldn't

recall a single face or name – could only open for him and grip his fingers with a cunt that was on the verge of coming. He had me flopping like a fish, utterly out of control and in dire need of completion – and then he ran his tongue down my quivering midsection. When his lips found the ones between my legs, I cried out, thrusting into his face to relieve the burgeoning ache inside me. Meeh drank deeply, sucking and licking and opening my petals like a brazen bee seeking every last drop of nectar.

So frenzied the sensations became that I passed out. When I blinked back to consciousness, he was wiping his mouth on my linen napkin, chuckling as he glanced at my chest. 'Red's a good colour for you, my Rose. How fitting, for a woman of that name who's come to seek her fortune in Satan.'

Stained with the raspberry juice, my two breasts now sported blatant, wet peaks of scarlet. I laughed aloud, out of sheer amazement. 'How do you do this to me?'

And then I dared look him full in the face, directly into tawny eyes that gave me pause. 'And how did you know there'd be a gold rush?' I whispered. 'Grant's letter travelled thousands of miles, yet it arrived just as the first ships returning from the Klondike docked in San Francisco and Portland.'

He held my gaze for a moment, then slid off the side of the bed. 'An astute question. I admire your intelligence, Rose, and I look forward to all the time I can possibly spend with you. Most who come here have no idea about the whys and wherefores of this place. Nor do they care enough to question them.'

As he approached the window, I knew I'd get no real answer from him. Odd, since Meeh liked to boast about himself and his accomplishments. After a glance outside, where the darkness was softened only by the crimson shine of the street lights, he smiled in my direction. 'Auditions begin at ten, my dear. An usher will escort you to my balcony box, so you'll have the best possible vantage point.'

'I planned to find Grant Galloway first, so I could –'

'Make him wait. As you devise your audition, consider how best to astound and amaze him, when he sees the woman you've become. Some of his own girls are competing, so he'll be in the audience.'

Some of his own girls. I didn't need Meeh to clarify a phrase that told me what Grant's letter hadn't. Had my old flame hoped to entice me into *his* establishment? The thought dimmed my enthusiasm, for I'd assumed he wanted me and me alone. Yet it served as incentive, too. By God, if he ran a whorehouse and hadn't bothered to tell me that part, Rosie DuBris could show him a few of her own accomplishments!

'I'll leave you to your meal now.'

'Thank you,' I said, my mind already alight with possibilities. I would give an audition like the wild wantons of Satan had never seen. These people didn't know me now, but my name would be on their lips for days after I made my appearance on that stage.

I was expecting an usher in evening wear to whisk me up a back stairway when I arrived at the already crowded opera house, for I sensed Meeh was keeping me as his own secret. I was *not* expecting the imposing woman who sat beside him in his private box, and who towered above him when they stood at my arrival.

'Miss DuBris, how lovely to see you,' the elegant little man said. He wore a tuxedo of black brocade trimmed in gold that twinkled like his ring and his monocle. 'May I present my close associate, Venus? And Venus, this is Rose DuBris – the guest Grant Galloway has invited to Satan.'

In the dimness, all I could make out were the whites

of eyes and a malicious grin. When Venus stepped towards me, into the light from the wall sconces, her skin had the gloss of dark chocolate. How was it that everything associated with Devlin Meeh left me momentarily stunned? This woman – an Amazon beside the diminutive doctor, and his opposite in every physical feature – stood head and shoulders above me, yet moved with a feline grace that left me feeling awkward in comparison. Her gown, a rose-coloured satin, dipped low to expose the tops of her breasts. The biggest diamond brooch I'd ever seen nestled in the crack of her impressive cleavage, and matched the earrings that dangled from her large lobes. She wore long gloves of rose satin, and her ebony hair was swept above a tiara of diamonds and rose quartz, to fall in ringlets from her crown.

Venus was at once outrageous and intimidating.

'How nice to meet you,' I murmured, trying not to wince when she gripped my hand.

'*Nice* isn't in my vocabulary,' she barked. 'And don't think everything's going your way, just because Devlin's made you his special guest. He owns this town and made Satan what it is, but Venus rules. Understand me?'

How could I not? Her obsidian stare bored right through the most vulnerable spots of my soul, sapping the confidence I'd felt after Devlin's encouragement this morning.

'Anyone can see you're the queen,' I replied. 'No doubt in my mind that the citizens of Satan toe your royal line.'

Not a smile nor a softening of those hard, shiny eyes. Only a smirk, twisting lips that blossomed with a hint of rouge. 'Everything has its purpose, little girl. And the way I see it, *debris* should be disposed of.' With that, Venus placed her fingertip on my birthmark and pushed me back towards my seat, until I couldn't help falling into it.

This wasn't the first time someone had mocked my last name, but Venus's affront was more than insulting – it was unpardonable. This bitch knew nothing about me! I'd done nothing to provoke such rudeness. Yet I nipped my lip against a retort, for I sensed the blond man observing us was keen on my reaction. I sat as still as my anger would allow, my flared skirts hiding feet poised to kick her. I kept my eyes focused on hers, until Venus sat down.

As though this were the signal for everyone, the opera house went quiet. The final whisperings from those in the rows below us *hissed* like doused coals. Dr Meeh took his seat between us, and I perched on the edge of mine, poised to catch every performance from his box just above the end of the stage. Violins and horns squawked like jungle birds, tuning, and then silenced at the tapping of the conductor's baton. The heavy curtains parted in the middle, inching into the wings to reveal a backdrop of scarlet sequins. With the slow, suggestive beat of a deep drum, the auditions began.

I sat spellbound as sylphlike ladies – scantily clad and accentuating their assets – announced their names, and then strutted and stretched and ground their hips in the age-old dance of seduction. One buxom redhead was clad in peacock feathers that swirled around her bosoms and barely covered her bush, jutting up behind her like a plumed tail. Another – this one a lovely blonde – danced with abandon, her lithe body clearly visible beneath a filmy harem-girl costume as she accented the beats with her finger cymbals. A third contestant, jet-haired with a slender black mask, drew raucous applause and whistles for strutting out in a tight black harness, which left all her attributes on display as she cracked a riding crop against the stage floor.

Meanwhile, the orchestra was playing to incite the audience, and the responses grew louder with each performer. The men clearly preferred the harnessed contestant, yet I'd seen nothing that sporting girls everywhere didn't do – and from the corner of my eye, I judged Devlin Meeh's reactions to be just as lukewarm. Venus looked downright bored, but what did *she* know? She'd written me off as trash before I'd said a word!

And as the morning's final applicant undulated in a belly dance, wearing a fake emerald in her navel and not much else, I felt I had a fighting chance at Pearly's position. The orchestra's fanfare called all the contestants out for one last bow, to which Meeh responded by standing at his balcony and waving benignly to the overflowing crowd in the opera house. A man in a tuxedo announced a two o'clock resumption of the auditions, and then everyone thronged the aisles to leave.

'What do you think, Miss Rose? See anything that inspired you?'

I smiled at my host, who looked like a fair-haired choirboy dressed for a wedding. His eyes latched on to mine in the dimness of his candlelit opera box. What brazen, outrageous behaviour would convince him I deserved to replace Pearly Gates?

'I've been thinking about it, yes, and –'

'Pardon me. I have things to do,' Venus cut in. She caught Devlin's head in her broad hand and kissed him soundly, her chocolate nearly overwhelming his vanilla. He dismissed her with a swat to her bustled bottom. It was the first time I'd heard him laugh, the first time I'd seen him on the receiving side of aggressive affection.

I suddenly knew how to win this competition. 'If I hadn't left my pack in the blizzard –'

'My driver picked it up while we were getting

acquainted,' the little man replied, his eyes following Venus out the box's back door. 'But I confess, the contents of that sled surprised me.'

I smiled, for the next surprise would be mine. 'Good,' I replied, standing tall with the idea I had in mind. 'I'll be needing a kitchen, and some milk and sugar and eggs. And an audition time.'

His monocle flickered when he grinned. 'I'll schedule you as the last contestant. And you may have the run of my private kitchen and pantry. You've got my curiosity up, Miss Rose – what do you hope to accomplish here in Satan? What's your wildest, fondest fantasy, my dear?'

I leaned down to kiss his freckled nose. 'I came here to reunite with Grant Galloway. But now, I want to be the madam at Le Coq D'Or, Dr Meeh. More than that, I want to be the most celebrated, talked-about madam in Satan – or the whole world! I'll see you this afternoon, sir. I'm bubbling like a pot on a stove and I'll have this place boiling over, I promise you.'

Bold words for a little nobody from Oblivion, Oregon. But I had talents those other hookers couldn't hold a candle to – and I had something to *prove*, to Meeh and the surly Venus as well.

As the contestant before me completed her act – some impressive stunts, done naked on a trapeze – I scanned the audience from behind the stage curtain. The opera house was huge and I was guessing it seated six hundred, with some spectators standing in the back aisles as well. Who could've known such an outpost existed at the northernmost pole of the earth? And why had Grant Galloway ended up in a town that was one thriving den of iniquity after another? He'd come from such a respectable, prosperous family – cornerstones of their Denver community.

But then, who could've guessed this farmer's daughter would've ended up a whore? As the orchestra ushered the trapeze artist from the stage, I had no time to ponder such philosophical questions, however. I'd vowed to capture Meeh's vote and take his town by storm. I smiled at the stagehand beside me, nodding for him to drag the claw-footed bathtub to the centre of the stage.

A hush fell over the house. People leaned forward in their seats, curious about the brunette taking her place at one end of the unusual prop. I untied the sash of the white silk robe I wore and then shrugged to make the fine fabric whisper all the way down my bared body. Then I stepped languidly into the tub, gazing out over the crowd with my best, bravest smile.

'My name's Angel-Face,' I stated, allowing time for my low voice to carry to the back rows, 'and I'm standing in the world's largest bowl of chocolate pudding.'

I reached down to scoop up some pudding with both hands, and then spread it around my breasts with slow, circular motions. 'It's so fresh it's still warm ... with a meringue topping that's light and sweet and airy.'

Again I dipped down, to place a handful of the froth on the peak of each chocolate-covered breast. For effect, I closed my eyes and ran my extended tongue up my palm – then looked back at the crowd. 'Of course, the best part of warm chocolate pudding is tasting it, letting it fill your mouth with that deep, sweet creaminess. And if that's not enough to tempt you –'

I slowly lowered my whole body into the tub and then stood again, so the dark, rich pudding drifted down my breasts and my stomach and my legs. I caught some of it above each knee and ran my fingers up through it, leaving white trails in the chocolate that followed the curve of my inner thighs, trails that ended at my pussy.

'– then think of me as a live chocolate lollipop who wants to share herself – and her pudding – and become Satan's new sweetheart,' I enticed. 'Now which of you boys'll give this naughty little Angel-Face the licking she deserves?'

The clatter of a baton filled the stunned hall, and damned if the conductor wasn't the first to hurry forward! The stagehand and the announcer came next, their tongues extended in their excitement. As those three mouths claimed my breasts and my backside, the aisles of the opera house clogged with all the men wanting a taste of me.

Pandemonium broke out. I was vaguely aware of boots thundering up the stairs and a rush of male bodies surrounding my tub. By then, it was a challenge to avail myself to everyone demanding an inch or two of my coated flesh. Again and again I was dunked, sloshing the chocolate over the sides of the tub as my enthusiastic admirers drew me up to lick and suck the sweetness from my skin. I was giggling uncontrollably, a victim of my own come-on being passed from hand to hand. Some laved my nipples, while others slurped between my legs and any other piece of me they could reach.

'Angel-Face! Where you been all my life?'

'Lemme at her! Gimme a taste of that chocolate pussy!' they brayed.

Again I was dunked, and again I was covered with mouths lusting after my butt, my breasts, my elbows – the darling of a good-natured group who couldn't get enough of me. When I noticed Devlin Meeh approaching from the wings, I smiled: his expression was downright gleeful as he made his way through the boisterous crowd. My hair had fallen askew and was saturated with pudding, and parts of my body sported teeth-marks I'd nurse for days. But I'd created quite a stir! And I was enjoying it as much as anyone else.

Then I heard the voice that had deepened some since my childhood.

'Rosie!' he called out, making me swivel my head to find his face in the crowd. 'Rosie DuBris, you ornery puss! Why didn't you come find me when you arrived?'

It was like the parting of the Red Sea for the Israelites: at the sound of that commanding voice the revellers stood aside, so I had a straight shot at his face as he strode up to the stage.

Grant Galloway had matured into a striking man, with feline green eyes that could still see through a girl's clothes, and a lean face accented by deep, vertical dimples. Judging from the crowd's reaction, my old flame had indeed assumed a mayor's place. His expression bespoke a fellow who was pretty impressed with himself, as well.

I was still being held between four or five admirers, who set me gently on my feet in the tub. My heart was pounding so hard the pudding dribbled off the tips of my nipples. Here was the man I'd left Oregon – my entire known world – for. But I wouldn't come running just because he wagged his finger!

'Beg pardon?' I replied. 'I couldn't hear you for all the slurping.'

The opera house fell silent, everyone caught up in the exchange between Grant Galloway and this woman he'd called by a different name. He hooked his thumbs into his back belt loops, calling attention to hard, slender hips and an alluring bulge in the front of his black pants.

'I *said*, why did you ask where I was?' he demanded. 'I invited you here as my guest, Miss DuBris. I had no idea you'd give yourself to every other man in town without at least saying hello first.'

I crossed my arms, to keep them from flopping nervously at my sides. This pushed my pudding-coated breasts at him in blatant invitation, but I kept my voice dead-level serious. 'I travelled more than two thousand miles, nearly vomited myself overboard on the ship, and almost froze to death in a blizzard to get here, Grant. Seems the least you could do was come to Satan's gate to greet me.'

A murmur went through the men around us as they sized me up with new interest, and then turned to catch Grant's reaction. His face hardened, but he recovered quickly when he saw Devlin Meeh on the other side of the stage.

'This conversation's best held in private,' he said in a low voice. 'You can usually find me at the Brazen Lady, but maybe Angel-Face'll be too busy running her own house to visit mine. That'd be a shame, after all the years I've worked my way up the ladder, hoping to share a finer life with you, sweetheart.'

He turned on his boot heel and strode off, leaving behind a crowd of murmuring men who'd cooled like the pudding in the bottom of my tub. I wanted to hurl a pithy remark after him but didn't, when I saw Devlin Meeh coming towards me. This time my admirers stepped back further, acknowledging the supreme leader of Satan – a man who inspired as much fearful respect as he did admiration.

'Well, Miss Du – or shall I say Angel-Face? – you've certainly taken Satan by storm!' he declared, chuckling with the crowd around him. Then he raised his arm ceremoniously, addressing those in the balconies and in the main theatre.

'It's clear this young lady would make a fitting replacement for our beloved Pearly Gates,' he called out, 'and she's displayed a delightful sense of playfulness, along with the level-headed savvy required to run Satan's most illustrious parlour house. However –'

The opera house grew as silent as a church at prayer.

Myself, I stood up to my ankles in pudding, my body smeared with the remains of my licking, suddenly apprehensive at the turn of this man's phrase.

Had I disappointed him somehow? Did he disapprove of the way I'd treated Grant? If I'd insulted the Mayor of Satan, perhaps I'd also cooked my goose with the town's founding father. Perhaps I'd just written my own ticket back to Oblivion, only a day after I'd arrived, by shooting off my smart mouth. I swallowed so hard my throat clicked.

'– after assessing the auditions of all our candidates, I've decided my assistant Venus will best replace the madam of Le Coq D'Or –'

A murmur snaked through the crowd, punctuated by the 'Go fuck yourself!' that drew all eyes to the balcony box. The woman in question glared down toward the stage, her body stiff with anger.

'– because I have other plans for this lovely new angel in our midst. Thank you all for your participation,' he crowed, both arms raised in benediction. 'Make our new madam welcome, and we shall spend the evening in celebration!'

As the excited crowd made for the doors, and the orchestra struck up a triumphal march, Meeh stepped up beside me with a smile I didn't know how to interpret. Once again that monocle flickered, and I was filled with awe and fear at the glimpse of Jimmy Crystal's face, looking cold and tired and unshaven this time. Why did that damn lens make me go all funny inside, seeing things I couldn't explain, things that simply could not be?

'What does this mean?' I murmured, gingerly taking the hand Meeh extended.

'It means I have a new mistress. And Satan now has an Angel.'

7 A Threat and a Promise

I stood there in the tub, on that opera house stage, basking in the glow of a golden-eyed gaze like I'd never known. Devlin Meeh still held my hand, as though he were about to lead me into the centre of a ballroom for a grand waltz ... as though I were dressed in finery like his own. Like a queen.

Then his face lit in a grin. 'Coat yourself in the last of this pudding, Angel. I can resist just about anything in this world, except chocolate. And the thought of eating it off your luscious body excites me in ways I haven't felt for *years*.'

That was awe I heard; the same sort of exuberance I'd felt when I came up with this brazen idea, and then had all those men rushing up to devour me. The pudding was only ankle-deep now, so I lowered myself slowly, holding his eyes with mine as I wallowed in the dark, creamy chocolate. With a sultry laugh, I scooped the pudding over my breasts and then cupped it against my pussy, delighting in the way those tawny eyes followed my every move. When had I ever had such an ardent admirer?

I stood then, letting the soft pudding drift down my body. Over my curves it slithered, dripping from my nipples and down the hollow of my belly to catch in the coarse hair between my legs. For several moments, Devlin drank me in with his eyes as though I were too beautiful for words. Again he took my hand, to stroke my palm with a dainty, catlike lick that made me quiver inside.

'Why are you doing this?' I murmured, sighing with the sensations of his mouth closing around each of my fingers. 'I'm nothing special, you know. Just your average –'

'Ah, but that's where you short-change yourself, my dear. Not only are you lovely, but you've displayed an indomitable spirit I find extremely attractive. You have a power within you akin to my own, and I simply must explore it. Nurture it.'

His lips wandered up my arm then, lingering in the ticklish spot inside my elbow until I giggled like a little girl.

'You see, Angel, most people in this world – including those who come to Satan – limit themselves to the lives they're familiar with. They dream of *what* they can become, rather than whom,' he went on in a mystical voice. 'Why be just the madam of my finest parlour house, when you can be my queen? Why be at the beck and call of every man who wants to fuck you, when you can belong to one who'll bestow great wealth and favour? Most of our residents must abide by Satan's irrefutable rules, but you, Angel-Face, have been lifted above such things. If you'll give yourself only to me.'

Devlin Meeh focused those insistent eyes upon me again and I sucked in my breath. His monocle glimmered in the candlelight, with the briefest suggestion of Jimmy Crystal's frost-bitten face. He was asking me to forsake all I'd had with my former partners – and all I'd hoped to know about the man who enticed me here.

'I'm to swear off other lovers? Completely?' I breathed, watching in awe as his mouth moved over my shoulder, preparing to claim my breast.

'Yes. For the privileges I'm about to share with you, that's a paltry sacrifice, my dear. If you can't agree to my terms, speak now or forever hold your peace.'

It was a vow I hadn't anticipated. Yet here in the

land where the midnight sun wouldn't show itself again for weeks, so far from all I'd known in Oregon, what did I have to lose? Grant Galloway's arrogance had sorely disappointed me, so I felt no allegiance to him whatsoever. After all, I hadn't *asked* him to pay my way or invite me here. I'd endured illness and the brutal elements – a great physical ordeal – to discover, in a few short sentences, that the dream which had kept me trudging those thousands of miles would never come true.

'Thank you,' I murmured. 'I accept your most gracious offer, Dr Meeh. I'll be yours and yours alone.'

I blinked then, realising he'd held that magnificent ruby ring in my line of vision ... recalling the warning in Ace Manley's goodbye, about this man not being what he seemed. And yet, as I felt my fate being sealed, I also believed I'd raised myself to new heights – in a land of limitless possibilities and pleasures!

'Let me take this stunning tuxedo off you,' I whispered. 'Let me fondle you and please you the way you're teasing at me.'

Meeh stepped away, grinning. 'Later,' he said in a voice lush with promise. 'I haven't finished with your initiation.'

With that, he stuck out his tongue and flicked my nearest nipple into a hard bud that ached with excruciating need. I moaned, letting my head fall back, longing for fuller contact over my entire body from a man who seemed intent on bestowing pleasure that might last the rest of the day. No more 'slam-bam, thank you, ma'am'! No more brief couplings that sated male lust but left me feeling empty and used!

'Step out of the tub, dear heart,' he whispered. 'Brace yourself on your arms and part those long, lovely legs. That's it – stick your brazen little backside in my face.'

How I endured his thorough mouth and the sensations that ran amok, I don't know. Meeh went for all my sweet spots, teasing behind my knees and lapping at my pussy lips from behind, making ravenous little moans as he cleared my entire body of the chocolate pudding. I couldn't stop laughing, gasping at the exquisite torture of his tongue as he licked and laved and made me shiver with exhilarating need. My cries echoed in the empty opera house, each one louder than the last.

'Now, turn around and sit against the rim,' he instructed softly. 'Lean back and spread your legs, Angel. Open yourself to me, completely.'

As though entranced, I followed his command. I balanced my weight carefully on the edge of the tub, gripped the rim behind me and then exposed myself to his gaze as he knelt between my spread knees. I marvelled at how he'd cleared most of my body of that dark brown pudding yet hadn't gotten a single drop on his snowy-white shirt or his tuxedo. And then I clenched with anticipation as his fingertips grazed the insides of my thighs, and his pink, extended tongue approached my pussy. Suddenly I was wet with a cream far more pungent than chocolate, and Devlin Meeh seemed ravenous for it.

When he touched my clit with the tip of that tongue, I screamed. My legs flew apart, inviting – no, begging – him to suck and nip and nibble until I collapsed with a climax. But Meeh was nothing if not the ultimate tease: with delicate strokes, he parted my cream-coated folds, cleaning each with a control that threatened to send me over the edge.

'Please,' I pleaded, unable to keep myself still for him. 'Suck me harder. Lord, Devlin, just stick that tongue up me and fuck me with it!'

With a low laugh, he continued his slow, torturous attentions, running the point of his tongue around the rim of my hole to incite more inner riots before taking occasional aim at my clit. The little shaft was so engorged it was poking out from beneath my thatch, between quivering lips that burned for more solid contact.

'So responsive,' he whispered, chuckling as I bucked against his curious fingertip. 'So pink and pretty down here, aren't you, my sweet? So fucking lovely, I might just keep you hanging on the edge for days –'

'No,' I moaned.

'– unless you beg me to finish you,' he added, keeping my tension high with the lightest circlings of his manicured nails. 'I want you to come so hard you shoot your juice all over my face, Angel.'

How many times had I been splattered that way, when a man shot his wad after withdrawing from my mouth? To have someone request such a climax from me seemed a bit daunting, for I'd never consciously squirted anyone. Yet as my muscles clenched and squeezed with my desire for completion, I knew I'd do anything Devlin Meeh demanded, to gratify us both.

And moments later, when he lifted my fleshy pad higher to expose my folds, and then thrust his thumb inside me, flicking his tongue against my clit, I let go with a colossal surge. Cream spurted from deep inside me. I kept pumping because I couldn't stop, writhing with a climax that came over me with a desperation I couldn't restrain – a force that took me by storm and left the evidence of my pleasure dripping from Meeh's nose and upper lip.

The little man rocked backward until he sat hard on the stage, his laughter ringing around the vast expanse of the opera house. He licked my cream from his mouth and then wiped his monocle with his bright yellow handkerchief.

'Good show!' he crowed, his body shaking with his

mirth. 'My God, girl, if there's ever a fire, I'll send you to put it out!'

I laughed, still weak from my climax, somehow more pleased with myself than I'd ever been. I'd gushed all over him and he loved it! I was about to reply with my appreciation, when wild applause broke out from the orchestra pit.

I thought we were alone. So engrossed in Meeh's mesmerising attentions I'd been, I had no idea we'd played to an audience of bright-eyed blondes – three perky young women who were so much the spitting image of each other, they had to be triplets.

'Bravo!' one called out, while the centre reveller placed her thumb and forefinger to her lips to give a loud, shrill whistle that filled the hall. The third girl kept clapping, and then stood to lead their ovation before the rows of empty theatre seats.

From the corner of my eye, I thought I saw the bustle of a rose-coloured gown disappearing out the side door. But I was too drawn in by the accolades of our admirers to wonder if that was Venus, and if she'd had something to do with positioning these three ladies while I was caught up in the throes of my initiation.

Devlin, meanwhile, was rising to his feet, observing our observers with an expression I couldn't read. He seemed as surprised as I that we'd been watched, yet that shuttered look of utmost control had now replaced his previous glee.

'Good afternoon, ladies,' he said in a courtly voice. 'You've been a most courteous, attentive audience. How kind of you, to regale my mistress with your applause.'

'We wanted to be –'

'– the very first –'

'– to greet your new queen,' they responded, going from left to right in rapid succession, without pausing for thought or breath.

I put my legs together, gaping at them. They made an impressive trio, decked out in gowns of emerald that brought out their expressive green eyes, with every golden head of hair coiffed alike and adorned with a large pink rosebud.

Meeh cleared his throat with an indulgent little bow. Then he smiled at me. 'Allow me to present the Titzler triplets – Zelda, Nelda and Esmerelda. Three of Satan's more ... provocative citizens.'

They tittered, pleased to be noted as notable. Their eyes swept over my nakedness, as though they, too, had a taste for chocolate but knew better than to partake while Meeh was present.

'And this, as you know, is Angel,' he went on in a purposeful tone. 'And she – as you know – is mine.'

Something about those last words struck me as odd. Yet as the trio rose to go, their faces radiated a childlike glee.

'We're also the KlonDykes – the stage band at the Brazen Lady,' said Zelda and, as she bobbed in a curtsy, Nelda added, 'We hope you'll come hear us play.'

The ripple of triple curtsies continued, and then Esmerelda chimed in.

'You'll never guess where we wet our reeds.'

All of a piece they exited the pit, their gowns shimmering in rhythm as they walked quickly up the carpeted aisle, arm in arm. 'Doesn't *she* look tasty?' one murmured.

'How'd you like to make those wings –'

'– flutter like an angel afire?' the other two remarked. The three of them giggled as one, each one's voice indiscernible from her sisters'.

We watched until they left the hall, and then Meeh picked up my white robe from the stage. 'Let's get you home before we attract another audience. You'll be the subject of enough gossip, once word gets around about your new status. The world that's walked in darkness is about to see a great light.'

Out back we went, to Meeh's plush carriage. The ride through Satan seemed tamer than my initial entry, perhaps because people had gone home to prepare themselves for another evening's revelry – or to ponder the result of the auditions. I had trouble telling what time it was, for during these winter months near the Arctic Circle, the sunless days were as dark as night. My body longed to rest, to catch up after my difficult journey as well as recover from my debut at the opera house. But my host refused to let me drift off.

'There it is, Angel, your new home,' he said, pointing out the window towards the foothills at the end of Main Street. 'You'll have your own suite, of course, and complete freedom to come and go as you please. My first order of business will be to clear out Venus's personal effects, but after that you'll be queen of my castle!'

And quite a castle it was, rising up like the pointed peaks of the misted mountains behind it, in turreted towers and fortresslike walls of stone. No doubt Meeh could host events for the entire population, large as the place was, yet it seemed shrouded in more an aura of warning than of welcome. I shivered, taking in the fiendish glow of the ruby-shaded lamps that lit our way up the winding road.

'A hot bath and a good meal will cure what ails you, my pet,' Devlin murmured, kissing my temple. 'My maid will see to these things while I help Venus pack. Faren Poole's a darling girl. She'll make you a perfect servant.'

Servant? Lord, I'd never thought to have one of those! And when she greeted us in the entry hall, bowing low enough that her budding breasts showed in the gap of her low-cut black uniform, I was immediately taken with her. Shiny auburn ringlets bounced around her impish face, which was freckled and free of cosmetic enhancement. In a place like Satan, such innocence shone like a beacon: refreshing, yet I wondered how much longer she'd be spared the wicked ways of this hedonistic little world.

'Faren, this is my Angel, and I'm trusting you to take the best care of her,' Meeh said.

'It'll be my pleasure, sir. She's all the talk, after whipping up that vat of chocolate pudding in the kitchen – and winning the competition, of course.' Faren beamed at me like a schoolgirl who felt herself the teacher's pet. 'You'll be quite comfortable here, Angel. I'll see to it myself.'

She held out her hand, like a child wanting to show her mama a secret hideaway. Her grip was firm and her pace a lively one as our steps echoed in the cavernous entryway. When we came to a marble staircase, I ascended at a trot to keep up with her. In her black dress and ruffled white pinafore, with her slender legs bare above white knee-high stockings and shiny black shoes, Faren looked like an Irish doll in French maid's clothing. Yet something in her manner bespoke maturity – and if Meeh had put her in charge of his queen, I had to think she'd been in his service for quite a while.

She flung open a white door at the end of the second-level corridor and gestured for me to enter. I stepped inside, on to plush carpeting of purest white, into a room that resembled heaven. The walls, the crown moulding and all the furniture and linens were white, too – so breathtaking I found myself whispering, 'For me? I'm to have this beautiful suite?'

'And anything else you desire.' Faren leaned against the door to close it, studying me with a speculative once-over. 'Between you, me and those bedposts, Angel

– I'll take *great* pleasure in serving you. Venus has a cruel streak, and it was a relief that she preferred to bathe, dress and coif herself, and expected no further ... satisfaction from me.'

The tone of that childlike voice made me return Faren's thorough gaze. Beneath that freckled face lay a secret that intrigued me, to the point I decided to ask about it outright. 'What brought you to Satan, into Meeh's service? He's told me everyone here is fulfilling a fantasy.'

'I'm very, very *good* at servicing,' she replied with a catlike smile. 'And in return, I'll never have to grow up. Or grow old.'

I blinked. Such a response convinced me further that this saucy redhead was no more a child than I was, yet she stood only to my shoulder. And in that juvenile uniform, which hid the mere suggestions of breasts ...

'How old *are* you?' I demanded.

Her green eyes glistened. 'No one knows. All that really matters, here at Meeh's palace, is that everyone he loves receives the utmost in care and attention. I've already surmised that, unlike Venus, you won't let your elevated station make you a pain in the ass. I'll run you a bath and fetch your dinner, milady. You'll feel like a new woman after Faren Poole sees to you.'

She crossed the room, past the magnificent four-poster festooned in white lace, through another doorway. The sound of water running into a tub beckoned me, into a bathroom where the walls shone like the white porcelain fixtures and the steamy air was scented with heather. In the corner stood a sink and a water closet with a wall tank and pull chain – far more modern than most places I'd lived – and a shorter porcelain seat with a faucet on the front. I studied this as I unfastened my robe.

'It's a bidet,' Faren explained with a lift of an expressive red eyebrow. 'A French invention for washing up after sex. Useful for other needs as well.'

With that she left me, and as I gratefully climbed into the tub filling with hot, foamy water I pondered what she might mean. I'd heard of those contraptions, and a woman of my ilk could certainly appreciate the convenience of washing up between customers. I let the rest go, however, content to drift in the hot water as it rinsed away the remains of my chocolate audition.

I was nearly asleep when voices on the other side of the wall jarred me from my languid state. Devlin Meeh's tone brooked no argument, but Venus was giving him a heated earful, anyway.

'You'll be sorry you treated me this way! I'm not some common whore –'

'You're who I've made you, my obsidian princess.'

'– who'll take your orders lying down –'

'Then stand up. You're certainly the mistress of many positions.'

Something shattered against the wall behind me. I hugged my knees, as though this might shield me from any other missiles, yet I listened intently, too. Such a fight between the master of Satan and his paramour could prove enlightening, considering how I'd replaced her in ways I had yet to figure out. Faren entered the bathroom then, and leaned down near my ear.

'Venus's suite adjoins this one, and she's refusing to leave,' the girl whispered. 'You've caused quite a stir, Angel-Face, because Her Majesty in Black has ruled Satan alongside Meeh since any of us can remember.'

'I didn't *ask* to be his –'

'Doesn't matter. Devlin has a very strong reason for his decision, and everyone – even the high and mighty Venus – must bow to his wishes.'

Another crash against the wall made me wince.

'Such behaviour doesn't become you, Venus.' Meeh's

voice sounded steelier now – far different from the way he'd talked to me. 'I've decided upon a new path for the people of Satan, and I'm working this purpose out with Angel. If you won't take Pearly's place, go below to oversee my salt mines.'

'Like *hell* I will, you conniving little –'

'Then your only choice is to leave. *Now*, before I become any angrier with you.'

There was a pause. My heart fluttered uncomfortably.

'Consider this carefully, my ebony princess,' Meeh went on. 'Here, you've spun a web that keeps your appetites appeased, whereas beyond the gates of Satan you'll be a misfit wandering in an unforgiving wilderness. Now, what'll it be?'

Venus let out an unladylike snort. 'Your little angel won't fly so high once her wings get clipped. You'll cast her aside, once I –'

'I always win, Venus. Never forget that.'

I held my breath, awaiting the hostile woman's reply. Somehow, the silence rang louder than their argument.

I shivered in bath water growing cold, pondering what I'd just overheard – and the many unexpected things I'd encountered since Dr Meeh rescued me from that blizzard. How could this pocket of civilisation escape the harsh climate of the Klondike? And how did Meeh exert such absolute control over an entire town – and especially over a militant, wilful woman like Venus? What did those mysterious images in his monocle mean, and why was I obeying the outrageously attired lump of a man who wore it? So far, the picture of Satan that Grant had painted in his letter rang true only on the surface: I sensed a dangerous undercurrent here, which would trap me in its undertow if I weren't extremely careful.

And how could Faren Poole remain a child – at least in appearance?

As though she'd caught my mental cue, the maid's coppery ringlets quivered as she removed her pinafore. 'You're thinking too much, Angel,' she murmured. 'It's best not to let your mind wander beyond certain limits. Better to play out your pleasures, as I've learned to do. Here – let me show you.'

8 **Brazen Ladies**

Without a hint of coyness, Faren stepped out of her short black uniform and stood naked before me. I could only stare, for she had the undefined features of a young girl: those little buds on her chest had been arrested before they could bloom, and her abdomen gave way to a hairless pink cleft between her legs. She smiled with all the wiles of a practised courtesan, yet when she stooped to remove her white stockings, I saw that her backside, too, was flat rather than flared with womanly curves.

'Here's the best use for a bidet, Angel,' she said with a confiding grin. 'Not nearly as messy or demanding as a man, and every bit as satisfying because we can control the sensations. Determine timing and pressure – even temperature – to suit our bodies' whims.'

I sat riveted, watching her straddle the short porcelain fixture, facing me. With illicit glee, she cranked the handles until water shot into the basin. 'Me, I like it hot and hard against my clitty. I wiggle into the best positions, while the water pummels my puss until I can't help screaming. It seems to go on and on when I bring myself off this way. How about you, Angel? How do *you* like it?'

I was too astounded to answer. I hadn't known this curious creature for even an hour and she was describing, in great detail, how she liked to climax. She awaited my reply, but it didn't stop her from fondling herself, slipping her fingers between her parted legs to spread her wetness around the pouting pink lips of her slit. A telltale rosiness coloured her cheeks, and I felt my own temperature rise despite the cooling of my bath water.

Faren squatted then, positioning her privates near the stream of hot water. With forked fingers, she raised her bare cushion of flesh and then splashed her exposed petals, which flushed a deeper shade of red. While I'd seen other sporting girls undress and titillate themselves to arouse their guests, I'd never witnessed such blatant stimulation – or seen, in such intimate detail, those intricate folds and a clit stiffening above a tight, flexing hole. When Faren slapped herself, fast, with the flat of her hand, the splattering sound filled the bathroom and made my inner muscles bunch.

What sort of fascination was this, that I couldn't look away? The maid seemed oblivious to my stares. Her hips wiggled forward and back, allowing the water to stimulate the sensitive flesh from her clit down past her hole, and then quickly back again. Her moans started low and crescendoed. She turned the faucets as far as they'd go, making the water rush against her with even more force. Her body tightened, and those little pink nipples rose like rounded buttons. Faren sounded close to coming – so close, my own fingers found a similar path. My inflamed pussy closed and clenched around them.

With a flick of her hand, the redhead flipped the faucet upward, then hunched above the driving spray as though she were humping a hot, hard erection. Her whimpers grew desperate, filling the steamy room and leaving me no choice but to whisper my own need for release as I squeezed my engorged folds. I was ready to explode when Devlin Meeh stepped in.

He was naked, as chubby and boyishly built as I'd guessed, with a miniature prick that went straight for

Faren's open hole. She screamed when he entered her from behind, and the two of them thrashed and writhed and splashed hot water all over the bathroom. His hands spanned her chest, catching those baby nipples between his splayed fingers. He rutted rapidly against her backside, as though his speed and stamina might compensate for his lack of size.

Devlin's eyes squeezed shut. His monocle tinkled to the wet floor. 'Faren ... my darling, my little princess,' he murmured, clutching her hips against his crotch. With an excruciating grunt, he climaxed. Then he crumpled against her back to catch his breath.

With surreptitious fingers, Faren flicked her clit and then got caught up in her own spasms. I surged against my hand, thrusting deep inside myself to seek a release quiet enough not to attract attention. On and on I throbbed, until I exhaled and fell against the back of the tub.

When the maid shut off the tap, the bathroom sighed with silence. Meeh released her, reaching for a white towel that hung by the sink. He dried himself with light, fastidious pats, lingering over the balls beneath his little paunch. Then he retrieved his monocle, patted his reddish-blond hair into place, and let out a sigh of utter satisfaction.

'Let's dress and go out on the town now, Angel,' he said. 'I'll show you around, so when I'm occupied with other business, you can amuse yourself.'

He stepped towards the door then and, with a wink back at the maid, he said, 'Thank you, Faren. You're a dream come true.'

The streets were thronged with people seeking an evening's entertainment – yet I wondered how, in this season of perpetual darkness, they distinguished between night and day. When did the citizens of Satan sleep? Indeed, it seemed everything about this town went against the rules governing the universe I knew.

As I strolled along on Devlin's arm, accepting the compliments and congratulations of those we met, I got an inkling of how it felt to be queen. Never before had I worn such finery: a stylish gown of patterned satin in scarlet, set off by a dazzling sapphire choker. Faren had arranged my hair around a nosegay of red roses and brushed my cheeks and lips with rouge. For the first time in my life I felt beautiful. And for the first time, I realised what power came with such physical perfection, because attractive people I'd never met admired me openly, as though eager to do my bidding.

'I've made the right choice,' Meeh said, patting my hand. He himself looked extremely dapper in a suit of deep green, with a cream-coloured shirt. 'Venus has always commanded respect, but people react to her out of fear rather than a desire for her friendship. You'll do well here, Angel. I knew you would.'

And what price will I pay? echoed in my mind, but I pushed the thought aside. Best, as Faren had said, not to ponder serious realities too long. Especially since I was eager to see this empire Meeh had created in these wintry hinterlands, where we could walk the streets in late November wearing no wraps. It was as though the ruby street lamps kept the fierce Arctic weather at bay – a magic similar to Meeh's monocle, which I sensed I didn't understand, and sensed I should never, never question.

'And here we have the bank,' Devlin was saying with a grandiose gesture. 'Not that anyone requires money in Satan. I see that all their needs are met – fulfilling the fantasy that they have the means to buy anything and everything they might possibly desire. Or to lose huge sums at the gaming tables and suffer no ill effects.'

'And what do they do in return?' I couldn't imagine a life where money was only a prop. I'd had to work hard for the few things I ever attained.

'They follow my rules: they invite their friends to join them here, and they indulge and enjoy themselves – but only to the point that it doesn't interfere with anyone else's fantasy.'

'And when it does?'

'That's where Venus comes in.' His cherubic face tightened, perhaps as he recalled his argument with the dark virago, but also with a wicked glint of satisfaction. 'She's devised an ingenious method for dealing with those who disrupt others' happiness. A unique brand of punishment that convinces most backsliders never to disobey again.'

'And if they do?' We were passing a row of gaming establishments, alight with coloured lanterns and humming with musical entertainment, as well as an ambiance of splendour.

'They go below, to work in my salt mines.' Meeh looked up at me, his boyish face utterly serious beneath that thatch of shiny hair. 'That's where I've made my fortune, Angel. All the world needs salt, and vast veins of it lie beneath this region.'

'Like the gold the prospectors are after?'

He smiled indulgently. 'Only fools lust after that stuff. Long after their false hopes have sent them home, I'll be prospering off a much more precious commodity, my dear. But I won't mislead you – the slaves who mine it suffer a bleak life in the bowels of the earth, as punishment for not following my rules. I sincerely hope you'll never find out first-hand.'

His warning, couched in courtly phrases, was certainly clear enough as he held my gaze. Then his monocle twinkled with his grin. 'We've come to Grant Galloway's establishment, the Brazen Lady. Why not have a look inside while I see how Venus is settling in? I'll return for you shortly.'

Devlin lingered over kissing my hand, and then sauntered across Main Street, greeting everyone with cheerful handshakes and claps on the back. While I didn't relish meeting up with Grant again, after the way he'd snubbed me at the opera house, this was the perfect opportunity to see how well he'd done for himself – to see if he'd written me the truth, and perhaps figure out the real reason behind his letter. He'd paid my way here, after all. He'd wanted something other than to say hello again after all these years.

I opened the door, noting THE BRAZEN LADY and GRANT GALLOWAY, PROP. in gold-leaf script on the glass panel, and stepped into a world like Jimmy Crystal could only dream about. The massive carved bar took up an entire wall to my right, glimmering with hundreds of liquor bottles and a bevelled glass mirror that spanned most of its length. Crystal chandeliers hung from the ornately painted ceiling, and the dark-scarlet walls and carpet bespoke an ostentatious elegance. Several well-dressed men sat sipping drinks, their smiles speculative as they figured out who I was, and why I might be here.

From the rear came the clittering of dice thrown against craps tables, the drone of dealers calling for bets at roulette and Twenty-One, and announcing numbers for keeno. At the very back of this immense establishment a stage spanned the wall, and ladies wearing beaded Indian headdresses and artfully arranged feathers were dancing to the suggestive beat of a stage band.

I strolled that direction out of sheer curiosity, to survey Grant's domain, and to observe the Titzler triplets before they caught sight of me. Even the smoke from choice cigars and fragrant pipes bespoke wealth, drifting in a lazy haze above the tables where gentlemen placed bets that could've fed the entire town for a year.

Why wasn't I surprised that the trio of sprightly blonde clarinet players was as scantily-clad as the ladies they played for? Zelda, Nelda and Esmerelda wore fringed leather vests that exposed their bare breasts and arms. When they stood up, marching in a tight circle to bring the song to a raucous finale, I saw gun belts buckled above their bare bottoms, with holstered pistols strapped to their thighs. They blew a final chord, and then turned to face the audience.

My jaw dropped. Between their legs, they were as bare as Faren.

'Well, if it isn't Satan's new Angel!' the one farthest to the left crowed.

'Here to bless us with her heavenly presence –'

'– and maybe flutter her pretty pink wings at us!' the other two concluded. In a twinkling they'd laid their instruments on the stage and surrounded me, their smiles bright with anticipation.

'I – I only came to say hello,' I stammered.

'We KlonDykes only know one way to get acquainted,' the triplet in front of me hinted.

'Like dogs sniffing one another –'

'– so we can identify you by your personal scent.'

Bad enough that these three looked so identical; I couldn't discern Esmerelda from Nelda or Zelda. When the blonde at my right lifted the hem of my gown, grinning wickedly, I kicked at her hand. 'Stop it right now, you –'

I gasped when a pistol pressed into my back. The two girls I could see reached for their guns, too. Their lush breasts bobbed in the vees of their rawhide vests as they grabbed me with their other hands. 'We're not going to hurt you, Angel. We're only –'

'– living out our fantasy as lawless robbers, roaming the streets –'

'– raping and ransacking,' the blonde facing me finished. 'But the people here are so eager to play along, we've never taken anyone against her will.'

My heart pounded as I tried to reason out their rapid-fire dialogue. Devlin Meeh's warning about hindering people's happiness rang fresh in my mind. But what about *my* happiness?

'Fine and dandy,' I retorted, 'but *my* fantasy is to be the world's most illustrious madam, which means I don't have to let just *anyone* paw at me and –'

'Well, you're certainly dressed for the part, Rosie,' a male voice vibrated from across the room. 'Now what seems to be the trouble? I won't tolerate any cat fights. The players here wager great amounts, and they can't be distracted.'

From the grips of the Titzler triplets, I glared at Grant Galloway. He cut an impressive figure in his white tie and tails, the black tuxedo hugging his body as he stopped before me, his hands on his hips. He looked so lean and mean his dimples could've been cuts from a knife fight, and his eyes – a luminous, silvery-green – took on a feline glimmer in the low light from the chandeliers.

'Call off your dogs, dammit,' I muttered, trying to shrug out of the triplets' grasp. 'They're sniffing at me like bitches in heat and –'

'And you haven't seen the half of it yet, sweetheart,' Grant replied. 'Anyone who sets foot in my establishment plays by my rules.'

He flashed the girls a grin then, obviously enjoying this unexpected turn of events. 'Have your way with her, ladies – your reward for being such a fine stage band, and such a feisty band of outlaws! It's not every day we entertain Satan's Angel, and we'll show her our best hospitality.'

I shrieked when they tipped me backwards, to be caught by the triplet behind me while the other two flung my skirts up over my head. My struggling only spurred them on: within seconds, they'd yanked down my drawers and stepped between my stockinged legs. The first touch of a tongue on my bare thigh made me cry out in rage.

Grant lowered the dress from my face so I could see his smug smile. 'What seems to be the problem, Angel-Face? Why, just yesterday you bared yourself before everyone in town!'

'I was auditioning for –'

'Slut,' he muttered, his expression growing cold. 'I had special plans for you, Rosie. You see now what you could've shared as my partner, but no – you had to fall in with Meeh first!'

'He plucked me out of a blizzard! And where were *you* when –?' I yelped and squirmed, dodging the double tongues headed towards me. The ladies between my legs were lapping gleefully, wetting me with loud, wet kisses as they giggled against my bare flesh.

'This little game with the Titzlers is the *least* humiliation you deserve, after the way you accepted my money and then took up with another man,' Grant mocked. 'You haven't changed a bit since we were kids behind my father's store. Cock-a-doodle-doo! Any cock'll do!'

The tip of a tongue tickled my clit and I cried out. Never before had I been held helpless – by a pack of randy *women*, no less! – and I for damn sure wasn't going to go down without a fight! I kicked against the hands that held my thighs apart, blinded again when Grant flipped my crimson dress back over my face.

'Let me hold her while you take your turn, Zelda,' he said to the triplet behind me.

I was then pinned tightly against his chest as Galloway gripped my forearms. Inquisitive fingers parted the halves of my ass from beneath me, and when a tongue found my puckered hole, I writhed upward, against the hot mouth of the lady in waiting. Her insistent lips parted mine, and she thrust her tongue into me. From around us came the murmurs of onlookers, encouraging Nelda – or was it Esmerelda? – to suck the honey from deep inside me. I heard the chinkle of money – wagers being placed against how many minutes it would take before I came – the rumbling of Grant's chuckle as he held me, while those three bandits stole my last scrap of dignity.

'That'll be enough. You've had your fun, girls.'

Devlin! His voice remained calm, yet I detected an undertone of irritation as he continued. 'Pull up her drawers and put her down. Meddling with my Angel again will get you caught in Venus's web –'

'You don't scare me! This was Venus's idea!' one of the Titzlers quipped.

My feet hit the floor with a thump, and when my skirts fell into place I saw pink spots in Meeh's chubby cheeks. His gaze was enough to cow the three blondes into returning to the stage for their clarinets, while the Indian dancers scurried off to start another song. The gamblers, too, turned back to their games as though nothing had happened, avoiding Devlin's censure.

Grant, however, stood firm behind me. He'd released me, to cross his arms defiantly, and the hatred in the glare he gave Devlin Meeh would've sent a lesser man slinking away like a cowardly dog.

'You know better than to cross me, Galloway. The mayor's not above punishment, you know.'

'The girls were only having their fun,' he countered

tersely. 'And since when is the likes of Rosie DuBris exempt from honouring the others' fantasies?'

'Since I said so. Since I proclaimed her my Angel.'

Grant's catlike eyes narrowed to slits. 'Does this mean I must find another?'

The blond man beside me reached up to smooth my rumpled hair. Then, in a gesture of eloquent concern, he tenderly touched the birthmark on my cheek. 'Yes, it does. I've got a special ... purpose in mind for this angel, so I'll not be sharing her.'

Devlin's smooth face brightened then, like the sun shining from behind a cloud. He offered me his arm. 'Come along, my dear. I have a special gift for you, to compensate for this unfortunate nonsense.'

All the way back to the castle I contemplated the incident with Grant Galloway and his girls. Zelda, Nelda and Esmerelda obviously had no fear of Venus – and were seemingly in cahoots with her. There was no love lost between the man who'd invited me here and the one who'd claimed me, either, and their mysterious conversation left me wondering why I was now being played like a pawn in some devious game of acquisition. It was one thing to bare myself on the opera house stage, and quite another to be held and tongue-fucked while onlookers bet on my surrender.

Surrender ... it seemed my fate, despite the way I'd come here assuming I had everything to gain. Grant Galloway had lured me with fond memories of our lust, but now refused to speak to me – except in scorn. Devlin Meeh had put me on a pedestal for a taste of chocolate, yet had placed me in danger of retaliation from his dethroned queen. And I had no doubt that the Titzler triplets would take every opportunity for mischief at my expense.

I went to bed exhausted, wondering what my benefactor's gift would cost me.

9 **My Guardian Angel**

I dreamed of Jimmy Crystal, so vividly that I smelled his rugged musk and felt the scrape of his chest hair against my breasts. I tasted whiskey on his lips before he whispered, 'Love me, Rosie. I need your body tonight! I need *you*, honey.'

I turned on to my back at his gentle insistence. His kisses caught fire and made me burn for him, between legs that spread in welcome. There was no moon, but in the crimson glow from my window I saw his rakish smile and the shock of dark blond hair falling across his brow. His shadow loomed on the wall, black against the flocked wallpaper, set off by the pale red light. When he straddled me, the silhouette of his erection jutted across the wall. My pussy clutched at itself, wanting Jimmy so badly I raised my hips to urge him inside me.

And oh, the solid feel of him! The warm, satiny smoothness as he slid into my wet slit, filling me so full with his cock that I began to writhe. He made me very aware of how long I'd gone without good loving – and how badly I missed the man I'd left behind. His shaft pulsed in my sheath, and I could feel his thick head bumping my inner wall. I sighed and grunted with each thrust as we moved together in the rhythm we established years ago.

He suckled my breasts, tickling the sensitive skin with his moustache. I giggled, tossing my head with the ecstasy of holding him again, brushing my lips along the side of his face. Lord, he was good! Jimmy was in the mood to make it last all night, and who was

I to deny him? When he raised my legs so my feet rested on his shoulders, I moved against him with my head tilted back, taking in the entire, magnificent length of him, feeling the ridge of him rub me deep inside. I'd soon be gushing from the perfect pressure he alone knew how to apply there.

'Oh, Jimmy ... Jimmy, please ... yes, right there ... ohhh, Goddd ...'

'Go with it, Rosie. Ride it sweet and slow, until you can't hold back any longer.'

The spasms made their lazy ascent, intensifying ever so subtly. Then he thrust against me and held it, gyrating against my wet folds to craze my clit with the coarse hair at the base of his cock. My mouth fell open, and I went with the fine, satiny madness that would soon swallow me whole.

'Yes, Rose, fly with it now – fly like an angel ... *my* Angel.'

Like summer lightning my climax struck, so startling that I sat up as I called Jimmy's name, grabbing him in a hug –

But the body was wrong. My eyelids fluttered but, even without looking, I knew it was Devlin. My hips quivered against him, gripping the fingers he'd filled me with, shoving against the thumb that had found my desperate nub. I came hard, shooting like a fire hose. My nectar filled his hand and dribbled on to the sheet. And when my body sank back on to that wet mattress, I was so embarrassed I might as well have peed the bed.

'Devlin,' I murmured, fully awake then and realising that I slept in my suite's white four-poster rather than the lumpy little bunk above Jimmy's bar.

'You sounded desperate,' he replied softly.

'I – I don't know what to –'

'No need to explain, Angel. My cock's not as big as

the one you long for, but you'll not lack for anything while you're mine.'

There in the darkness, with his soft hands and gentle voice soothing me, I could believe Meeh's assurances. I could tell myself that many – including Grant Galloway – had treated me far worse, and that I'd improved my lot by agreeing to be this powerful man's lover. Yet, as the wispy remains of my dream dissipated, I felt a hollowness inside. Could only Jimmy fill it?

Come morning – or what passed for it, when Devlin got out of my bed – I told myself this Klondike wilderness would not be my undoing! Nor would the people here in Satan, who seemed determined to make me pay for a sin I'd unknowingly committed by accepting Grant's invitation. I bathed and went downstairs to breakfast, joining Devlin in a dining room that felt ridiculously huge for two people.

He sat at the end of the mammoth table, rising when I entered. 'You look absolutely gorgeous in that shade of jade, Angel. All decked out for the Christmas season, and ready for this gift.'

Christmas? Had the months passed that quickly?

I sat on the edge of the chair he pulled out for me, blocking out simple holiday memories that felt suddenly painful. Had Jimmy gone to the woods for a tree? Would he string popcorn and hang French letters on the branches? Devlin's caress lingered on the column of my neck, pulling me back into the present.

'Before Faren brings our breakfast, I want you to have this, Angel – this crystal talisman that symbolises my regard for you, and sparkles like your sweet charm. It carries the power of my protection,' he added in a low voice.

He reached into the pocket of his purple velvet jacket, bringing out a piece that glimmered in the light from the chandelier. It was a tiny angel – a head flanked by wings, perfectly proportioned and about half an inch high. I would've sworn it was a diamond, the way its tiny facets lit with multicoloured fire as he shifted it on his fingertips.

'Oh, my, I ... it's beautiful, Devlin.'

'Like the lady who wears it.' He lifted my chin, grinning until his monocle winked at me. Then he pressed the back of the crystal into my cheek, where my birthmark was.

What was I to say? When Meeh held the angel there, a deep heat penetrated my skin. And when he let go, and then gently polished the crystal with his handkerchief, I sensed I'd been branded as surely as a cow got marked by a cowboy.

'Look in the mirror, Rose. No one can ever doubt you're a special woman now, with her own guardian angel standing watch at all times.'

I walked to the massive sideboard as though in a trance. I'd unwittingly labelled myself when I took the stage name of Angel-Face for my audition, playing upon Grant Galloway's flirtatious reference to my birthmark. The glittering crystal piece covered my defect, yet made it all the more prominent.

I couldn't tell Devlin that, of course. His expression belied an underlying motive, an intention to mark me as his. Why did I suspect this would make me even more of a target?

I forced a smile as I gazed at my reflection. 'They say crystal has powerful properties that attract good fortune and ward off evil. Is this what you've given me?'

'There's that astute wisdom again. Just one of the reasons I find you so attractive, my dear.'

'So this will protect me from the triplets' mischief? And from Grant's retaliation?'

'If you believe it will.'

I was pondering this, when Faren carried in a tray of

warm, fragrant fruit breads with butter and jam, and paper-thin egg pancakes wrapped around sausages. Although I'd been famished when I sat down, my appetite ebbed when I caught the expression on the maid's face. Absolutely appalled she appeared, as she stared at my cheek.

'Begging your pardon, sir, but didn't that crystal belong –'

'I've given it to Angel for Christmas, as a symbol of my affection and esteem,' Meeh cut in smoothly. 'It suits her perfectly, don't you agree?'

The rest of what Faren intended to say came out in a forceful sigh. 'If you insist. Why, yes – it's lovely on her, sir.'

This only confirmed my suspicions, and made me wonder who the piece belonged to before – and who would lash out when she saw it emblazoned on my face. I knew better than to ask this of my host, however, for he was heaping his plate with crepe-wrapped sausages as though he'd given me a whole new life in that one chunk of jewellery.

'You know what I've been thinking, girls?' he queried gleefully. 'I can't get the sight and the taste of Angel, coated in that chocolate pudding, out of my mind. Wouldn't it be even more outrageous if the *two* of you smeared each other with chocolate? What a time we could have!'

Devlin was forking down hearty bites while I picked at a piece of nut bread, watching Faren's reaction to this suggestion. Her arched eyebrows almost made me laugh – almost let me forget how threatened I felt – until the butler entered the room bearing a silver salver. He was a cadaverous man with skin so pale the blue veins crisscrossed his neck like a road map; a fellow who performed his duties as though skulking around in the shadows of the palace. He bowed at Meeh's left, offering an envelope.

'So sorry to interrupt your meal, Dr Meeh, but I've an urgent message. I'm to await your reply, please.'

'Thank you, Jarold.' With a flicker of distaste, the baby-faced blond broke the wax seal and skimmed the folded note. He scowled. 'I'll see to this myself. To nip it in the bud, before anything more comes of it.'

Tossing his napkin on the table, he glanced at Faren and me. 'Excuse me, ladies, I must attend to a matter of immediate concern. I'm looking forward to whatever you cook up with that chocolate fantasy I've mentioned. The sooner the better.'

He bussed my cheek and hurried from the room, leaving us to wonder what crisis he was heading off – and leaving his butler wide-eyed at the sight of my crystal tattoo. As though sensing I was about to quiz him, however, Jarold pressed his lips into a lugubrious line and hurried off as though he'd seen a ghost. A ghost of someone he'd rather forget.

My stomach churned around what little I'd eaten. 'All right, Faren,' I said in an agitated whisper, 'you have to spill it! I haven't even left the house yet, and I'm being stared at like I've dressed in a dead woman's jewellery. What'll it be like –'

'Actually, Miss Angel, you have.'

'– when I go out among other people to ... What do you mean, Faren? Who did this crystal belong to?'

The redhead's freckled face paled. 'That's not for me to say, miss. Bad luck to speak ill of the dead, you know. And in your place, I'd be more concerned about the most recent woman to wear it.'

'Who is –?'

The maid busied herself putting Meeh's dishes on her tray. 'It's just like him, to cover our flaws – to turn them into points of interest that render us attractive. He did that with me, you know. I was pug-ugly when he brought me here – mousy brown hair and a body stunted by a childhood disease, so I'd never develop into a desirable woman. But Meeh transformed me into a little girl who plays to his tastes. I'll be forever in his debt ... and forever young. You'll profit, too, if you follow his lead.'

I listened closely, studying her smooth, freckled skin and the juvenile body beneath her black uniform and pinafore. 'So who am I supposed to watch out for, Faren? Who won't like it that I've inherited her crystal?'

'You'll have to excuse me, Angel. I've said too much as it is,' she whispered. 'Just watch yourself when you're out and about, all right? Stick with Dr Meeh and it'll be the talisman he claims it is. I'll see to getting that chocolate ready for us –'

She was disappearing into the kitchen, leaving me alone in that cavernous dining room with the remains of my breakfast taunting me. This was the woman who'd unabashedly brought herself to climax on my bidet, baring herself in more intimate ways than anyone I'd ever known, so her fearful reaction to this crystal boded ill for my future in Satan. I'd been left alone with more questions than answers, about a subject crucial to my well-being.

I wasn't one to shy away from superstition, but I didn't like it that Meeh had given me a piece belonging to someone of obvious importance ... a woman who'd died – perhaps under dubious circumstances? I trudged up the stairway, wondering who had made such an impression on Meeh's staff, and who the crystal belonged to after she passed on. No wonder the little angel pestered me! Every time I spoke or chewed or yawned, the gemstone reminded me it was there, embedded in my flesh. Surely whoever wore it before didn't have to contend with the pulling sensation Devlin had subjected me to, the constant reminder that I was now his.

I entered my suite and shut the door, needing time to think about the unexpected things I'd encountered in Satan. On the surface, everything seemed as idyllic as the picture Grant had painted in his letter – which I got out of my valise and reread with many a shake of my head. How gullible I'd been to believe his pretty fibs! A woman in my position, who'd heard so many men boast about deceiving their women, should've seen through such a ruse!

But I was here, and I would make the best of it. After all, I'd somehow found favour with the man who mattered most in this odd little outpost. So who could prevail against me?

I sat stock-still, not breathing. Was someone in the next room, where Venus had once lived? Dr Meeh was tending business, and I doubted Faren or Jarold wanted to be anywhere near me until they recovered from seeing my new facial decoration. Which left me alone upstairs.

But no, that was definitely the sound of drawers squeaking as they got yanked from cabinets, the hurried rifling through their contents, along with a disgusted muttering. The voice was low and muted by the wall between us, but I had no doubt the intruder was after something specific – and was quite peeved about not finding it.

Considering my maid's reaction and warning at breakfast, I decided to sit absolutely still. No point in confronting someone who wasn't supposed to be here ... perhaps the someone who'd written that note, to get Meeh out of the house? This thought disturbed me. Only one woman I'd met had the nerve – and motive – to challenge the man who ruled.

I rose silently from my vanity bench, instinctively gripping a poker from the marble hearth, my heart hammering. As though on cue, the door to my chamber of heavenly white burst open, and in walked the tallest, darkest, most menacing woman I'd ever met.

Venus looked fierce in a glimmering gown of hellfire red, which pushed her ample breasts upward until they nearly spilled out of its daring, dipping neckline. She slammed the door behind her, advancing on me like a panther intent on fresh prey.

'You've been in my room,' she accused, her dark eyes narrowing to wicked slits. 'And you've stolen something that's *mine*, bitch!'

'No – and no, again,' I replied as calmly as I could. Little good it did to tap the poker on the floor in warning, when I was too paralysed to raise it in my defence. 'Except for what arrived in my pack, Dr Meeh has given me everything I –'

'Doctor, schmoctor,' she taunted. 'Devlin can't even heal himself, so don't expect miracles when he claims – my God, it's on your face! That's *my* crystal, you bitch! He made me leave my jewels behind, but I have my ways of taking them back!'

I brandished the poker when she reached for my cheek. 'I don't know anything about that!' I cried. 'If you've come back to steal from Meeh, that's *your* business! Take this angel from my face, and you're dealing with another force altogether!'

Venus smirked, grasping the sides of her crimson hips. 'So he told you it was a talisman? That it had supernatural powers to thwart those who want you *dead*?' she sneered. 'Well, aren't you just the pussy's pyjamas? And aren't you just another one of Devlin's fools?'

Her hand snaked forward, but I struck it with my poker, wondering where such bravado came from. This woman glared down at me, a full foot taller than I with a body as sleek and sinewed as a warrior's ... an Amazon accustomed to taking what she wanted. Suddenly she grabbed my weapon and pulled me so close our noses touched.

'Enjoy your days as Satan's angel, because they're numbered. Meeh only keeps his mistresses around while we amuse him, and debris from the streets soon rots,' she muttered. Her breath reeked of an odd, cloying sweetness – opium, perhaps? – that made me shake my head to clear it. 'Then you're *mine*, Nosy Rosie. And then you're *gone*.'

Once again her finger found the birthmark, but this time when she shoved me backwards, I felt no need to remain polite. Perhaps it was the pain, a surge of heat that pierced my face, which prompted me to push back. I slipped a foot behind her ankle to send her sprawling against my bed, a scarlet stain on my pristine sheets. The she-devil sprang to her feet, her appetite for vengeance whetted.

'So you want to play dirty, you smelly little skunk?' she cried, leering at my decorated cheek. 'I'll keep that in mind, for sometime when you least expect it. Meanwhile, you better watch your yellow back.'

So much for the protection of Meeh's mystical crystal! After Venus left, I gingerly fingered the jewel in my face, wondering what kept it embedded there, not daring to pry at it. Like a faceted scab it sparkled, covering the mark I'd been born with, yet announcing to friend and foe alike that I was no common whore now: I was Devlin Meeh's whore. I had indeed gotten my wish, and could consider myself a far more illustrious sporting girl than Oblivion, Oregon and Jimmy Crystal could ever afford.

But it didn't feel nearly as fine as I'd anticipated. At least two other mistresses had worn this glistening angel: one of them was dead, and another seemed determined to kill *me*. Fantasy fulfilment was getting to be a dangerous game, and I wondered if anyone would win it.

10 **Snatched!**

'I've always adored the taste of chocolate, and the smell of it wafting up from my cup. And now I love the *feel* of chocolate!' Meeh crooned. 'Chocolate coating my body, chocolate slithering down my limbs. My God, is there anything like this sensation of sitting in a fresh chocolate pie?'

Devlin sat immersed in my tub, which Faren and I had filled with chocolate pudding. I'd never seen a man so deliriously happy, so enraptured by the scenario I'd created onstage, in which he himself now starred. The childlike blond dipped his hands into the pudding's dark richness and then watched it dribble down his arms. At that moment, it didn't matter that he ruled a kingdom where fantasy reigned supreme: his present reality seemed the reason he'd lived his entire life. Wallowing in warm chocolate was his dream come true – and he'd never known it, until now!

'Happier than a pig in shit,' Faren remarked with a chuckle. 'And he resembles one, too!'

'You're just jealous, little girl,' he shot back. 'You're dying to join me, aren't you?'

'Haven't been invited,' she replied with a nonchalance that betrayed her arousal.

The maid then ran a hand through the pudding, making a sultry show of sucking her fingers clean, one after another. As Devlin watched her pink tongue flick between her digits, I realised he wasn't wearing his monocle or that huge ruby. He was merely himself, without those mystical objects I'd become wary of. After all, who could say whether their powers came from Meeh, or if I'd only imagined the visions within the lens and the odd sensation of losing control when he flashed his ring at me?

'Well – since this whole idea was originally mine, I'm not going to *wait* for an invitation,' I announced, unfastening the sash of my dressing gown. 'I want a chocolate massage, I want a *fucking* chocolate massage – with four hands going at me at once!'

Devlin's face lit up, and he laughed as I stepped in with him. The pudding oozed between my toes, covering me to my knees with its velvet warmth. Grinning, I scooped up a handful, propped one brown-coated foot on the rim of the tub, and then slapped the pudding between my parted legs as he watched.

'But first, I want you to eat me, Devlin,' I challenged in a low voice. 'Show Faren what she missed at the auditions. Show me again how you love licking chocolate from me.'

His hands were already running up my coated leg, he was so eager for me. Small splotches of pudding dropped on to his round, boyish face as he leaned towards my dripping pussy, his tongue extended. A few quick flicks around my clit made me gasp with the excitement of this game, and then his mouth pressed against me in earnest, groping my folds to suck the sweet pudding from my slit.

Faren looked ready to faint dead away. Her green eyes were riveted on Meeh's mouth slurping my pussy, while she shed her pinafore and popped the buttons from her uniform. With her hairless mound and two suggestions of breasts, beaded in pink, my maid looked like a life-sized doll. Definitely ready to be played with. Her ringlets quivered as she stepped closer, itching to join in, yet not wanting to miss a moment of my excitement.

'I've got to watch this,' she breathed. 'Lie back in the tub and hook your knees over Devlin's shoulders. I want to see every nip and nibble, Angel. I want to watch your pussy lips flutter around his tongue.'

From that moment, we became three of one mind. I eased down into the warm pudding, and Devlin was so hungry for it he was already lifting my hips to position me. With my back against the tub I sank lower until the chocolate sloshed up around my shoulders, glancing from the man who licked between my legs to the girlish maid who looked on from over his shoulder. Faren was gnawing her lush lower lip, straining to see every intimate detail – and then she, too, stepped into the tub.

I gasped when she took my big toe into her mouth, which gave her a straight shot at what Meeh was doing to me. With a groan, he leaned into his work, sucking noisily and kissing my nether lips as his tongue darted between my folds. Faren lapped at the sole of my foot, making me howl and writhe in Devlin's slick hands – which in turn got him to giggling. He thrust his tongue inside me then, his mirth vibrating all the way through me.

'Let me see!' the servant squealed, and then I felt her hands on my inner thighs, pushing them open around Devlin's head. Damned if she wasn't wrapped around Meeh from behind! Her arms were thrown over his shoulders, and her hips wiggled in a telltale up-and-down against his bare back.

'You horny little pusss!' I hissed, catching her eyes in a blatant gaze. 'You just *wish* you could taste me! You'd just *love* to lap my cream and –'

'And I will!' she retorted, leaning closer. 'I'm going to pinch your clit and make you come before you want to. But don't you dare let Devlin have it all.'

With that, Faren raised her hips to cradle his blond

head, and then she began to thrust. This shoved Devlin's tongue further up my passageway and made him moan, which reverberated against my flesh until I began to shake uncontrollably. I'd never taunted another woman into this sort of play, and my response shot ahead of me as Faren stared daringly down at my bare body. I was coated with brown cream and crushed between Meeh and the back edge of the tub, my legs splayed and flailing crazily.

Just as I felt the first spirals rising like the steam from a tea kettle, the maid caught my clit between her thumbs. My scream echoed around the white tiled walls, driving Devlin to tongue me harder. His sucking, and the furtive slurping of our bodies in the muck, made a strangely erotic music as we struggled and strained with my rising excitement.

The first wave hit me, and then Faren tickled my desperate clit from its underside. My climax propelled me up out of the pudding, spewing juice and chocolate all over Devlin's face – which only prompted him to laugh and lick at me faster. Merciless, the maid was, and with a wicked giggle she pumped me with her thumbs until I blanked out. I collapsed, suspended by my knees from Meeh's shoulders, splattering chocolate pudding with a loud *smack* as I landed in it.

The man between us brayed with laughter, wiping muck from his eyes. His soft body shuddered and, as I recovered enough to focus on him, I sensed I was seeing a Devlin Meeh few of Satan's citizens ever knew.

'Faren, you naughty girl!' he said between giggles. 'Does Daddy have to spank you?'

'Smear my ass with pudding first,' she murmured, despite an artful widening of her emerald eyes. Then she wailed, 'Please, please! Anything but a spanking, Daddy! I promise I'll be good.'

'Too late for that. You know the routine, little princess.' He ducked his head, scooting between her legs towards his end of the tub, so the maid stood between us. 'Lean over, and brace yourself on the rim. And if a few smart smacks don't set you straight, we'll let Angel devise your punishment. I bet she's good at it.'

I watched in awe, not knowing how this little scenario might play out. I'd heard of people who craved discipline – men who delivered loud, firm swats on the backsides of women who pretended to be penitent, yet nearly burst with their need for release. Devlin stood up, the chocolate slithering down his short, slender legs, as his contrary 'child' positioned herself. From where I sat, I got quite an eyeful of her pebbled breasts, and on past that to the notch between her spread legs.

Meeh took his time, ceremoniously rubbing the chocolate around her butt.

'Please, Devlin,' she pleaded, 'I'm sorry I overstepped and made Angel come all over your face. I'm a rude, spoiled little girl. I'll do much better next time!'

Was that honey dribbling from her hole? My Lord, Faren was shaking all over, closing her eyes as the blond behind her palmed pudding in circles around the halves of her ass. What interested me more, however, was my view of Devlin: his sac swung between his legs as he rubbed, and that little prick stood straight out, pointing at me from the vee of her thighs. It was a slick, shiny pink, like a little bald head, and I swore that yellow eye winked at me with each throb.

The first *smack* took us both by surprise: Faren squealed, her cunt convulsing towards me, while I sank lower, as though avoiding similar punishment. From this angle, I looked up from the pudding at her two rosy nipples – and reached up to pinch them between my fingernails.

'You bitch! That's not fair. I –'

Faren cried out with Meeh's next smack, and I

laughed. 'You pinched me, so I'm getting you back,' I crooned. 'And now I'm going to slather pudding all over your puss, but there'll be no one to lick it off. You'll have to suffer that slow drip, without being able to wipe, or –'

'No!' she howled, and then clenched after another firm slap to her backside.

I rather enjoyed this game! Still holding her nipples between my fingertips, I put my feet together to use as a scoop, raised them carefully, and then pressed the tops of them into Faren's slit. She humped like a dog, exhaling with a wheeze – but I left her hanging, with chocolate cream dripping from her.

Devlin sucked air, his cock rigid as he raised his hand. 'Met your match, Faren?' he asked in an unsteady voice. 'Ready to offer yourself up as penance?'

'Yes! Please fuck me – please –'

'Open your naughty hole and beg me.'

'Oh, Devlin, I'm dripping! I need you to –'

'Wider! If I don't see your pussy lips lapping at that pudding, Angel's going to smear you with more until you do it right. Aren't you, Angel?'

From between Faren's quivering legs, I saw Meeh's boyish grin – and a wink.

'I think she needs to suffer,' I replied, and before our victim could protest, I scooped pudding into my palms and splattered it against her chest. When she jerked in surprise, I repeated the process with my feet and her pussy again, making her howl anew.

'Oh, quit your whining,' I muttered, playfully shutting her up with my pudding-filled palm.

Faren licked the hand I closed around her mouth, a tickling sensation that made me giggle – and then I went for the pudding that flew in tempting droplets from her shuddering chest. First one little bead I lapped, and then the other, circling with my tongue until the maid was shuddering violently with need.

'Please, Devlin, please, oh God, just ram it up me,' she wheezed.

She got her wish, for the man behind her looked just as rampantly desperate to sate himself. He lunged, burying his stub within her, making the chocolate splatter between them. His balls shivered and shimmied, clearly within my view – and far too tempting to just watch.

Once again I scooped, and this time I pressed the chocolate-coated tops of my feet against the juncture of their rutting bodies. Their groans rose in a hoarse duet as Faren's slender body quaked and returned thrust for thrust. With the upper bones of my feet pressing into her, I could feel the vibrations intensifying, could rub pudding against her clit until she whimpered, while my toes grazed Devlin's shimmying sac.

He inhaled fiercely and then surged, bucking as though he couldn't get it out fast enough. The maid screamed, so I moved my hand and let her wails fill the bathroom in a back beat to the rhythmic slapping of their bodies. Hot juices dribbled down my feet. I pressed upward, urging them to further completion, until Meeh and his maidservant thrashed themselves to a breathless finale.

Devlin pulled out, to sit against his rim of the tub. Faren panted above me, her arms so rubbery from bracing herself that I gently eased her down into the chocolate. Like a child she wrapped around me, resting her weight between my legs and her head on my shoulder.

'I'll get you for this,' she whispered.

'Ah, sweet revenge!' Meeh replied, scooping up some pudding. His eyes glimmered like gold as he ate it, drinking in the sight of us cuddled against the opposite end of the tub. 'I've enjoyed this immensely, ladies. Once we catch our breath, I think Angel deserves that massage she wanted ... and we'll see what else comes up. I don't intend to waste a drop of this marvellous chocolate!'

The next three weeks were spent in pleasure, with various combinations of partners in several rooms of Dr Meeh's ostentatious home. He and Faren apparently shared a secret agenda: to keep me off the streets and out of harm's way. Each day, they devised more scenarios with chocolate, or with elaborate costumes – for Devlin had a wildly colourful collection of clothing and shoes and jewellery – and between them they kept me from dwelling upon the crystal angel on my cheek – and the freedom it was costing me.

By the time Christmas Eve rolled around, I'd been gifted with eye-popping pendants, lush Russian furs, gowns from Paris and London, and enough sinfully delicious food to fill out the hollows caused by my long trek to the Klondike. These diversions took the edge off my dreams about Jimmy Crystal: startling nightscapes where my senses were so keenly attuned to him, I swore he was in bed with me. Sometimes Devlin brought me off, and sometimes he let me stew in my own juice.

I didn't mention the man in these dreams to Meeh or my maid, for what good would it do? I'd forfeited my past and the kind, gentle barkeep I'd left behind to answer Grant Galloway's call. I was living out a lot of women's fantasies as Devlin's mistress, so I had no room to complain – nor anyone but myself to blame for a heart that echoed like the vast, unoccupied rooms of this mysterious man's mansion.

And on the night before Christmas, he made a droll,

notable St Nicholas, decked in red velvet trimmed in ermine, with a white wig and beard wreathing his youthful face.

'Don your gayest apparel, my dear,' he quipped, 'for tonight we ride the streets of Satan, with gifts for all! With you beside me in the sleigh, we'll make a magnificent spectacle. I've never had a Christmas Angel, so it's sure to be a night of enchantment.'

The dress Faren brought me stole my breath away. White it was, of a shimmering iridescent fabric that clung suggestively to my curves. The voluminous wings, fashioned of ostrich feathers, gave me an angelic glow, completed by a halo that would shine when it caught the light. I felt like a fairy princess as I gazed in the mirror, soaking up the maid's admiration. Never had I been so beautiful, even if the angelic vision was a ruse – even if that crystal angel on my cheek taunted me every time I smiled or spoke. I was truly excited about getting out of the house, for what could befall me with Devlin Meeh at my side?

As though he'd consorted with Mother Nature, a light snow was falling as we boarded his luxurious sleigh. Why wasn't I surprised that Devlin pastured a team of reindeer year-round for his annual pageant? And who else could've produced a large stash of wrapped gifts, as though by magic, to hand to everyone lining the streets to greet us?

And oh, those smiles! And their adulation as they reached into the sleigh to clasp my hand! I was indeed the Queen of the Evening – the Christmas Queen – because I was Satan's Angel. My heart swelled with the joy I saw on those hundreds of faces as my admirers greeted me and accepted a gift from the St Nicholas guiding the sleigh slowly through town.

We stopped at the Exquisite Inn, where Devlin had arranged for a feast to honour the proprietors and managers of Satan's businesses. The dining hall was arrayed in festive greenery garlands, and the tables draped in scarlet brocade with star-shaped candles flickering in their centres. Down a red-carpeted aisle Devlin escorted me, my white angel's arm tucked around his bright red one.

I'd never seen him look merrier, or more pleased – for he had a benevolence about him, despite the absolute control he held over his city. He seated me at the head table while the honourees filed in behind us. Then he excused himself to make final arrangements with the chef.

I felt awkward, seated on the dais, watching the madams and merchants and bankers take their places with Satan's other civic leaders. I'd had no chance to meet them, since I'd spent most of my time in seclusion, so they glanced at me as curiously as I stole glimpses at them ... wondering, of course, if the mayor would appear, and if Venus sat in the shadows.

The crystal angel prickled on my cheek, catching the light from my table's candle to shoot tiny rainbows whenever I moved my head. Low conversations lulled the room, but no one spoke to me. Perhaps they knew Devlin Meeh would introduce me in his own good time.

Waiters in crisp black tuxedos filed out from the kitchen then, bearing platters of delicacies to begin the meal. I received mine first, and sat gazing at glazed apricots and pâtés moulded into wreaths; herbed crackers and paper-thin slices of smoked salmon fanned out around fresh watercress and plump red grapes. My stomach growled, but as forks clinked around me I waited for Devlin's return.

A commotion at the door caught our attention. I grinned, thinking our host had devised an amusement for our first course – Meeh was the ultimate showman, after all. A hiss of exclamations arose with the clamour of hooves, and damned if three horses didn't sashay through the front door and up the aisle! They were headed straight towards me – I was to be a part of the revelry! Everyone in the hall was stuck to their seats by surprise, as I was.

Three masked bandits thundered through the room, wearing black cowboy hats and brandishing pistols. When they shot out the chandeliers, people ducked under their tables, their squeals of delight mingling with the crash of glass.

Too late I recognised them. Still, my heart pounded with the novelty of it all, because Devlin would be coming at any moment to congratulate these marauders on their inventive performance. The leader of this trio flashed me a wicked grin as she went by, her breasts bobbing beneath her black leather vest. But as I watched her gallop past, I was lifted from my seat by the other two, who rode on either side of the dais and hooked me under the arms.

'Put me down!' I screeched, kicking the air. 'This is all in fun, I know, but –'

'Oh?' the blonde on my right replied. 'I'm taking my assignment quite seriously. Aren't you, Nelda?'

'Damn right, Esmerelda. A lot's riding on it, so to speak.'

They urged their mounts forward, until I was tossed like a sack of flour on to Nelda's lap. Her sister then fired shots behind us, over the heads of the startled crowd, and let out a loud war whoop.

'What in God's name are you –'

'God has nothing to do with this!' My captor laughed. 'We take our orders from a much lower power – the folks who truly control Satan when Meeh's not watching. We've been worried about you, Angel. Thought maybe he'd screwed you senseless and left you for dead.'

'Now *there's* an idea,' her cohort crowed. 'But we'll have to wait our turns, I suppose.'

She ducked to ride through the hotel's back door, which Zelda was holding open. The three of them cried out like wild Indians after a massacre, and off we went at full gallop, accompanied by gunfire. The horses' hooves clattered on the streets, and with each step I was pummelled against the hard pommel of the saddle, praying we didn't have far to go, hoping it wouldn't take Devlin long to rescue me.

Who awaited us at the end of the ride? A green-eyed tiger? Or an elusive ebony menace?

11 **Away in a Manger**

'Whoa, Dancer! Easy does it, boy,' Nelda crooned as she guided her horse between those of her sisters. Zelda dismounted and opened the wide, creaking door of what appeared to be an abandoned stable. I saw stripes of Satan's red sky in the cracks between its weathered boards, and the heavy scent of old hay made me sneeze.

We'd had a wild ride to the far end of town, through alleys and behind buildings I'd not seen before, and I hadn't heard anyone following us. The other dinner guests were as startled as I when these masked bandits rode boldly through the dining hall, and they were probably awaiting us as part of the show's finale.

But the KlonDykes had no intention of returning me to the Exquisite Inn. They took me inside the decrepit building and tossed me on to an old hay bale, which crumpled beneath me. One of them – Zelda, I thought, for she seemed to be their leader – struck a match to start a fire in what looked like a blacksmith's forge. Why on earth had they brought me *here*?

'How quaint – how appropriate! – to come to the stable on Christmas Eve,' one of the sisters remarked. They were taking off their bandanna masks, all of them dressed in those fringed vests of black buckskin and men's denim pants that hugged their bodies with an indecent allure.

'Yes, and here's our babe in the manger –'

'– wrapped in swaddling clothes,' finished another sister.

'Or is she an angel, fallen from the roof of our

creche?' the fire-lighter queried, grinning maliciously. She was sliding an earthenware pot towards the flames, which licked at kindling arranged beforehand . . . they'd obviously plotted my abduction for the evening they knew Devlin would show me off. 'Meeh's mistress might be arrayed in white, but she certainly passes for a fallen angel in *my* book!'

'Make no mistake, my ladies.' A man spoke from the doorway. 'I met Rosie DuBris way back, when my pecker first needed a nest, and that innocent-looking white gown doesn't fool me, or anybody else!'

My stomach knotted at the sound of Grant Galloway's voice. He stood silhouetted against the crimson sky of Satan, lean and hard and tall, like a gunslinger from frontier days. Like the handsome young man who'd plucked my cherry and told me he loved me – thus leading me down that primrose path so many girls took when a boy made them feel special. He pushed his broad-brimmed hat back further from his face to reveal a feral grin. His long dimples flickered in the light from the forge's rising flames.

He offered me a hand up, but I didn't trust him enough to accept it.

'Fine, then, we'll play in the hay, like when we sneaked off to the livery stable in Denver. You never asked for much in the way of amenities,' he remarked with a derisive snort, 'and nowadays, you don't require much from the company you keep, either.'

'Is that why your doxies have taken a shine to me?' I retorted. 'Tarnished goods, am I? Well, you're not the Grant Galloway I knew back then, either! *That* boy would've come after me, rather than expecting me to trudge two thousand miles, alone, to tickle his fancy.'

'There were hundreds of fortune-seekers trekking north, Rosie. And you never met a man you didn't like.'

That line slapped me with the memory of my gallant

Mountie, Ace Manley, and I bit back a scalding remark. I was ridiculously outnumbered. Better to keep my own counsel and think about how to get out of here, before I found out what that crock had in it.

But Grant had other ideas. Swift as a panther, he hauled me up from the hay bale and grabbed the dipping neckline of the white dress – as though to rip it off my body in one nasty swipe. But instead, he nestled his fist between my breasts, kneading the exposed flesh, watching the firelight play upon my bare skin.

'Ahh, I've made her cry,' he taunted. But then he took a closer look. 'Well, well now – isn't *this* interesting? Girls, did you see what Miss DuBris is wearing on her cheek?'

My throat closed as the Titzler triplets crowded around to behold his discovery.

'Ooh!' Nelda squealed. 'Does Venus –'

'– know you've stolen her sparkly little toy?' Esmerelda finished.

'Her favourite instrument of torture?' Zelda leaned closer to study the crystal, laughing low in her throat. 'You'll never –'

'– *never* guess where she wears it!' Nelda completed the conversational circuit.

I yelped when the nearest triplet tried to pry a fingernail beneath the gemstone. She jerked back as though her hand had been bitten. Or burnt.

'Maybe you shouldn't mess with her magic,' I warned, shielding the angel with my fingers. 'If she's so fond of this crystal, she wouldn't want *you* wearing it!'

'She's given us free rein,' the blonde to her left boasted.

'Told us we can do anything we like –'

'– as long as we *snatch* you!' Zelda finished with a raucous laugh. 'And, honey, trust me – your snatch will never be the same after tonight! Are we ready, girls?

Let's get on with the plan, so Grant can have *his* turn at her.'

Before I could bolt, I was grasped by one set of hands while another tore the gorgeous white gown from my body. I struggled, wondering what nasty things they had in mind – or what indecent expectations Galloway had when the Titzlers were tired of me. He just stood there, arms folded across his chest, watching the feisty blondes bind my arms to my upper body with an old harness strap – grinning lasciviously when they criss-crossed the leather so my breasts bulged forward in lewd invitation.

Meanwhile, another triplet had stripped off my silk underthings, making a great show of sniffing the slit of my drawers. The tormentor standing behind me then tightened another length of old leather around my waist – and damned if her sisters didn't each grab a leg! They'd positioned me between hitching posts once used to hold the horses being shod here and, with the agility born of thinking exactly alike, they flipped me backwards, on to the hay bale again. My legs flew up and got bound with the leather strap, which they looped through the hoops of the two hitching posts.

This left me lying spreadeagled, facing Grant and the farrier's forge, which now glowed with a flickering fire. All this had happened within seconds, leaving me stunned enough not to identify what Zelda was now stirring in her pot, eyeing me as though she was enjoying this torture immensely.

'Let's get naked, ladies,' she suggested slyly. 'Angel-Face has been such a sport, we should at least show her a little hospitality –'

'Not to mention our three prime examples of –'

'– the bushless beauty for which we're famous!'

The Titzlers stripped quickly, casting aside their denim trousers to reveal those smooth, hairless mounds beneath their hip-hugging holsters. My pulse pounded weakly. Whatever was in that crock would bring a lot more enjoyment to *them* than to me, and it would be useless to beg Grant's intervention. He'd seated himself on an old wooden bench, settling in for whatever festivities his exuberant employees had cooked up. His grin looked wickedly smug.

'How about some Christmas carols, girls?' he suggested. 'Something to make the season even brighter before we give Angel-Face her new look.'

Giggling, the triplets trotted behind the forge to pull out the clarinets they'd stashed there beforehand – just another part of this insanity to make the waiting more unbearable for me. The hay was scratching my bare back, so I hated to wiggle even the slightest bit. But being ogled by this onerous quartet was enough to make any woman nervous.

'I'll wet your reed if you'll wet mine,' one of them said brightly.

'I'm sure Angel wants to watch this part –'

'– from her uniquely advantageous position!'

They gathered near my head, one straddling to face me while the others formed the rest of a tight triangle. Identical naked pussies, with deep mulberry folds and clits that protruded beneath bare mounds, opened above me as they stood with their legs parted. In that respect they resembled Faren, but my maid had never been so blatantly ribald about her hairless state. The KlonDykes had taken their clarinet reeds and were rubbing them against the slit of the triplet to the right, making their holstered pistols bump against their bare thighs. Working up quite a scent, they were, plying each other's folds and teasing their clits with the slender strips of reed, until drops of dew dripped on to my face.

I squeezed my eyes shut, rolling my head to avoid

this fragrant rain, but one of these naughty girls simply straddled my head and held it between her bare ankles as the warm-up continued. I saw the wetness gathering around a hole that pulsed and grew carmine with her excitement. Fat splats of juice fell from her, and she shook with her impending climax.

'Play me,' she rasped, clenching her teeth. 'Play me hard and make me sing.'

Her siblings immediately placed both of their reeds between her spread legs while Nelda – or maybe it was Esmerelda – worked her own reed frantically between the two of theirs. She cried out, spurting her nectar on to my chest and face, her taut thighs flexing with each surge of satisfaction. The other two were near the edge as well, and it became an urgent matter for the three of them to climax in rapid succession, just like they talked. The stable rang with their cries, which sounded more like the yowling of cats than caroling – until Galloway shoved them back.

'My turn,' he breathed. And when I opened my eyes he was standing over me, magnificent in the flickering shadows, with his cock sticking out at least ten inches from his half-masted pants. 'Play me a song now, girls – maybe "O Come, O Come, Emmanuel". And I'll be Emmanuel, of course.'

He stroked his cock, extending it further as I watched, wondering what he was about to do with it – and to me. I squirmed beneath him, dripping with female wetness I couldn't wipe away, knowing the worst part still awaited me. Meanwhile, the KlonDykes tuned their clarinets and began circling like Indians around a campfire. The first strains of the song Grant requested made him laugh with the irony of it.

'Do you swallow?' he challenged, fondling the ridged length of his prick.

'You should ask if I bite,' I retorted, although it was a

foolish thing to say. Large as he was, Grant Galloway could easily choke me in this defenceless position – even though he knew better than to harm Devlin Meeh's mistress.

Or at least I was counting on that. I had to grasp any straws I could, considering my predicament.

And as he lowered himself, in rhythm to the triplets parading around him, my insides tightened in spite of the awful way this man had treated me. Weeks had passed – months, actually – since I'd seen such a randy, handsome cock and I wasn't immune to the need Grant created by flaunting himself. Closer it came, that enormous erection. I licked my lips. A drop of fluid appeared in its little eye, glittering like a jewel in his bulbous, crimson head.

'Tickle me with the tip of your tongue,' he ordered.

I raised my head, my tongue extended in a curving point towards that hole. When I touched the salty drop, Grant sucked air – but drew back with a laugh.

'Shall I shove this up your cunt? That's what you really want, isn't it?'

Visions of Devlin Meeh's wrath overrode the desire flaring deep within me.

'Cat got your tongue, Rosie?' he taunted, inspiring the triplets to blow a mocking cat-call with their horns. 'I know how you love to fuck, honey – how you pump yourself crazy on a man's cock because you love sex like few women know how. And the man with the monocle doesn't have squat for your pussy, does he?'

Once again he lowered that throbbing head, pressing it into my lips this time. I opened my throat and swallowed him whole, closing my jaw to trap him there, the nasty bastard! I'd done nothing to deserve this sort of humiliation, and I knew how to take my revenge.

He chuckled, but it wasn't a pleasant sound. 'Need your help here, girls,' he said to the circling blondes.

'When you were wetting your reeds, you forgot to offer Rosie *her* satisfaction. I bet she's never had three women working her at once.'

'I get her pussy!'

'Save her clit for me!'

'I get sloppy seconds, then – after Grant fucks her!'

I was suddenly besieged by blondes, two of whom tossed aside their clarinets to ravage my spread pussy. One knelt between my legs, levering my hips up with her hands so her sister could get at my clit while she herself stuck her tongue up my hole. I screamed – which of course freed Grant's equipment. He rose quickly from his squat.

When he saw the third girl watching us, rubbing the mouthpiece of her instrument between her legs, he snapped his fingers and pointed towards my head. 'None of that, Nelda, when you can have an angel lapping at you. Sit on her face. And don't get up until she makes you gush.'

It was almost more than I could handle. My poor clit was being licked and tickled by a giggly Titzler, while her sister thrust her fingers in and out, and then lapped at my juice like a ravenous cat. Nelda was squatting above my head, lowering her sleek, hairless slit.

'Kissy-kiss,' she crooned, parting the folds with her fingers to expose the extended stem above her deep-pink petals. 'I like it hard and fast, Angel-Face. Curve your tongue around my nub and give it a rubbing.'

I had little choice, for her wet lips were on mine – as insistent as Faren's, but plumper and with a muskier scent. Her two sisters had me quivering, however, working me down there so mercilessly that I got desperate for release. I began nicely enough, for Grant was watching. But when a spasm ripped through my abdomen, I clenched with its intensity.

'She bit me!' Nelda yelped.

No sooner had she jumped to her feet than I found myself suspended by the ankles at the hitching loops, with Zelda and Esmerelda standing stiffly on either side of me, their pistols pointed at my face.

They wouldn't dare shoot Devlin Meeh's queen ... would they? The stable echoed with their unsteady breathing, yet the barrels of those guns didn't quiver. I swallowed hard, still panting from the beginnings of a colossal climax. 'I couldn't help it! I had to thrust and – and –'

'I'll make you *thrust*,' Zelda muttered.

My heart stood still when she yanked the other gun from her holster, her bare thighs flexing. Any of the triplets could do me in, trussed up as I was. Yet when I saw this weapon, I could only gape: it had a mother-of-pearl handle that matched her handgun's, but the part hidden inside the holster was made like a cock, so thick it put Galloway's to shame.

Without further ado, she stuck it up me. I gasped with the cold, hard girth of it, determined not to let these outlaws win. But my tormentor cunningly pressed the inside curve of the handle against my clit as she pumped me. My whole body rocked with the brunt of her punishment, making the hay whisper illicitly as it scratched my bare backside.

The other three watched with wicked grins, knowing how convincing this Titzler could be, thus armed, and the flames kindled by my previous climax flared again, consuming me this time. I screamed, thrashing in my leather wrappings, helpless to do anything but convulse again and again.

'Wax her,' Grant grunted. 'It's getting late, and we've had our fun.'

'But you haven't come yet –'

'– and I haven't gotten to lick it out of her,' the other two protested. But a glare from Galloway shut them up.

'We'll do that next time,' he said. 'We've got to be gone before they come looking for her. Zelda, you and Nelda do the honours. Esmerelda, you keep watch – and I'll keep her quiet.'

What on earth were they up to now? Nelda fetched the pot from the forge while her sister grinned maliciously at me, letting her gaze linger between my spread legs. Grant quickly removed his boots and pants, then straddled my shoulders with his shirt-tail flapping around his backside. His cock loomed huge above my face as he lowered himself – until he raised up enough to chuck me under the chin.

'Bite *me*, and you won't live to tell about it, Rosie.'

My eyes widened and I knew better than to sass him. I obediently opened my mouth to take in the full length of his erection, but the joy was gone from it. What had happened to the playful young man who'd initiated me? Why was he now using my lust for lovemaking against me?

The first searing of hot wax between my legs drove out all sentimentality, however. Like lava from a volcano, it clung to my skin, making me squirm and whimper around Grant's cock. He slid in and out slowly, the tip of him going down my throat, while Zelda's molten madness formed a burning circle around my slit. I strained to keep from clamping down, clenching my eyes shut . . . wondering if I'd survive even if I *didn't* bite this crafty cocksman.

Endless minutes went by, with that shaft sliding in and out as the wax cooled and solidified. I tried not to think about what happened next. Why did the Klon-Dykes find this torture worthwhile, to achieve that bare-pussied look they seemed so proud of? The man in my mouth moved faster, his breath catching in his throat.

'All right. Let's do it,' one of the girls whispered.

The pain was like a lightning strike, bright and blinding, when they yanked the wax, along with my coarse, curly hair. I screamed silently, muted by Grant's huge cock, inserted so far his sac slapped my chin. His movements became frantic. I was thankful for all the large men who'd taught me how to handle such pressure – and, indeed, I saw some of them as my life passed before me. The ordeal between my legs became a blur and then, mercifully, Grant climaxed. His salty seed filled my mouth – and then he pulled out to empty himself on my face. He saved the last splash for the crystal angel.

'It is finished!' one of the girls announced.

'Yes, it is,' Grant gasped. He smirked at the mess he'd made of my face and hair, and then quickly climbed into his pants. 'Lovely seeing you again, Rosie. Now that you've come to Satan, it'll be just like old times. Never thought you'd be the pussy-kissing type, but it adds a certain –'

'Someone's coming! I hear horses!'

'Scramble!' Grant barked. 'They can't catch us if we head off in different directions!'

He bolted towards the main door, while the girls scurried towards their horses. Visions of being found like this, naked, with leather traces around me and my feet strung up – not to mention a gooey face and a pussy as pink as a singed flamingo – would've made me cry if I weren't so sore and angry. But, Lord, did I have a story to tell to whoever rescued me!

I kept quiet, though, as the KlonDykes mounted up. I tried not to smile as I thought about what Devlin would do to my abductors.

Hoofbeats thundered across the dirt floor towards the other end of the stable and the far door opened with a loud squeal. A draft whistled in, but I was too hot on preparing my story to feel its chill.

Then, however, one of them rode back. She hopped down and quickly stashed the black pants and the clarinets in a lidded feed bin. Then she slipped a knife from her vest pocket.

'You're cutting me loose?' I asked, for I heard the approaching hoofbeats now.

'Hah!' she replied with a toss of her blonde head. 'This looks way too easy. If they want you, they'll have to find you.'

12 **Lost Souls**

The road to Hell is paved with good intentions, but the road out of Satan was a bumpy ride. I had no idea where we were going – and, silly me, I imagined myself overpowering my abductor along the way. But Miss Titzler had only unfastened my feet – not the strap binding my arms – and hastily wrapped my ruined gown around me before shoving me up on her horse, to flop like a rolled-up rug in front of her saddle. I didn't know if that was a pistol or her dildo jabbing me in the back, so I didn't argue with her.

Again we rode past places I'd never seen, and soon we ran out of places, out to where snow-capped foot-hills and frozen wasteland were all I could distinguish in the darkness. The horse's breath wreathed us in vapour as the temperature grew suddenly colder.

'They'll never find you,' she crowed. 'Their Angel-Face will be gone without a trace – without evidence of whoever whisked her away.'

We headed into snow at that point, a driving white wall of it. I knew then that we'd left the city limits, for within Satan's walls that mysterious lack of winter weather had insulated us from Klondike reality. What was this wicked triplet planning to do to me? And how did she think she could get away with it?

'Get off, and good riddance!' she exclaimed, and with a shove she unhorsed me. 'Grant doesn't need your kind of trouble. Not when he's got the KlonDykes to keep him entertained.'

I slid awkwardly down the horse's side, landing on

my feet with a sharp jolt before stumbling backwards. As I fell into a snowdrift, horse and rider thundered back towards town, leaving me out in the middle of nowhere with just the whistling of the wind and the sting of snow against my exposed skin. My tattered white dress had come partly unwrapped, and with my arms tied tightly to my sides I was damn near helpless.

But long before I became Satan's Angel, Rosie DuBris had determined she would never give up or give in. Facing adversity from those who scorned me – which included do-gooders, and drunks who stiffed me when they couldn't rise to the occasion – was simply part of a sporting girl's game. I knew I'd better find shelter soon, or I'd become frozen food for the wolves.

I struggled to my feet and began to walk. The only light in these twenty-four-hour Klondike nights was the snow, which threatened to freeze my eyelashes together. Squinting ahead, I searched for the red glow over Satan. We hadn't ridden very far from the back side of Meeh's city ... so if I could wander close enough, any search party he sent would soon find me.

But what if Devlin didn't send anyone?

For all I knew, he was testing me – or had tired of me. Or had decided he wanted Venus back. Lord knows that dark-skinned dilettante knew more sophisticated tricks than I; something to tickle that little dick's fancy after Meeh got his fill of chocolate frolics.

If that were true, I'd wander, lost, until I keeled over from the cold.

Shaking those thoughts from my head, I stumbled forward. I could no longer feel my arms and my feet were frostbitten. Small consolation that my stripped pussy was so cold I didn't notice the burn from the Titzlers' waxing. I had to believe that Faren would take my side. Had to believe that the KlonDykes would be punished for dumping me – as would Grant for his part in their heist. The lust for revenge often flared hotter than the lust for a good fuck, after all.

I heard movement, I thought – or were my ears ringing from the cold? When I squinted into the dark, windswept distance, I could barely discern someone ... or something ... moving very slowly. Coming towards me.

I stopped to catch my breath and consider my options. Unless my brain had iced over, that was a human form, hunched into the wind, with a scarf whipping about his head. If he were a man of ill intent, I was defenceless. But then, most men of that sort wouldn't be out wandering this wasteland, would they?

'Are you lost?' I called out, and then felt stupid for asking.

The figure stopped, straining forward. No doubt I was quite a sight in my white rags and black leather straps.

'Have I made it to Satan?' he replied above the rush of the wind. 'Got caught in this damn storm. Set my sights on that hellish glow, hoping to get there before I froze to death.'

I turned, astounded to see the reddish light he spoke of, off to my right. I could've wandered right past my destination and never known it! 'You've made it to Satan, all right,' I replied, 'but you might wish you hadn't.'

An odd choice of remarks for Devlin Meeh's queen – especially since this poor fool was as desperate for shelter as I. Yet I felt I should warn him about what he was getting himself into, like I wished someone had forewarned me.

He loomed closer, to where I could hear the wheeze in his breathing and make out a powerful body beneath his blowing clothes ... a body a woman would enjoy a good tumble with, in better conditions.

When he held his scarf to one side to better see me, I sucked air. That dark hair and those sparkling blue eyes ... but it simply couldn't be –

'Rosie? Rosie, honey, is that you?' he cried.

'Collin? My Lord, Collin Cooper, what're *you* doing out here?' In my excitement, I hobbled forward too fast and fell against him. 'You've already found your fortune in the gold fields and you're headed home!'

Enfolding me in the welcome warmth beneath his overcoat, the young man laughed ruefully. 'Oh, Rosie, it's disgusting. This whole trek's been a bad joke, a total hoax. But let's get out of this wind before I tell you that sad story. My God, woman, you're not wearing enough to cover – what the hell happened to *you*?'

I buried my face against the thick silky beard he'd grown. 'Now there's a sad story, and yes, a disgusting one. I was dressed to the nines, at a fine Christmas Eve dinner, and abducted from my table. On horseback! I – I can't go into what those KlonDykes did to me, except to say ... my feet are freezing, Collin. I'm not sure I can walk back to –'

Bless that handsome man's heart; he slipped an arm beneath my knees and cradled me against his midsection as though I were as light as a child ... a child he was extremely glad to see. Collin tugged the sides of his coat around us to shield me from the fierce wind, and then started walking towards the crimson glow that glimmered in the night sky. I was so exhausted and frozen, I lay limply against him, conserving our energy by not talking.

I drifted back ... to my room above his father's mercantile, which seemed half a lifetime ago, after all I'd been through ... saw him holding the bucket in front of my face, on the ship ... recalled the wild night we spent in Ace Manley's Mountie outpost ... the treacherous rapids as we travelled in that little boat towards Dawson City and our parting of ways. What a wild coincidence, to meet Collin Cooper again, just when I needed him like never before.

Or was it really happenstance? Since I'd met Devlin Meeh, I wondered if coincidence really existed. Too many inexplicable things happened when he was around – things I could ask about, but for which I got no direct answers. And if I learned that Collin had come all this way, on my encouragement, and then found out there was no gold – and never had been – how would I live with myself? I'd taken him away from his father's store, and a comfortable life. All because I believed that romantic clap-trap in Grant's letter.

I drifted to sleep in Collin's arms as he trudged through the snow, powerless against my exhaustion ... vaguely made out voices awhile later ... felt myself being shifted to somewhere blessedly warm where I felt free ... where my sleep deepened into oblivion. If I was to die, I hoped my kind, blue-eyed saviour knew I checked out a happy woman, basking in his body's warmth.

I shimmered with exquisite exhilaration, realising it was a dream and hoping I'd never waken – or was this heaven? Had I passed to the other side, to forever flow in this vibrant warmth that radiated from deep inside me? Somewhere, in some former life, I recalled my days as a sporting girl and thought I'd found a reward far more stunning than I'd dared anticipate: I felt hands worshipping every inch of my skin ... smooth, velvety palms following my curves, lingering in the sweet spots that sent a delicious tingling through my limbs.

I shifted, but only so these incredible sensations could spread to my front, up the flat of my belly to caress my breasts, and then down again, hesitating before touching more lightly, as fingertips would stroke a newborn ... along the crevice where my inner thigh joined my body, slick and smooth and ever-so-sensitive, then between my nether lips, which opened like the petals of a rose, begging for this ecstasy, this silken seduction I hoped would never end.

I sighed languidly. 'Please ... yes, there,' I murmured.

I couldn't see my dream lover, even though I knew it was his warmth, his body, his light, lovely touch that was now spinning me in a slow, ethereal pirouette, rising higher, lighter, keening inside for completion, yet wanting to make it last on and on. His finger found my wetness and spread it over my folds, so lovingly I wanted to cry with the beauty of it.

I parted my legs, and with my hand I guided these fingertips between my deepest folds, and then into the hole that constricted around them, pulsing and singing around the soft, solid probes. My body rose of its own accord, undulating like a snake coiling up from a basket at the sound of some charmer's horn. A surge of inner heat drove me higher, ever higher to that sweet pinnacle of release ...

'Please, take me,' I whispered, desperate to be further filled. 'I think I'll die if you don't.'

Which didn't make sense, if I were already afloat in the spirit realm. But I was too far along to question myself – or the one who did my bidding. Beside me, a large, warm body shifted, kissing my neck and shoulders, positioning himself between my spread legs, touching my nub with the head of his hard cock, then entering me oh, so slowly ... innn so deep, and ouuut so smooth ... innn again, making me writhe upward to meet the root of this wondrous, thick member now driving me towards insanity.

I let go, let my languid body ebb and flow and surge with the one loving me, rubbing high against my clit, his weight centred there as he ground gently against me.

'Oh God, Rosie ... God, you're so perfect ... pink and slick and smooth, sucking me deeper inside you.'

Whose voice? Not that it mattered. Such perfection was not to be questioned – not by a woman of my ilk, who usually took whatever came up because it was her job to give more than she received. Yet here in heaven, I mused, I'd found the perfect cock with the perfectly considerate lover attached to it. Far be it from me to waken and bring it all to an end.

But the spirals were tightening. I grimaced in my sleep, thrusting in that slow, hypnotic rhythm, gripping the shaft that sank itself to my very core, searching for the woman who would welcome him, and convulse with him, and then go mad with him and take control by losing it.

Shivers ran through me, along the deepest, secret channels of my being. Then I climbed higher, rising towards that peak – gripping him with a sheath born to complete him – seeking that sweetness as I thrust upward to swallow him whole. I couldn't fight it: my hips quivered and took on a life of their own. Sucking air, I tightened around his cock and rocked mindlessly, endlessly, ecstatically, until he surged into me with smacking sounds that sent our wetness all over the bed.

He rested against me, sighing.

'Please don't go,' I murmured, kissing his ear. He smelled clean and male and very familiar – was this Jimmy Crystal? Had he gone beyond the veil, as well, and met me in the hereafter? If so, my life – the loss of it – had not been in vain.

I drifted to sleep again, content and at peace.

'Angel? Angel, come to the surface now and talk to us. Your eyelids are fluttering, my dear, so you might as well open them,' a different voice coaxed. 'You're the only one who can tell me how you came to be wandering out in the cold, wrapped only in a black leather strap.'

The image startled me back to reality. Yes, I recalled it now – so vividly my mind tried pushing it back in favour of summoning that lover who'd made me climax so exquisitely. But when I opened my eyes, blinking, I faced a pudgy strawberry blond whose monocle glimmered in the light from the bedside candle.

I know this man ... but what is he asking for, really? And why does Jimmy look like warmed-over death in the reflection of that lens?

I coughed, cottony-dry, and a glass of cool water was placed at my lips – where my skin pulled around the edges and felt very sore and tight. Indeed, my entire body ached, deep within my muscles, as well as a stinging over all my surface. I composed my thoughts, glancing around a room entirely of white. Yet I sensed it wasn't the heavenly vision of my dreams.

'Talk to me, Angel. When I find out who did this to you, there'll be hell to pay.'

The intensity of his voice frightened me: was he talking about the lover I'd had last night? How had he known of my dreams?

He gently stroked my face, his expression softening. 'I didn't mean to scare you, my dear. But when I saw you were missing from our table at the Exquisite Inn, and no one had followed your trail, I damn near panicked. It's not a feeling Devlin Meeh ever intends to experience again.'

Devlin Meeh. The table at the Exquisite Inn. Christmas Eve, when those hoofbeats had thundered towards the dais ... and then all that followed came back to me in a gut-wrenching rush.

And more than the soreness of my chapped, wind-burnt skin, I was keenly aware of a different sensation between my legs. I looked down and gasped. I was totally naked, stretched out on my bed – and I was bare down *there*! When I shifted my legs, I could see the tip of my clit and my outer set of petals pouting from beneath my hairless mound.

A sharp intake of breath made me look beyond the blond who stood at my bedside, to a familiar bob of auburn curls. 'Faren,' I murmured.

'Hello, Miss Angel,' she gushed, clutching her hands as though to keep from touching my puss. 'We were so worried! It's so good to have you – but how did you come to be a pinky like me?'

Pinky. *Like a singed pink flamingo.* My face prickled with humiliation. 'I – damn, but that wax was hot! And when they pulled it away to remove the hair –'

'Who, Angel?' Meeh insisted. 'I have my ideas, but only you can confirm it before I mete out their punishment.'

I sobered at once. 'You don't like it. You don't want a naked angel.'

'Oh, I can't *tell* you what sensations you've caused, my love. And it's been a full-time job to keep Faren from eating you alive,' Devlin said in a raspy voice. 'But first things first. No need to fear retaliation, Angel, because I'll never again leave your side. *So* lovely you were, in your white gown that night! But we found it in tatters, and you were trussed up like a turkey. It was sheer luck another lost soul got you back to town before you died of exposure.'

I recalled it all too well, and discussing it would only bring my humiliation back to life. But Devlin was right: he wanted to punish my abductors, and this need for revenge was the only thing that had kept me from lying down in a snowbank and dying.

'It was the KlonDykes,' I murmured, shifting beneath

Faren's avid gaze. 'When you went into the kitchen, they rode their damn horses right into the dining room, snatched me by the armpits and hustled me out the back, before anyone could believe what they were seeing. It came about so smoothly, I thought I was the evening's entertainment – thought I'd be returned to our table, laughing at the colossal joke they'd made of me.'

Meeh's brow furrowed. 'The triplets did this?'

'They galloped out to a dilapidated stable, with a farrier's forge,' I continued quietly. 'They'd planned it all out – had their clarinets stashed in the straw, and then bound my arms to my sides and tethered me to hitching posts, with my legs spread. They ... fondled themselves to wet their reeds, and paraded around playing Christmas carols while Grant made me ... suck him.'

'Galloway was in on it? But he was there when I escorted you to our table.'

'All a part of their plan,' I murmured. 'Meanwhile, Zelda had lit the fire and was stirring something in a pot ... and while they took turns tormenting me – while Grant shot his wad all over my face – I felt wax being spread, like molten lava. Then they let it harden and yanked it off –'

A squeal filled the room when Faren clutched her crotch through her uniform.

I smiled ruefully. 'That's exactly what I said! And then they laughed at me. And when Nelda heard hoofbeats approaching, they scattered – except one of the triplets returned to remove me and the rest of the evidence. That's when she dumped me outside of town. In the snow, without any clothes.'

Devlin considered this, stroking his chin as the thunderclouds gathered along his pale brow. 'Only one sort of punishment suits this occasion!' he rasped. 'I'll tell Venus to take immediate action –'

The blood rushed from my face, for I'd neglected to mention that the Titzlers said *she* had instigated their mischief.

'– and you will see for yourself how those who cross me come to regret it,' he muttered. 'Perhaps they, too, shall be cast out into the wilderness, when they're too weak from Venus's wrath to save themselves. This is unforgivable!'

He stalked towards the doorway of my room, intent on vengeance – but then turned to me again. 'That handsome young fellow who brought you here – you knew him, didn't you?'

I couldn't help smiling. 'Yes. That was Collin Cooper, my partner when we took off from Seattle. He was coming back from the gold fields, empty-handed, and got caught in that storm.'

Meeh's lips curved slightly. 'Funny, the way things fall into place sometimes.'

And then he was off on his merciless mission.

13 **Our Little Secret**

'Will you be wanting a bath now, Angel? You smell like you got rode hard and put away wet, if you catch my meaning.' Faren stepped to my bedside, her fingers trembling visibly as she rested them on the sheets.

My eyes widened. 'What day is it?'

'Twenty-sixth, miss. Devlin was heading out the gates with a search party, late Christmas Eve, when Mr Cooper stumbled into sight. Once we tucked you into bed, you slept through Christmas!'

An alarm went off in my mind, telling me my dream lover – that lovely man! – hadn't been a dream at all. I was indeed sticky between the legs, and if Faren had smelled it on me ... and Meeh most definitely had *not* been the man plunging deep inside me ...

'A bath would be wonderful,' I murmured, hoping to cover my troubled thoughts with my smile. Devlin had set himself on punishing Grant and the KlonDykes, so perhaps he hadn't caught the telltale scent of sex between my legs. Or perhaps he understood that I'd been deep asleep when my mystery man came over me ... and inside me.

'It'd be my pleasure to bathe you, Angel. But first I'll give you a belated Christmas gift.'

Her green eyes shone like fiery emeralds, and intuition told me it wasn't a present wrapped in paper. After taking my breath away with her gaze, she let her focus linger on my bare breasts and then flow lovingly down my stomach to the naked cleft that seemed to fascinate her so. Faren let out a sigh, licking her lips.

'How very lovely,' she breathed, removing her ruffled pinafore. 'When I first saw it – when Devlin had Mr Cooper carry you up here to bed – it was all I could do not to touch it ... taste it. And then when your friend slipped in here last night, I got so damn horny watching him plunge that gorgeous cock into it, I had to pleasure myself with Meeh and then spend the next hour on your bidet.'

'My friend?' I queried, watching the black dress fall away from her budded breasts. If she'd kept Devlin occupied, perhaps he was none the wiser about my midnight visitor ...

'Oh, Collin. Now *there's* a pole I'd like to climb!' Faren giggled. She stepped out of her puddle of clothes, then reached tentatively towards my bare thigh. 'But he'd be second-best, Angel. Any man would. That's just the way of it with me, and there's no sense pretending otherwise.'

I'd gathered that, these past weeks while this maid and I had entertained Devlin with our chocolate delights. But she was wiser than her girlish looks suggested: Faren always, always danced attendance on Dr Meeh when he was with us, reaching for me as part of his pleasure. Now, however, with lust radiating from her face, there was no mistaking her preference, and her knowing stroke between my wet petals made me forget my fears about getting caught; made me open my legs and watch as first one and then another of her gentle fingers circled my slit to make it quiver in anticipation.

'I want to lick your pretty puss, Angel,' she whispered, pleading with her eyes. 'I want to taste you, and Collin. I want to feel those slick pink lips on mine, kissing me back, and then – when you can't hold back any longer – I want to rub your stiff little clitty with mine, until we're howling like the insatiable pussies we are. We'll make so much juice, I'll be changing your sheets and airing out your bed! We're kindred souls now, you know.'

Such talk, from someone who looked about twelve! But her words spoke to the part of me she was stroking, ever so slowly, as though she knew I was unable to refuse ... knew which folds and throbbing little knobs most wanted to make her whispered wishes come true.

When she climbed on to my bed, her body softened by the candlelight, I slipped a pillow between my back and the head board, so I could watch her take her delight. Faren extended her tongue, kneeling between my knees with her hands splayed over my bare thighs. My heart stood still, quivering in its place as she lowered her mouth to my naked mound ... a part of me that still looked foreign this way, yet held a novelty I hadn't anticipated. At the first touch of her tongue, my legs spread themselves further apart, and I was lost.

Faren lapped delicately at first, savouring the taste of mingled sex, male upon female. Laughing low in her throat, she teased me from the base of my hole all the way up the underside of my clit with one smooth stroke of her tongue tip, tensing every muscle in my body. I was incredibly close to coming, even after such minimal stimulation – I suppose because the rapture on the maid's face was more than I'd bargained for. When she settled her flattened tongue between my folds, to rub up and down with firm, wet strokes, I spread those slick pink lips with my fingertips, opening myself more fully to her than ever before.

With a moan, she licked me in earnest – and then I realised it wasn't just Faren I'd heard. Collin stood in my doorway, his cornflower eyes riveted to the sight we made – red ringlets bobbing between the spread legs of a woman brazenly offering herself up for more, her plump butt wiggling in the air, teasing at him ...

displaying another naked slit and the honey running there.

'Come in,' I breathed. 'Faren was just telling me how much she'd like to climb your pole, Collin. And I see it's growing taller, even as we speak.'

He let out his breath in a rush, his hand going for his belt buckle. He'd shaved since I saw him out in that blizzard, leaving a close-clipped beard that followed the arc of his cheeks down from his moustache and along his jaws. His raven hair was longer, nearly to his shoulders now, and it shone soft and clean in the candlelight as he approached my white canopy bed.

'I must've died and gone to heaven,' he rasped. He glanced at Faren's juvenile features and then watched with more interest as she laved my open folds with her quickening tongue. My clit was clearly visible, sticking up in the pale pink cleft of my mound, and the maid's lapping sounds were driving us all to distraction.

I shuddered with the first wave of my climax, thrashing on my pillow. At my extended moan, Faren rose up, wiped her chin with the back of her hand and grinned at our guest.

'You'll have to wait your turn, Collin. I promised Angel a seeing-to.'

His clothes continued to fall around him as he watched her pivot between my legs, until she faced away from me. Angling herself so her ass stuck up, she rested her weight on the backs of my thighs, and with a finger she found my slit again. I convulsed, wetting her, for I could see the honey gathered around her own puss. I could already imagine her spreading it over mine, with those grinding thrusts she used on Devlin to get the best from his little prick.

'Stick out your clit and fuck me with it,' she commanded, rocking against me.

I had no choice, for my body was too wired to deny

her. Thrusting out my nub, I strained to make the best contact with her pussy and the fingers she slid between us. My wetness welled up and, without any hair between us, we were slipping and wallowing against each other with that sexual insanity of those who need release more than food or water or even air. Our yelps intensified this wiggling, making the honey run between us until we were sloppy with it.

Then we found the right spot – that pressure point where the rubbing was right for both of us. Our clits became greedy with need. Like crazed animals we moved, groove to groove, until Faren burst into a wailing frenzy and convulsed. The sight of her backside, flexing and shimmying above her exposed pink folds, sent me over the edge as well.

'Don't you vixens *dare* quit before I get my turn!' Collin rasped. With one broad hand, he shoved Faren towards the foot of the bed to create a space between our writhing bodies.

His cock had shot out like a telescope, throbbing a bright reddish-purple at the tip, which he then thrust into the maid's open hole. She'd landed with her face against the mattress, ass in the air, and this new stimulation got her going all over again. Collin heaved himself against her, indenting her fleshy hips with his fingers. Grimacing, he thrust with increasing speed, making the bed rock wildly along with their guttural moans.

What a sight he was, that man – all broad chest and bunching, muscled hips as he slapped against her with his sac dangling. Faren cried out, raising up on her knees to sit atop that pole she'd admired, until she could handle no more of it. She danced like a manic grasping an electrical wire, and then fell forward, exhausted from her second climax.

But Collin wasn't done – he'd saved himself for me!

And when he turned on his knees, the look on his rakish young face was almost as titillating as that randy, rampant shaft now pointed at my sex.

'Open wide,' he teased in a husky voice. 'You girls've got me going now, and I'm not nearly finished!'

My vow to Meeh vanished when Collin's broad, bulbous tip pressed my pussy. While I'd spent countless days with this man, travelling to the Klondike, I'd been too indisposed to fully arouse him – or so it seemed, from the look of him now. Collin towered above me, his dark hair flowing around a face taut with passion, his body flexed to take its pleasure. That he'd merely whetted his appetite on the maid fuelled my desire, and I opened to swallow him.

Deep inside me he slid, making both of us grunt and grab for each other. Hot and hard and fast he went after it, squeezing his eyes shut, letting his jaw fall slack so he could pant with each push. I squeezed him and then released, squeezed and then released again, revelling in the feel of such a solid cock working me to another peak. I came from out of nowhere, from the core outward, and as I felt his hot seed filling me I strained towards those final, satisfying vibrations that would top me out.

He fell on his elbows, his chest moving against my belly as he caught his breath. Faren crawled alongside me and stretched out too, wrapping her upper leg and arm around us from the side. A stillness settled over the room.

'Well, I've done it now,' I sighed, running my hand along the soft skin of Collin's back.

'I won't tell if you won't,' Faren replied.

Our handsome guest raised up to give us a questioning look. 'You can't tell me you didn't *want* that.'

'Oh, the wanting has nothing to do with it,' our redhead replied with a brittle laugh. 'But Dr Meeh's a possessive one. When he takes a wench under his wing, he expects her total fidelity, in exchange for his devotion and protection.'

Collin considered this. 'I thought it was a fellow named Grant you came here for.'

Bless him, he wasn't judging me, nor did he seem skittish about staying in our arms. 'Seems the gallant Mr Galloway invited me here to fill his quota,' I said quietly. 'That's why I warned you about coming here to Satan. The rule in this peculiar paradise is that you have to convince someone else to come, or be banished to Meeh's salt mines as his slave.'

'So I've fulfilled your obligation,' Collin said with a shrug. He touched the crystal angel with his fingertip. 'After all we shared, making our way up here, I couldn't allow you to suffer that punishment, Rosie. You're the best gold I've found on this trek.'

'It's not that simple, sweetheart.' I worded my reply carefully, not wanting to repel such a considerate man. 'Dr Meeh took me as his mistress before Grant had a chance at me, which is why Grant allowed his girls to abduct me and ... wax me.'

'And throw you naked into the snow? That was your reward for travelling two thousand miles for that no-good –?'

I stroked his face – but we couldn't let his anger get us in trouble. 'Devlin will deal with it in ... an appropriate manner,' I insisted quietly. 'Satan is his town, Collin. He makes and breaks the rules, at his discretion. But why were *you* out there? Something about a hoax?'

Collin's mouth snapped shut; his colour deepened. 'Came all this way to find out there's no gold – or at least no claims available. By the time those fellows toting the gold nuggets disembarked at Seattle, before we left, all the available land was staked and claimed.'

The bottom dropped out of my stomach. 'But they were talking as though –'

'Talk's cheap, Rosie. And desperate fools will believe anything. Especially if it's too good to be true.'

'But Grant's letter said –' I swallowed the rest of that sentence like a bitter pill, not daring to think back on the hardships we'd endured to come to the Klondike. 'God, I'm sorry, Collin. I goaded you into coming here –'

'You were the right woman at the right time,' he interrupted, watching me with those soulful blue eyes. 'Had somebody else come along with the same information – and they would have, within a few days – I'd have been on my way just the same.'

His face and voice softened then. 'Like I said, Rosie, you're the only treasure I found on this trip. Other fellows got nothing but a broken soul and their dreams yanked out from under them – and the prospect of making the long trip home when the weather's fit.'

My thoughts went back to the Mountie outpost, where hundreds of other prospectors passed through each day, and where Ace had warned us we'd be stranded for the entire winter, once Lake Bennett froze over. 'So this means thousands more are camping, waiting to get up here, come spring.'

'And the only profit anyone'll turn is mining the miners. Selling them supplies or services at devil-get-crewed prices.'

Once again I got an odd feeling about the nature of Satan, with its gaming dens and stores and whorehouses, and the man who ran it. *Funny, the way things all into place*, he'd said. But now that I'd heard the truth, and could only imagine the ramifications, come May, this whole situation seemed anything but funny. wondered again if this end of the earth turned on a lted axis, following a plan envisioned by a twisted, manipulative architect.

And I had a feeling I'd been putty in his hands.

14 **Oh, What a Tangled Web**

'All is ready, Angel. The Titzlers and Galloway have been rounded up and will soon receive their punishment. I thought you'd like to watch.'

The glee in Devlin's voice should've warned me about the spectacle we'd witness, but I did want to watch that foursome take their medicine. Collin and Faren came along to one of the rooms in the far reaches of Dr Meeh's splendid palace – an area I'd not seen because I hadn't noticed the passageway that tunnelled towards it.

Downward we walked, on a ramplike hallway lit by crimson candles in sconces spaced far enough apart that their light glowed eerily. Something sinister lurked here, like the disembodied spirits of those who'd been punished before, mocking us as we attended this event. Devlin had suggested we wear our best clothing, and he'd given Collin a starched white shirt and a new tuxedo. Meeh himself was decked out in a red satin suit with lapels draped in holly: Saint Nicholas wearing a vee-shaped wreath. He made a droll figure, escorting us into a room with ampitheatre seating, yet the pervading mood remained dark and ominous.

We took places in the centre of the front row, before a stage with black velvet draperies overdrawn with sparkling, weblike motifs – as though spiders spinning diamond thread had designed them. Devlin slipped his hand around mine. 'If this particular punishment doesn't produce apologies from the KlonDykes and Grant, they're off to my salt mines,' he whispered. 'No one's immune, you see. Even the mayor can be brought down a peg or two.'

My heart faltered at the nasty edge in his voice. Meeh clearly enjoyed meting out the consequences, when Satan's citizens broke his law – which made me wonder if he *knew* about my episodes in bed with Collin, and was putting on this show to prepare me for my own doom.

A squeal of pulleys and the stately parting of the stage curtains drew me from my musings. The lights dimmed, drawing my attention to the backdrop for what appeared to be a play ... about a giant spider. Here again, the weblike designs spanned the back wall in delicate arcs and peaks, glistening silver against the black velvet that resembled a night sky.

Was that weeping I heard in the wings? Voices I recognised made me smile, for Nelda, Zelda and Esmerelda could have killed me with their treachery. Yet the desperation underlying their pleas gave me pause.

'It wasn't *my* idea to abduct her –'

'– or to dump her in the snow, beyond Satan's gates!'

'We were following orders. Grant's orders!'

Their excuses rose to a shrill pitch as they approached from offstage, and a scuffling sound told me they were struggling against whoever escorted them, just as I had tried, in vain, to escape the Klon-Dykes' connivery in that stable. Whimpering came next, and when they were shoved ahead of the three burly guards who steered them, we got our first look at Satan's latest criminals.

It was a pitiful sight. Gone were the vests and bandanna masks and holsters the girls wore with such bravado: they were naked, with their hands cuffed behind them, which forced them to walk onstage with their breasts thrust forward. Their blonde hair had been hastily bunched atop their heads, held loosely with pins that might fall out at any minute. With their tear-streaked faces and their bushless pussies on parade before us, they might've been students at a girls' school caught skipping their evening vespers.

Collin leaned over to whisper, '*This* is who abducted you? They don't look capable of –'

'They rode in on horses,' I reminded him, unable to take my eyes from the struggling trio, 'and with six pistols tied at their thighs, and the element of surprise, all the odds were stacked in their favour.'

'I know what *I'd* like to do to those bitches!' Faren hissed on Collin's other side. Yet she was gazing at the bare clefts between their legs with unmistakable hunger, squirming in her upholstered theatre seat.

Meeh leaned forward to take us all in his gaze. 'Venus will give them more than they can handle – believe me! She has tricks up her … sleeve that only those who break my rules find out about. Now they'll realise it's a bad idea to cross Devlin Meeh. Very bad indeed.'

The ebony queen he spoke of stepped into view then, strutting in a gown of iridescent silver that left her sleek, powerful arms bare and plunged in the front to push her lush breasts into full view. The dress hugged her curves, flaring at her hips into a swirling circle; cascading diaphanous layers whispered and swished with her every step. Never had there been a more royal vixen than this stunning virago with her dark hair coiled above a jewelled tiara.

I was glad I wasn't her victim. Her smile alone banished all hope of escaping with even a shred of self-respect.

Without a word, she pointed to the triplet nearest the centre of the stage, and then to the backdrop of shimmering, silver web. That guard nodded, steering his blonde captive in the direction of Venus's imperious gesture, holding firm against the girl's struggling. He turned Miss Titzler to face us, and with the furtive click of a key released her handcuffs. He then raised one of her pale arms, and Venus leaned forward with a pitching motion – and before my eyes knew what they were seeing, that triplet's arm was fastened to the glittering web behind her.

She screamed, and as the guard struggled to align her other arm, I saw a slender thread, with little silver balls on each end, snake through the air at lightning speed. It wrapped itself rapidly around her wrist and a thread of the web.

'Zelda! Esmerelda!' she cried. 'Help me! This bitch is going to –'

But Nelda's words turned into a squeal as the web began to revolve, raising her up off the floor to hang by her extended arms. With two more quick flicks, Venus sent her balled ropes through the air with dead-centre accuracy, and the first victim was now attached to the web by her wrists and ankles, spreadeagled and squirming. Her hair came loose on one side and fell over her face, making her shake it from her eyes.

At a finger signal, the second guard shoved another Titzler toward Venus's web, filling the theatre with a caterwauling that made my skin crawl. 'Zelda! Zelda, what'll I do?' she cried.

But the stoic leader of the KlonDykes could only watch in amazement with the rest of us as her sibling got stuck to the slowly turning web – this time facing away, with her arms stretched wide, like her legs, which left her wiggling backside in full view. As Esmerelda fought her bonds, those pink petals between her legs quivered like a delicate open rose afraid of an approaching storm.

'Don't think you're getting away with this,' Zelda muttered – perhaps to her guard as well as Venus – as she too was shoved towards the web and uncuffed.

This time the spiteful spider queen caught her blonde bug with wrists directly above her ankles, facing away, so that as the web revolved, Zelda drooped inelegantly with her butt bobbing lower than the rest of her body. Nelda now hung suspended upside down, with her golden hair dangling below a face reddened by rage and the rush of blood – with her breasts quivering above her chin. Esmerelda, in the twelve o'clock position, hadn't been bound as closely to the netting so was slanting sideways, on her way to the downward curve.

Venus looked quite pleased with herself, but I saw an obvious gap. 'Where's Grant?' I muttered. 'He arranged this whole mess, after all.'

The woman in silver turned my way, wearing the wickedest grin I ever saw. 'Come out now, Mr Galloway,' she called into the backstage area. Her voice rode low and smoky around the theatre; Venus was bent on retribution, knowing she couldn't lose. 'You know our bargain: you must fuck each triplet until you come, squirting where we can all see it. Failing this, you'll be bound to my web just like the ladies – and I take over from there. Understood?'

Grant's laughter preceded him, and when he stepped into view, unclothed and cocky, I wanted to slap him.

'It'll be my pleasure to perform for you, Venus,' he boasted, taking himself in hand. 'What man wouldn't want to be in my place right now, ordered to service these three delectable ladies? A fantasy come true!'

He looked directly at me, stroking his prick to an incredible length, as though thinking I'd be too jealous or aroused to remain in my seat. In that short interval, however, the triplets rode a few more degrees around their carousel, and I began to see the sort of contest Venus had devised. Climaxing three times would challenge even the randiest man, but to come with each of the girls – on that moving web spun of gossamer threads – would require nothing short of a miracle.

He turned to look at the web then, which was spinning Nelda into a sideways flight nearly within his reach. His body flexed, lean like a pale panther's, in just enough light to enhance the flat planes and masculine lines I'd savoured in my imagination for lo, these many years.

I had learned, however, that time doesn't improve all things. It was Jimmy Crystal I missed at such a moment because, for all his boring predictability and reluctance to change, I knew my gentle barkeep wouldn't even consider the Titzler triplets. He'd take his punishment, silently, like a man, and then he'd return to *me*.

Grant, however, had something to prove. As Nelda rode into the lowest position on the rotating web, he trotted towards her, his cock bobbing ahead of him. 'Suck me, sweetheart,' he crooned, aiming the shiny reddish head at her mouth.

But the blonde turned away. 'I'm going to be sick,' she wheezed, her stomach rippling with a suppressed heave. 'And even if I weren't, I'm disgusted with you. *You* should be spinning on this damn contraption!'

'But none of us go free unless – you've got to cooperate!'

His commandeering attitude got him nowhere, however, and meanwhile Nelda was rising too high to take him in her mouth. She slapped her knees together, too, with a sound that echoed around the rafters.

'Fine! I'll get you next time,' Galloway muttered. He wrapped his hand around his pecker again, to meet the oncoming Esmerelda. Since she was facing away, with her arms and legs extended to form four points of a star, the only opening she could offer was from the back side.

Considering this, Grant calculated the movement of the web and waited for the outstretched blonde to rotate, so he could grab the silver threads above her wrists and then step on the ones beside her bare feet. This put him over the top of her sprawled body – not that she could cooperate. The strands of the web stretched, so each time Grant tried to thrust between her legs, the two of them swayed like monkeys on a vine.

'Would you hurry up and get this over with?' Esmerelda snapped. 'The sooner we're finished with this humiliation, the sooner we can start working at Le Coq D'Or. We're quitting at the Brazen Lady because Venus has offered us much better pay –'

'– for shorter hours, and fancier clothes!' Nelda piped up.

'And we don't have to toot those stupid clarinets, or put up with your bullshit!' Zelda added. This triplet was agitated enough – or just spoiler enough – to begin swinging her suspended backside, as though she were propelling herself on a trapeze.

The entire web rippled with her movement, causing Grant to stab repeatedly at the air between Esmerelda's legs while trying to maintain his grip. 'Traitors!' he called out, not sounding nearly as bold as when he'd begun. 'After all the times I've set things up so you could ride out your outlaw fantasies –'

'Oh, stuff it up your butt!' one of them jeered, and this set the whole trio into a chorus of catcalls and obscenities.

'What a fine idea,' Venus said slyly. She stood to one side, her arms folded beneath her bulging breasts, biding her time. Didn't seem surprised when Grant reached the top of the wheel's rotation and gingerly clambered backwards to avoid going down head-first.

This brought him, slowly and swinging awkwardly to find footholds, to where the third Titzler sagged from her bindings. She hung deceptively still now.

'Zelda, please,' he coaxed. 'You and I have always been able to reason with each other, to reach a compromise that benefits us both.'

He was wrapping himself carefully around her, positioning himself so he could straighten his legs and enter her from below. Just as he made this move, however, Zelda sprang to life again.

'I'm *tired* of being compromised!' she snapped, and she swung up with enough force to catch him in the crotch – which sent him flying off the web.

Grant landed in a heap, trying very hard to repress his pain and wrath. The dark virago standing beside him showed no mercy, however: Venus raised one silver-slippered foot and pressed it into his chest, flattening him against the floor.

'You've had three chances,' she said in a diamond-edged voice. 'So now it's my turn. And since it's my game, I can change the rules any time I please.'

Galloway was about to protest, but his captor undid the flowing skirt of her gown with the flick of a wrist. Down it slithered, on to his face and chest, with a shimmering sheen of silver. This left Venus clad in a sleeveless, trim-fitting garment that resembled a camisole fastened between her legs. And what legs they were, long and muscled as she stooped to remove the skirt from Grant's face, showing us an ass with hard curves, accentuated by the bands of her tight silver costume.

Grant's expression mirrored my own amazement ... and then it registered outright fear. Meeh's queen of discipline reached slowly, seductively, down her abdomen, keeping her high-heeled slipper on his chest as her fingernails sang a siren song along the fabric. Galloway's Adam's apple bobbed hard when he swallowed, his eyes riveted to the inevitable destination of those ebony hands.

'I'd like another chance,' he rasped. 'I promise I won't disappoint you this time. We go back a long ways –'

'Yours has never been long enough,' Venus said with a sneer. She spread those powerful legs to reach between them, to grip whatever had provoked Grant's sudden adjustment of attitude. From our angle, we saw the quick flex of hips, and I felt the tightening of Collin's grip on one side while Devlin Meeh suppressed a knowing chuckle on the other.

The wheel, meanwhile, had come to a halt, and all three KlonDykes swivelled their heads to see what was happening to Grant. Nelda went paler and Esmerelda gasped; Zelda, who hung as though slung in an invisible hammock, got eyes the size of saucers.

'Holy shit, would you look at the size of that cock!'

I jerked in my seat, straining to see what I couldn't believe. Indeed, Venus was holding Grant Galloway spellbound – or nailed to the stage in terror – with the thickest, longest, darkest erection I'd ever seen. Like a tree branch it stuck out, and I calculated that if she leaned over at the proper angle, she could rub that thing between her breasts.

Grant, as a man, probably had other ideas about where she planned to put it – and Collin's intake of breath confirmed this. He squirmed beside me, scooting his ass against his seat, as though to escape the fate he saw coming for Galloway.

Venus, however, lost no more time on first impressions. 'You know our deal, Grant,' she said in a sinuous tone. 'You didn't even get yourself inserted!

These girls can't *stand* you and your arrogance any longer! So now you all must take your due from –'

'But you've seen what Rosie's wearing on her cheek!' Grant protested, pointing desperately in my direction. 'She stole your favourite crystal, Venus! So why isn't *she* up here to get reamed?'

'Nice try. But it's not her turn yet.' With a snap of her fingers, the statuesque creature directed the guards to the man beneath her foot.

In seconds they'd grabbed Galloway and were shoving him towards the web, where the KlonDykes watched from their various positions. And, as before, Venus deftly flicked four more of those silver-balled strings through the air to whip-stitch him to the silvery strands in a most ungainly position: facing us, with his hands above his head and his legs hitched up at hip level, so his crotch bulged toward us, spread wide. His prick had withered to a pitiful thing, and I saw his asshole puckering in fear.

'Now you know why Venus thrives in a place like Satan,' Meeh whispered. 'Where else can a biological misfit be queen? Where else can a freak of nature live out the fantasy of dominating all she – and he – surveys?'

The crystal angel on my face grew hot. Venus's hint that my turn was coming hadn't escaped me, and the thought of being at this mannish woman's mercy filled my mouth with the coppery tang of fear. I sank lower in my seat, wondering what Venus would do to the four victims caught in her web ... wondering what sort of mistress this ebony spider had made for Meeh, and why he'd demoted her. It had to be more than love of my chocolate pudding. Had to be some sort of ploy, since he'd also implanted this weird woman's favourite crystal in my face.

'Isn't she a piece of work? Every muscle, every sinew

as sleek as steel. Built to go on and on and on ... the best of both sexes, in one incredible body,' the pudgy blond beside me remarked. Then he leaned closer, as though to share a secret. 'While Venus does indeed have a shaft, it's about the size of mine. That chocolate cock you're squirming at is a leather dildo designed to fit over her equipment, strapped in place beneath her clothing. Now you know why no one misbehaves a second time in Satan. Looks real, doesn't it?'

Real, indeed; as real as the hermaphrodite's wrath if she found out I knew her secret. Had I not already been concerned about what Venus planned for my future, perhaps I would've better understood Devlin's fascination for the arachnid who now mounted her web with quick, agile sweeps. She truly did resemble a spider with only half the usual number of legs, making her way toward Nelda with an incredible grace that barely made a ripple in the network of curving threads. She must've weighed as much as Grant did, with all her muscle and height, yet she crossed the gossamer silver strands as though walking on air.

Nelda had landed at the top of the circular web, which was no longer revolving, and watched Venus approach with horrified eyes. 'I don't have *room* for that thing in my –'

'You'll take it wherever I stick it,' came the tart reply. 'This is your punishment for mistreating Meeh's mistress, after all. Not a cakewalk.'

Without warning, Venus swung up between the blonde's legs and planted her dark mouth on the bared, spread pussy. Nelda shrieked, struggling so hard the entire web shimmied and set the other three victims rocking in their places, contemplating their own doom.

Did Venus bite her? As the shrill cries echoed around us, I shifted in my seat. The blatantly carnal sight had an odd effect on me: while I was horrified by what I saw, I couldn't look away. I had to watch every shudder of Nelda's lithe body; wonder about the texture and temperature of that tarantula's tongue as it probed her; listen for every furtive lick and slick flickering of Nelda's folds ... and hear the unmistakable change from terror to ecstasy in her protests.

'Oh no, not there! Please not – I can't stand any more of this torture! This – Lord, your tongue is all the way up my ... no, don't stop! You *cannot* leave me hanging this way, to –'

Venus raised up, smirking. 'So you want this big dick, do you?'

'Oh, yes – yes! Or even just your tongue. *Anything* but this cold, empty space!'

Nelda's tormentor swung up higher, to stick that extraordinary stinger where her tongue had been. Miss Titzler buckled, folding forward, wearing a grimace of sublime climax – until Venus pulled out just as quickly as she'd penetrated.

'No! You can't leave me! You have to finish this – this ...'

But the creator of that web moved on with a cruel laugh, nimbly swinging toward Esmerelda. This triplet, the most squeamish of the three, bunched in upon herself in an effort to escape invasion. With her limbs spread and her backside hanging free, however, she was defenceless against Venus's tricks. Without preamble, the ebony jester fitted herself against this triplet's backside and began humping like a large black dog.

Esmerelda's shrieks joined her sister's, lower in pitch but expressing the same initial shock and pain. She was dripping wet, however, for a copious amount of girl juice splattered the stage below them. Soon, she too was singing a siren song of desire that knew no degradation.

'Oh my word, yes – *yesss!*' she crescendoed, rising

into the upper registers of her voice as she writhed against the web.

Venus twisted then, giving us a profile view of the punishment she was putting out – the quick in-and-out of that prodigious cock pumping and grinding in a pussy that somehow took it all in. Esmerelda was tightening towards a climax that would fill the air with an outpouring of lust and obscenities I wasn't sure I could withstand, when Meeh leaned over to enlighten me.

'You realise, don't you, that the insatiable Venus is whetting appetites, whipping those girls into a frenzy – only to leave them unsatisfied,' he whispered. 'And, unlike most lovers, this queen of sensual excess can leave her partners wanting it, craving it, so dependent upon it that they suffer continual need for a climax that'll never see completion. They'll live in a state of constant peak arousal and not be able to come.'

Sporting girl that I was, I'd never heard of such a thing ... indeed, I'd sometimes *wished* for such a state of arousal. I crossed my legs hard, while on the other side of Collin, Faren had stuck her hand up her dress. She was staring, mesmerised, at the two Titzlers Venus had left hanging, her own wet scent wafting around us as she fingered her folds.

'How ... how does she do that?' I murmured, wanting to maintain some sense of perspective as I anticipated what Venus might do to Zelda.

Devlin chuckled. 'Just as her body is capable of male and female response, something about her juice produces an insatiable craving in those who receive it. Some of those she's punished have wandered about humping everything and everyone they see, like sex-crazed dogs, until they simply go mad.'

Insanity, he was saying. A burning desire so keen it couldn't be quenched.

'And then what happens to them?' I breathed. Venus was now lapping at the cheeks of Zelda's ass, and I didn't want to miss a single wet stroke.

'They eventually wander off.'

Into those brutal Arctic elements that would've been *my* demise, had Collin not come along. I squirmed, not wanting to know any more about this spider and her venom. Yet I tingled with the possibilities of having that huge cock inside me – fake or otherwise.

'It's for the best, really,' Meeh went on quietly. 'By then, they've lost their taste for food and haven't slept for days – usually suffer such extreme chafing of their privates that they can't wear clothing. All their bodies know is the constant throbbing of a climax that wants to go over the edge, and never quite gets there.'

To the cavalier observer, it would sound like the ultimate way to die – in such a constant state of arousal that nothing else mattered. I could already see, however, that the KlonDykes – that playfully horny trio of horn-players – were already approaching a frenetic state of need that resembled pain. Like having a wildfire case of poison ivy with no way to scratch.

And, like me – and like Collin and Faren seated beside me – the two blondes and Grant now watched Zelda stiffen with excruciating arousal as Venus slipped that cock inside her. They bobbed as one, the pale blonde fitted against bent black legs that flexed with each thrust, moving faster and higher with each stroke.

Was this the same woman who'd laughed while pouring hot wax around my snatch? She had nothing to chuckle about now. She was yowling like a ravenous cat, twisting within Venus's grip to get the best angle, straining and bearing down against that monstrous cock as though she couldn't get enough.

And she never did. The spiderlike hermaphrodite disengaged, leaving Zelda bawling like a lost calf, thrusting against air. She did, however, follow the domineering madam's progress towards Grant, who now sported a throbbing erection despite the horrified expression on his face.

'Get close to me with that thing, and so help me, I'll –'

His threat disappeared into the vast space above us, just as his cock got swallowed between the halves of Venus's taut ass. She'd pivoted nimbly and opened herself without any apparent thought – although her sly smile told us she knew precisely how to humiliate the great Grant Galloway.

'You were saying?' she mocked, rocking against him. With her head pointed our way and her lithe body back-thrusting between his two splayed legs, Venus resembled the centre of a brown-eyed susan springing out from two pale petals – but luridly evil.

Grant, meanwhile, got more caught up in the rush than he would admit. And once again Venus let her victim reach that near-peak state before pulling away – only this time she turned in place to go at him again. Galloway hollered long and loud when it was her cock up his ass – so she shut him up by hoisting her big bosoms out of her costume and into his face.

Set on vengeance, Venus skewered him in earnest, her breathing accelerating until it filled the theatre like a misbegotten wind out of the wicked hills. She squeezed her eyes shut, rutting like a buck, and then cut loose with a siren-like wail. Jism spilt out of Grant's backside, splattering with a rude noise as she pumped herself to completion, making poor Collin moan and shift from one cheek to the other while Faren gasped against her hand.

My seat was wet, and Meeh casually ran his hand up my thigh to bare it before testing my puss with an inquisitive finger. 'Do you want her too, my dear?' he murmured.

'*No*! I don't want to be crazy with –'

'Then heed my warning, Angel. The KlonDykes realise that the crystal piece in your cheek kept Venus's lovers safe and sane before ... because by placing it in the eye-hole of that dildo, she kept her juice to herself,' he explained. 'At her whim, she can also call upon the crystal's magic to reverse the ill effects of today's punishment. So, naturally, the girls and Galloway will *want* that sparkling little gem, as an antidote, but also as a peace offering to the goddess who now has them in her thrall.'

The faceted angel fluttered her little wings, pinching my face. Once again, I wondered at the powers Devlin Meeh possessed, wondered if my imagination were augmenting them, or if he really did control every little sigh and heartbeat in this mystical domain where he and Venus ruled.

'Why are you doing this to me?' I whimpered. Venus was climbing lithely down from her web, her breasts bobbing pert and proud while that cock remained rampant, despite her climax. 'What did I ever do to deserve –'

'All things are revealed in their own good time,' he intoned, wiping his wet fingers along my bared collarbone. Then he leaned closer, inhaling. 'Ah, sweet perfume of pussy. Even without any chocolate, you're the most delectable thing to come to Satan in many a blue moon, my dear.'

I swallowed hard, feeling as befuddled and desperate as my four tormentors, whom the guards were now loosening from the web's slender threads. 'What will keep me safe then?'

Meeh grinned, making his monocle wink – and in its

lens I caught the image of Jimmy, lying in a repose resembling death, in the snow. 'Never forget who you are, Angel. And whose.'

With that, he rose from his seat and eloquently gestured for Faren, Collin and me to precede him from the theatre. The show was over, and the moral of its story was strikingly clear: I was a marked woman, a pawn in some nefarious game that had yet to play itself out.

15 **Caught in the Act**

'As the New Year comes in, I want to come in *you*, Angel. I hope you're ready.'

I smiled at Devlin, for what else could I do? Timing a climax at the chiming of midnight was nothing new for me: Jimmy and I had delighted in it many times, even when it meant slipping away from the revelry of our friends in his saloon for a quick in-and-out. Meeh, however, was now inspired by my hairless puss. Couldn't seem to get enough of having his 'two little girls' pleasure him.

It was the 'little' part that bothered me – little, as in Devlin's dick. Now that I'd seen Grant as a grown man, and witnessed the chocolate-coloured log between Venus's legs, I wanted what I couldn't have: a nice long cock, filling me to the rim and overflowing.

Because Collin was such a willing temptation along this line – and because he better understood the consequences of my messing with him, after seeing Venus work her web – he'd taken a room in the Exquisite Inn. Faren and I missed him. He was young and handsome; wanted adventurous sex for its own sake, rather than as an obligation to hold over us.

So New Year's Eve found Faren and me naked in Devlin's boudoir, which he'd redecorated in crimson silk and sheeny-shiny green taffeta for the holiday season. He'd picked me as the woman to be in when the clock struck twelve.

'Here, kitty, kitty,' he teased, dribbling cream from his saucer of red raspberries on to Faren's budded breasts and down her stomach. 'Lap her up, Miss Puss. Lick her ... spread yourself above her so I can watch her tongue your clit. Now that I can see it all the time, sticking out with those pink petals from your naked pussy, I want to watch it from every angle, in every degree of arousal.'

He sat behind us, a pale, chubby potentate propped against crimson pillows in his black lacquer bed. Faren was lying on her back, with his feet resting on her shoulders so she could fondle them – he had a passion for feet, Devlin did. I straddled her, facing away, to give our benefactor the best view of the private parts he was so enamoured with.

At the first touch of my tongue on her tummy, the maid giggled, playing her part as the little miss. A long stroke with the tip, down the central groove of her midriff, sent her into paroxysms of childlike laughter and had her kicking like a baby getting tickled. I moved in quickly, to bring her to sharper focus and to put my own petals above her mouth. The nub in the notch of her naked cleft was chubby and pink like Meeh; I circled it with teasing flicks and then lapped at the white cream caught in her carmine folds.

Faren convulsed with laughter, which brought her head up between my legs. She grabbed the halves of my backside then, squeezing as she separated my folds with her tongue. Then in she plunged for a blissful moment, long enough to make *me* focus, and to prime my pump in a way Devlin wouldn't. Bless her heart, she wanted us to have a good time too, in spite of this being a 'sex to order' situation.

With an eye to the clock on the mantel, I flexed and gyrated for him, exposing all the slick petals Faren didn't have in her mouth. As her licking shifted, so did mine, for we enjoyed mirroring each other's attentions to make our own pleasure, without Meeh being the wiser.

'Oh my, Angel, you're going to drip all over Faren's face. Raise up and let me see how wet you are,' he instructed in a voice going edgy with desire. 'Oh, yes, I think you'll be oozing all over her soon.'

And with that, he inserted a finger, probing me until he found the sweet spot high up inside, which made me groan against him … made me close my eyes to savour the pressure building there … made my muscles clutch as the liquid heat boiled over. With a little cry I gushed, tilting my hips forward so more would drip on to Faren's chest than into her nose and eyes.

The quick shifting of the mattress announced Devlin's arousal: he was panting at the sight of my open, inflamed hole, tracing the folds and flaps with his wet finger as he positioned himself on his knees behind me. Faren, ever aware of where her bread got buttered, cupped his sac in one hand and gave my breast a squeeze with her other. She was quaking with the strokes of my tongue, begging me with each shallow breath to bring her off.

'Oh, Devlin, look how hard you are,' she murmured. 'And I get to watch you ram that thing into Angel's pretty puss. God, the sight of it, entering her … yes, go deeper, Devlin … shove it up her cunt.'

That high, childlike voice worked its magic on all of us, for I was far more enthused about this coupling than usual – perhaps because Devlin, all three inches of him, seemed harder and more insistent. He bumped against my hips, rutting rapidly as his maid caressed his balls. When the clock mechanism whirred, ready to strike, Faren slyly pressed her thumb to my nub and held it, knowing the contact there would spur me on.

With the first strike, I caught fire and quivered inside.

Devlin kept pumping, mumbling about how he was going to shoot like a cannon, while Faren got caught up in her first convulsions. Two ... three ... Grabbing my backside, she levered herself up to plant wild, hot kisses where my honey flowed, which pressed her mouth against the base of Devlin's cock as well – and prompted me to spread further, enhancing the contact from both of them.

Six ... seven ... I lapped Faren's juices with my full, flat tongue as she climaxed. Nine ... ten ... Devlin got downright desperate, his wails coming each time he pumped, mindless with ecstasy. Eleven ... twelve ... I curled in and came, compelled by the merciless pressing against my clit.

Meeh's final cry turned to delight and laughter as he fell back against his pillows. 'Good show, girls!' he crowed, panting as he held his privates. 'It's now officially eighteen ninety-eight – because I've declared it so!'

Humility had never been Devlin's strong point. Yet I wondered if there wasn't something more than boast about his statement, for it seemed everything he said and did had a direct effect on the events in Satan and the lives of its citizens. His citizens. As Faren and I rolled away from each other, I was keenly aware that I'd started this new year in basically the same way I had several others: sweating, and wet between the legs, and sated – at least for the moment.

But oh, what a difference the place made. And for all my aspirations upon leaving Jimmy Crystal and Oblivion, and becoming Satan's Angel, I couldn't really say I'd improved my lot at all. Not at all.

My growing dissatisfaction made me restless, and even as I tried to hide it from Dr Meeh, I realised I was knotting my own noose. He seemed to see all and know all, as though that crystal angel on my cheek opened my thoughts, my very soul, for his viewing. But he said nothing, of course. He simply grinned that altar-boy grin and gazed at my hairless slit, as though anticipating surprises he wasn't going to tell me about.

I was free to go where I pleased when not in his bed, so on a mid-January day I dressed in one of the more modest gowns he'd lavished upon me – blue, it was, like my eyes, fashioned from flounced taffeta and lace. Faren was making a rare trip into town for toiletries and massage oils, so I joined her in the carriage and we planned our outing.

'I can't believe you've never visited Satan's shops,' she tittered. 'They cater to a high-dollar clientele – but since no one's forced to pay their tab, who cares?'

'Meeh's merchants don't charge anything?' Yet another oddity about this town aglow with ruby streetlights at midday.

'Well, he owns all the stores, you know. And once we're here ... he pretty much owns us, as well,' she replied quietly.

Ah, yes – that again. The part of this paradise that chafed like a starched collar, despite the wealth and apparent well-being of everyone we saw. The streets of town were crowded with bejewelled ladies and well-dressed men, all smiling and going about their daily business as though it didn't *matter* that they marched to Meeh's music like the mice had followed the Pied Piper.

I'd have been better off to assume their complacency, their acceptance of what they'd lost to live out their fantasies here. My woolgathering gave way to more curious thoughts, however, when I caught sight of the Brazen Lady – and Faren's mind ran in the same direction.

'What do you suppose has happened to the Klon-

Dykes and Grant?' she mused aloud. 'I can't think Devlin would actually allow them to go *mad* with passion. Galloway's the mayor, after all. Has been since anyone can remember.'

'One way to find out,' I replied, knowing even as I said it, I was asking for trouble. Even though the angel that shimmered on my cheek was supposedly a talisman cloaking me in Devlin's protection, I was spitting on the devil's tail to even consider going into Grant's gaming room without Meeh.

Which was precisely why I wanted to. It was as though something lured me to those gold-lettered glass doors ... something as wicked as a whore wagging her finger to come hither, and then placing that finger in her slit.

'Do your shopping and meet me here in an hour, all right?' I suggested, thumping against the carriage ceiling for Jarold to stop. 'Then I think we should pay Collin a call. After all, Devlin said he'd be off tending to business all day.'

'I do miss that rakish face and those bottomless blue eyes,' the maid sighed. 'But you be careful, missy! They kidnapped you before, and heaven knows what they'll try if they're still humping everything in sight. And Venus isn't one to miss an opportunity, if she learns you're out alone today.'

'If she wants this damn crystal back, she can have it,' I muttered, scooting toward the open carriage door. 'I didn't come here to be an angel, after all. This place might be a paradise, out here in the wilds of the Klondike, but it's a far cry from heaven.'

My thoughts shifted back to Jimmy Crystal then, but they were fleeting. As I stepped into the Brazen Lady, I was again surrounded by sights and sounds and smells I considered far, far above me: wallpaper that glimmered with gold leaf; low, cultivated voices that spoke in worldly accents; the furtive scents of expensive Scotch whiskey and Parisian perfume and wiped-up sex; the rich rustlings of silk underthings and heavy linens as I passed between intimate tables where patrons ate – no, dined upon – elegantly prepared pheasant and exotic fruits I had no name for. All this provided by Devlin Meeh, not necessarily out of generosity. I knew him too well now to believe he truly loved these people. Or anyone, for that matter.

A ruckus erupted in the rear and I swivelled to take it in: Zelda, Nelda and Esmerelda stumbled to the front of the stage, clutching their clarinets, their six-gun holsters bouncing against their thighs. Otherwise, they were naked – and their faces, pale and strained, seemed filled with their large, very dilated eyes. Again I witnessed their reed-wetting ceremony, that three-way titillation that brought cautious laughter from a crowd who seemed as wary of their odd behaviour as I. When they finally began to play, they swayed at different rhythms – while each of them played a different tune, and didn't even realise it!

It was a sobering sight. Those three sets of wriggling hips suggested that Meeh's prediction was coming true: the KlonDykes were caught in the throes of orgasms they couldn't have, and mindless of everything else. So great was their need for release, perhaps intensified by their raucous music and half-dancing, that the centre triplet – Esmerelda, I guessed – finally placed her instrument between her hairless sex lips and rubbed frantically against it.

From out of the crowd, Grant Galloway approached the stage, scowling. 'You girls are finished!' he barked, pointing towards the stage curtains. 'Out! Now!'

Whimpering, the Titzlers tottered off, probably to scratch that maddening itch that hadn't gone away. I swallowed at the thought of this, wondering if I dared stay in this place – for Grant, too, looked harried and thinner, garbed in a white sheet like Father Time ... because his pants rubbed him raw?

I moved towards the shadow of a roulette wheel, not wanting him to spot me. Apparently the KlonDykes' jobs at Venus's parlour house had fallen through, or had been a bluff in the first place. And the man they worked for – who perhaps had kept them on to take advantage of their perpetual need – had somehow found me in my dark corner. Grant gazed ominously for several seconds before walking back to a table where tuxedoed customers played Twenty-One.

I exited quickly, grateful to inhale the outside air. But where would I go? I still had forty-five minutes before Faren was due back, and I had no desire to be the target of furtive stares from those wanting to catch a glimpse of my unusual facial decoration. I began to walk, however, thinking myself safer if I remained in plain sight, among others who strolled the street by the light of those crimson lamps. No doubt the perpetual darkness of the Klondike winter – the total absence of sunlight for weeks on end – was affecting me the way it did these other people.

The sound of giggling piqued my curiosity, and I peered down an alley towards its source. I saw a narrow door, open, behind the large, brick buildings, and in the darkness I could make out wisps of smoke ... smoke that swirled in fascinating shapes against the darkness. Or was this my imagination tricking me? I walked towards the laughter and inhaled a strangely sweet aroma, deciding to take a peek inside and then be on my way.

I realised then why the voices seemed familiar: Zelda, Nelda and Esmerelda sat on floor pillows, in a tight circle around a large hookah. Each of them sucked on a flexible tube with a mouthpiece, inhaling deeply before holding her breath. And when they exhaled, the smoke curled about them, caressing them in the dimness, before wafting towards the door ... approaching me like some Oriental dragon made of vapour, wearing a smile that concealed the flame it was about to belch out.

I'd seen opium dens before, but the condition of those who frequented them had served as a harsh warning. Intuition told me the triplets sought relief from that insatiable raging between their legs, and were indeed on the downhill slide Meeh had described. I turned to leave – and ran smack into Grant Galloway. He grinned, a slightly absent expression edged with venom.

'Do come in, Rosie,' he intoned, blocking the doorway. 'The girls have been wanting to apologise for their mischief on Christmas Eve. Perhaps if you tell Meeh they've repented, he'll undo this damn hex before we – they – become too insane to be redeemed.'

'I – I don't smoke, thank you.'

'Such an uncharitable attitude. If you were ever inclined to try it, now's the time. Meeh provides only the finest of the poppy, you know.' His lean face lengthened, making those long dimples downright lethal. 'And even if you decline, you owe us this chance to make amends. Why, if I didn't know you better, I'd say you've been hiding yourself, Rosie. Afraid of meeting us where Devlin couldn't defend you.'

A protest rose in my throat, which was precisely what Grant was trying for. Yet, with his sheet-wrapped body blocking my retreat, and the Titzler triplets watching with their wide, pied eyes, what choice did I have? I'd allowed my curiosity to lure me from Meeh's safe haven, and I'd gotten myself cornered. My only consolation was that Faren would be along soon, and she was well aware of my vulnerability.

So, I sat down on the plump pillow Nelda – or was it Esmerelda? – was patting, and before I could refuse it, a mouthpiece was slipped between my lips. Zelda's smile waxed predatory as she held the hose in place. Looking into her glazed eyes gave me the sensation of staring down a deep well and seeing only my own tiny, indistinct reflection in the distant water.

'I think she's here to see Grant,' the naked blonde stated, sounding vague despite the obvious purpose of her suggestion. 'I think she knows he has a constant hard-on, and she's been too fascinated to stay away.'

I'd been holding my breath, but was forced to breathe – and the first draw of that smoke made me choke. The other two girls surrounded me immediately, cooing their concern and encouraging me to try again. But I wasn't anybody's fool ... yet. They were there to prevent my escape.

The little den darkened when Grant shut the door. He unfastened his makeshift toga, letting it fall around his body – a body gone wiry with need and constant motion; still muscular yet not as imposing as when he'd straddled me in the stable. His erection, however, pointed at me like a pistol. It pulsed, reddened from recent wear, and when he stepped towards me the crystal angel on my face smarted so sharply I inhaled more deeply than I intended.

Already I knew why this foursome sought relief with the hookah, for my head was tilting in lopsided circles. The triplets didn't seem nearly so fierce, with their dishevelled yellow hair falling about their bare shoulders, and their breasts bobbing with each move they made, and those black leather holsters riding low on their ... seductive hips, while framing the ... pink, wet pussies that seemed to pout and beckon me closer ... close enough to sample the honey I could smell despite the heady perfume of opium now filling the closed room.

'You came to Satan because you still wanted me, didn't you?' Grant asked. He sounded sing-song, and I wondered if it was from the drug working on his voice, or on my ears.

I nodded, inhaling again before letting the mouthpiece slip from my lips.

'I bet you spent many a night, over the years, wondering what became of the kid who picked your cherry,' he continued, inching closer. That pointer between his legs claimed my full attention now, because a bead of moisture had formed at its eye, like a tear. 'And when you counted the money I sent, it didn't take you two heartbeats to decide.'

His arrogance should've turned my stomach, but I couldn't deny he was right. Couldn't deny that after these weeks with Devlin Meeh, the prospect of having this long, hard cock throbbing inside me – wherever Grant chose to put it – overrode my irritation with him. After all, I was closed up in some little closet where my benefactor would never find me, let alone find out what I'd done during my trip to town. These people knew better than to abduct me again, in broad daylight, for they realised Venus and Meeh would make good on his threats to send them to the salt mines if they transgressed against his Angel again.

I licked my lips, still gazing at the fine piece of male machinery poised mere inches in front of my face.

'Do you want to touch it?' Galloway breathed, tilting his pelvis forward. 'Do you want to taste it, Rosie? You've got a better appreciation for such fare now. Even a single lick around the head would compensate for the times you refused to try it, when we were kids.'

The room drew in its breath, waiting. The KlonDykes,

too, had focused upon me as best they could, stepping back so events would take their course.

The skin of his prick pulled tighter, slick in the dimness, and the little slit wept another tear. My tongue darted out to catch it. The wet, salty droplet slithered towards my throat, and before I knew what I was doing I opened my lips in invitation. My eyes closed when the tip of him met my mouth. As he eased the hard length of it over my tongue, a collective sigh rose around me.

What a rock he was! He moaned with each move, and I sensed he was restraining himself, savouring the feel of my willing mouth around a member so desperate for release. In and out he thrust, rocking to wet himself and to feel the pressure of my rounded lips, his rapid inhalations defining the beat of my own heart.

Gentle hands were undressing me, and I didn't resist. Grant's fingers framed my face and I rose on to my knees to better suck him. Where I'd felt apprehension moments before, I now felt challenged to bring this man the satisfaction he'd been unable to attain since Venus jinxed him. That was my calling, after all – satisfying a need. Feeding a hunger.

And as that hunger became my own, my body followed the path familiar to it: I became so engrossed in pleasing this man that I myself sought the same fulfilment. With the hookah's smoke drifting around us, and the triplets' whispered encouragements, I melted back into the pillows. Grant kissed his way between my legs, levered my hips with his hands, and dove deep within me. I hooked my ankles around his neck and pushed upward to meet him.

He grew longer and harder, if that were possible. Then he buried himself to the root, where his coarse curls tickled my bared, sensitive skin. My blood sang a siren song, racing through my veins. How many years had I wanted this? How many nights along the trail to the Klondike had I wondered if it would be as wondrous as I hoped?

Grant was groaning, near climax and rutting with an urgency that drove my own. I bent my knees at his chest, rubbing myself against his hardness, surging towards completion like a wildfire out of control. Never had my body wanted it so badly. Never had I felt so filled, yet so hungry for more; so aware of the consequences, yet so ecstatic to find myself in this position, at the command of the man I'd first fallen for. They say a girl never forgets her first love, and Grant Galloway was making all my fantasies come true, far as reclaiming what I'd lost with my youth and my innocence.

I convulsed, and then gave myself over to him with a cry. He drove faster, wetting us both with my honey, pounding against me to bring me to a shattering climax – probably in hopes of bringing on his own. I shuddered, thrashing in the pillows, grasping the hands that clutched mine as he struggled to match my level of ecstasy – and tried to shoot the wad that had been building since Venus hexed him.

His grimace grew tighter. His eyes became slits as his head fell back. He grabbed my backside and, with a low howl, he rocked himself toward completion while I did my damndest to help him over that edge. His panting filled the room, mingling with the excited whispers of the triplets, who were involved in their own intense stimulation. The den reeked of sex and opium and sweat, and when I felt his cock throb like a wild animal fighting its way out of a cage, I muttered, 'Do it, Grant. Fuck me senseless. Fuck me until you –'

The door flew open so hard it banged the wall.

'Well, Angel, you've done it now,' a familiar voice crooned. 'I gave you the keys to my kingdom and you've gone behind my back, to break the only promise I asked of you. You'll be very, very sorry you disappointed me.'

16 **My Descent into Slavery**

'What do you want from me?'

We were in Meeh's carriage, going back to the mansion, and I knew I'd better face my accuser head-on. No excuses. Devlin sat across from me, his round face expressionless beneath his shock of reddish-blond hair; harder of line than I'd ever seen him. If I begged, or tried to hold Grant responsible for what went on in the opium den, I'd only dig myself a deeper hole. Since Jarold was driving us, it was a cinch that the skulking, emaciated butler had informed his master of my whereabouts, and Meeh had let nature take its course.

'Bring me Jimmy Crystal.'

'*What*?' I gaped at the man across from me. Why did I sense he knew Jimmy, even though I'd never spoken Crystal's name here in Satan?

'You're obviously in love with him. He won't be difficult to convince.' Devlin stroked his baby-smooth cheek, lost in devious thought. 'Of course, since his business hasn't been too profitable of late, we'll provide money for his passage.'

Bait. My mind tilted in a final spin from the opium I'd smoked. I knew now how Galloway had gotten me here, but why had he enticed me to Satan, after all these years? Was I still shaken from being caught with Grant humping me? Or were all these recent events pieces in a puzzle? Part of a master plan this Machiavellian man had devised?

'Absolutely not,' I replied.

Devlin laughed nastily. 'You don't know what you're

saying, Angel. No one defies Devlin Meeh without paying the price. Haven't you suffered enough?' He raised his hand to flash that oversized ruby at me, twisting it on his finger to catch the reddish glow from the street lights we were passing.

I felt its unearthly power, its pull on my heartstrings. But I swivelled my head to stare out the opposite window. I knew his tricks now, and I refused to fall for them.

'You know you want him, Rosie. You'll never find another man like him.'

He spoke in the dulcet tone I would've associated with guardian angels; that still, small voice that might inspire confidence or courage. But I kept my eyes averted, thinking as quickly as I could, considering the lingering effects of the opium. 'I won't ask Jimmy to sacrifice himself, simply because I made that same mistake.'

Meeh barked another laugh. 'Better think about it, Angel. Now that you've disobeyed me, you're subject to the same rule as the others. You must bring someone here, to Satan.'

'I have. Collin's come in!'

'I want Crystal.'

'*Why?*'

Meeh crossed his arms, making the sequins sparkle on his outrageously striped suit of purple, green and orange. 'I don't owe you an explanation for anything I do. I don't owe you anything, Angel, for I took you as my own. I gave you a home – my protection when –'

'You set me up as a target!'

'– others would use you for their own humiliating purposes,' he continued tersely. 'Yet you've defied me by thinking and acting like a whore – prostituting yourself – when I've offered you a way out of that thankless, narrow state of being.'

I didn't ask to become your whore, I almost shouted, but I sensed I should protest no more. Meeh held all the cards, after all. At least while I was in his presence.

'All right, then – what's my punishment?'

'You'll not contact Crystal?'

'Absolutely not. I'd rather subject myself to Venus on her web.'

He grunted, his tawny eyes narrowing. 'Insanity's too pleasant a fate for you, my dear. It's time you saw my salt mines.'

I clenched my fists to keep from slapping that boyish face. The perpetual night, lit by the crimson street lamps, passed by outside the carriage. Dozens of residents who seemed so very happy with their lot here in Satan – with whatever fantasies they'd aspired to when they came – strolled the sidewalks, laughing and talking. Apparently they'd had no trouble, no crisis of conscience, coaxing someone else to join them.

When we approached the Exquisite Inn, I realised we weren't going back to Meeh's palace on the hillside. We were headed in the wrong direction, as though he'd been planning my punishment all along.

And of course he *had*. Devlin Meeh, always in control of his emotions, was ultimately in control of everything around him as well. So why should he look distraught about putting his mistress in her place?

By the light of the lamps at the hotel door, I caught sight of Faren Poole, glancing towards this familiar carriage – and she was talking with Collin! They looked chummy, standing close enough to whisper secrets to each other, like a couple who'd shared intimacies. I lurched towards the door to holler for their help, but Devlin caught me by the wrist.

'Too late for that, Angel,' he jeered. 'I've asked my maid to keep Mr Cooper occupied, and she's never let me down.'

And, of course, I had. And, of course, I would serve my time in the mines until I won back his favour. The first stirrings of panic played with my pulse, and when I saw the stable where the KlonDykes had taken me, I felt a flicker of doom.

'What will you be doing with me?' I asked, hoping this sounded like a rational question rather than a plea for mercy. 'After all, it was Grant who shut the door of that opium den while his girl gang stuck the hookah's pipe into my mouth. It wasn't as though I –'

'They've served my purpose as well,' he replied slyly. 'And Venus has doled out punishment enough for them, don't you think? You saw how desperate they were. Already wasting away. They'll eventually seal their own fates without any help from me – and, of course, I saw all this coming long ago.'

It was his smugness that enraged me, but I had no chance to strike back at him, for the carriage had stopped inside that ramshackle stable and Jarold was throwing open the door. His smile resembled a skeleton's, vacant and eerily threatening, as he helped me step down to the straw-strewn floor.

'This is where we enter the mines,' Meeh explained. 'My butler will prepare you for the descent. Then you'll see why you should've kept shopping, rather than letting your curiosity lead you astray. Curiosity killed the cat, you know.'

The butler spun me roughly around and grabbed the back of my dress with his clawlike hand and, in one swipe, he tore it open down the back. I yelped, looking over my shoulder at Meeh. But the blond in the striped suit was clearly enjoying the show.

'Jarold's been waiting for this opportunity ever since you arrived,' Devlin said with a low chuckle. 'He doesn't say much, but he watches and waits. He's seen you in bed with Collin. He knew what you were about when you suggested Faren finish her shopping, and he came to me like a fox licking his chops. A fox with a feckless hen backed into a corner.'

He grinned at his manservant then. 'Do as you will, Jarold. You've gone a long time without a woman, my good and faithful servant.'

This was the man who'd been so utterly charmed by my chocolate pudding audition! And so fascinated by my waxed pussy. Would he now hand me over to his morbid, ugly butler before banishing me to the salt mines?

Jarold again yanked the back of my dress and let it fall, so he could gawk at my camisole and drawers – and then he tore them from my body as well. I shivered, more from the thoughts of what this monster might do to me than from being stripped naked in the chilly stable. The butler's avid gaze followed the curves of my breasts down my front to lodge on the bare essentials between my shaking legs. A drop of saliva formed in the corner of his spectral smile, to dribble down his chin.

I looked away, unable to face him. I heard him unfastening his belt ... lowering his pants, and I could only shudder with revulsion at the anticipation of his touch. I braced myself, knowing Meeh would make things more difficult if I let my fear show – when the twinkle of his monocle made me look up.

'Hoofbeats,' the little ogre muttered. He steered me towards the back side of the farrier's forge, where the KlonDykes had stashed their clarinets. A brick he pushed on the side of the fireplace opened a door in the floor.

I considered screaming, so whoever approached would know of my struggle, but as the stable door opened for Collin and a small band of men, Meeh was ushering me down a flight of metal steps, into darkness.

'You'll not be needing Cooper's help – or anyone else's – from here on out, my dear,' he crooned. 'The mines are a world unto themselves, entered only with my permission.'

'And when will I leave?' I challenged. With the door sliding closed above us, I had little to lose.

Devlin struck a match to light a sconce, revealing his sly grin and the shining eyepiece that reflected my naked state. We were penned in by walls of intricately curling ironwork, painted white.

'Most mine slaves never make it out,' he replied blithely. 'I give them every opportunity to redeem themselves – as I will you, my Angel – but they remain bound by invisible handcuffs even after I've handed them the key. Human nature, I suppose, to stay with the familiar, even when it disgusts and humiliates them, rather than risk the unknown.'

His philosophy was lost on me, for when his mouth found my bare breast, I sucked air. He teased my nipple to a peak with his tongue, so effortlessly I despised my body's betrayal. But succumbing was all I could do. His warm hands framed my chest and he suckled in earnest, laving my flesh with his eager tongue as he'd done so many times in his palatial home.

I writhed in his embrace, more to avail myself than to escape him. Cool curlicues of grillwork cut into my back and I grabbed at the wrought-iron walls to keep my balance. By the time he slipped a finger between my legs to spread the wetness around my slick, hairless folds, I was rutting against his hand. Rubbing myself to reach the climax my body was begging for.

Like wildfire the need consumed me, and my cries filled the cell-like chamber. As I convulsed around the thumb he shoved against my sweet spot, I realised anyone in the stable would hear my ecstatic release, rather than any sign of desperation or pain.

To add insult to injury, Meeh knelt between my legs before I could recover from my climax. Deftly he parted my dripping folds – my legs spread for him, with their own traitorous anticipation – and lapped at the honey there, like a fat cat gorging on cream. The tip of his tongue knew just where to tease and then where to linger, with the perfect pressure in all the right places. I seeped with more juice, despite my efforts to separate myself from this irrational behaviour. I was indeed acting as his whore now, thrusting my hips forward to beg for his mercy – his exquisite attention in this form of fucking, which had always been my favourite.

I was soon screaming again, my wanton cries reaching a frenzied pitch as a climax more excruciating than the first rocked my body. I thrust mindlessly against his face, seeking out that salvation that only came from release ... a pleasure this little demon doled out so generously. After a particularly loud shriek, my entire body tightened into a knot of ecstatic oblivion: an orgasm within an orgasm.

Collin would think I *wanted* to be down here. With Meeh. Jarold would feed my young partner some tale about how I'd entered the mines by choice, because I cared more for Devlin than for the friend who'd gotten me to the Klondike alive. As I looked around what appeared to be an elevator shaft, I knew my descent would seal my fate. Unless I could find a way to outfox my captor.

Meeh pulled a lever and the cagelike contraption floated slowly downward with a quiet groan of pulleys and ropes. He wiped his monocle on his purple handkerchief and then adjusted it to his eye again.

'Such delicious prey,' he murmured, watching the jism trickle down my thighs. 'And such a willing victim. Lovely traits from *my* point of view, but they'll work against you in the mines, my dear.'

What could I say? As the elevator descended, I stood dejectedly with the run-off from two cataclysmic climaxes getting sticky. Making me feel dirty. I hadn't put up one iota of struggle. I hadn't once renounced my body's wayward needs, to argue for my freedom. Rather, I had confirmed Meeh's unspoken opinion of me: I was already his slave, and unlikely to change that. Whether in his opulent home or here, below Satan's surface, I had set aside the issues of Jimmy Crystal and my own future for the sake of sexual pleasure.

'Here in the mines, I require absolute silence and obedience,' Devlin said as our cage came to a halt. 'My slaves speak only to Venus or myself, only when we address them. You'll be assigned a cot in the dormitory and a place in the dining hall. And you'll endure whatever your overseer allots as your job, or your punishment. Without a word.'

Silence. It explained the eerie, tomblike air of the cavernous room we entered, even though I saw dozens of workers along aisles that branched out from this area like the spokes of a wheel. They were all naked, except for black leather harness straps that criss-crossed their chests and circled their waists. Some were attached to cartloads of shining white cargo: salt, in chunks that others had chiselled out and loaded. Like two-legged donkeys, they laboured beneath their loads. Even from this distance, I read desperation on their faces. A desperation they could not express aloud for fear of punishment.

'And here,' Meeh continued in a conversational tone, 'we have the Playpen. A unique form of correcting those who cry out from the whip or get caught talking, or in any way defy my established order.'

From floors of smooth, glistening white rose black bars similar to a jail cell, except this pen stood in the centre of the reception area. I guessed it would hold eight people standing close enough to touch one another, four abreast in two rows. I pondered it, wondering what punishment this could be, compared to the back-breaking fate of hauling salt. Yet my experience in Satan had taught me that every sword had a double edge, every word a secret meaning. Every day disguised a pervading darkness, like the Klondike itself.

'I'll offer you a last chance, Miss DuBris.' My escort spoke quietly. 'All you need do, to escape this doom and restore yourself to my good graces, is write Jimmy Crystal a letter, inviting him here.'

'What if I do and he refuses to come?' I hedged.

'He won't. Nobody can.'

I squeezed my eyes shut against yet another image of Jimmy glistening in my captor's monocle. This time, Crystal looked directly at me, imploring me, mouthing words I couldn't decipher. A look of gaunt anguish haunted his handsome face.

'No! I don't know why you want him, but it won't be *me* who sets him up.'

'Such a shame that your sense of honour rules your reason but not your body.' He cleared his throat, taking me by the elbow. 'Very well then, Rose. I'll present you to your overseer. He's new, but I'm expecting great things of him.'

So, I was no longer his Angel. As though the faceted crystal sensed my fall from grace, the spot where it was lodged in my cheek burned until tears came to my eyes.

'No whining!' he barked with the sternness of a Biblical patriarch. 'From now on, you speak only to Venus or me, when we address you. You eat and sleep when you're allowed, and you obey without question. Rather than bringing pleasure in a life of ease as my mistress, you'll be sweating out your days and nights like a mindless pack animal, producing the salt that supports my city.'

We'd been walking across the open entry hall with its high, smooth walls of glistening white – such a contrast to the constant darkness above ground, yet in its way a threat as well. Every detail was clearly visible here, without need for light other than the sconces along the walls. And I sensed that in its way, the unrelenting whiteness formed a backdrop for another sort of insanity: that of perpetual production, and fearfulness which defied sleep. Here, there was no place to hide. No place to go in solitude. No secrets.

Although the air was as pleasantly warm as the climate in town, I shivered. My nipples hardened, riding the crests of my chest with each step towards one of the corridors. I caught a glimpse of a large room with rows of long white tables, and then saw a chamber of the same size lined with Spartan white cots. Only one room, which meant both sexes slept in the same area. Naked. Visible every moment, waking or sleeping.

For a fleeting second, I almost relented. Jimmy, after all, would never expect me to serve out such a fate to save his hide. He hadn't wanted me to leave Oblivion, and he'd always relished the role of rescuer.

But I swallowed hard, determined to serve out this sentence for being caught in the crime of my passion, my moment of weakness.

We stopped at a room lined with pegs, where harnesses were hung – rich, dark, polished leather straps befitting matched teams pulling royal carriages. Devlin stretched up to bring one down, and with practised ease dropped the contraption over my head to fasten it behind me.

He stepped back then to admire the sight I made, trussed up with my breasts protruding around the black

X of straps and my bare pussy and legs quivering beneath a band around my waist. With another of those sweet, boyish smiles – a look I'd come to despise – he kissed the crystal on my cheek.

'Behave yourself, my fallen angel, and perhaps – *perhaps* – I'll check on your progress in a week or two. Or maybe a month. Time has little meaning here in the mines, you see.'

I resolutely clamped my lips together. If it was silence he wanted, silence he'd get!

Meeh turned towards the mine corridor, the only splash of colour in a world of white striped with black. 'I've a new slave for you, Galloway!' he called out. 'Come and get her!'

17 **The Playpen**

Meeh's elevator had barely disappeared up the shaft before I pivoted to glare at Grant. He'd changed his usual tight black clothing for a white toga that stopped short of his knees, showing his muscled legs to fine advantage – and which left no doubt about the erection beneath it.

'I thought you were the mayor, Mr Galloway. Seems you have your finger in a lot of –'

'Pies?' he finished haughtily. He slipped a hand behind my head and placed his other pointer finger against my lips, to insinuate it between my teeth. 'No, dear Rosie, pies were your forte before you came to Satan. Obeying the rules obviously is not.'

I scowled around the strong, slender finger he was now slowly pulling out, and pushing back in.

'Meeh told you, not thirty seconds ago, that slaves are to be silent. I could punish you for this but, considering the circumstances, I'll give you a second chance.'

The heat rose in my cheeks. This man, who'd lured me to the Klondike under false pretences and then broke my vow to Devlin Meeh, had now become my overseer, the man in command of my fate. With his finger sliding in and out, tickling the length of my tongue, I couldn't challenge him, much less plead for a reasonable explanation. Grant Galloway was in control of me, and he loved it.

'You see, Miss DuBris, my fantasy here in Satan is to be in charge – of anything, of everything. Suits me, don't you think?'

I couldn't answer. My lips formed a tight O around the warm, probing digit that mimicked a dick. I could only rivet my gaze into his and silently demand answers, knowing he'd probably not give them.

'Yes, when Devlin saw how neatly I'd cornered you with that hookah, he decided to use Venus's curse to our advantage. The ladies and I can now keep very close watch on you and your crystal angel – perhaps coax it from your face to cure ourselves. Meanwhile, there's no one we'd rather scratch our insatiable itches with. It will be our pleasure, indeed.'

I swallowed, which tugged at Grant's finger and made him grin deviously. Once again, just when I thought I'd figured out the rules, Devlin Meeh had changed the game: I was more than ever at the mercy of the KlonDykes and their boss. Thoughts of the three blonde pistoleers leering at me as I slept didn't set well. Not well at all.

'Life in the salt mines has its advantages,' he went on in a serpent's voice. He focused on the finger-dick, thrusting it faster, so I could barely breathe, much less follow these new developments. 'If you work well – if you give more than is expected of you and please your overseer – things could be downright pleasant for you here, Angel-Face. I think you know what I mean.'

His erection prodded my midsection as he talked, following the same suggestive rhythm as his finger. Here was a man whose need for satisfaction ruled everything he did now, day and night. Grant might *think* he was in control of me, but his insatiable desire for a hot, wet hole drove him to distraction ... a distraction I could satisfy better than anyone else, because the angel on my face represented his salvation.

And I'd be damned if I'd let him have that! Offering up my mouth and my sex was a small sacrifice indeed, if it meant this overseer was too busy humping to make me haul carts of salt. I no longer wanted to be his lover, and certainly not his slave, but humouring him would buy me some time and keep the KlonDykes at bay.

So I smiled around that probing finger, reaching beneath his toga to grip his petrified pecker. Grant's eyes closed in immediate gratitude and he rocked his hips, which meant he forgot about the digit in my mouth.

'Please, God, suck me,' he whispered. 'You can't possibly know the horror of being caught in that web. Condemned forever to crave the freedom of release.'

Never forget who you are. And whose. Those words took on new meaning with each new situation I found myself in. And right now, with Grant Galloway in my clutches, I might find the missing piece of this puzzle Meeh had trapped me with – now, before the Titzlers or anyone else saw me pumping my overseer in more ways than one.

'Why does Devlin want Jimmy Crystal?' I demanded in a whisper. Then I quickly knelt to give this man what he'd begged for.

As I sucked his hot hardness into my mouth, Grant groaned and clutched the hem of his toga up out of the way. I kept him wet, spreading saliva with my playful tongue until I saw his deep dimples flicker with a grin. Although he made a fetching sight, reminiscent of a Roman soldier – or Julius Caesar – he'd lost more weight. Here was a man who might literally fuck himself to death unless he found a way to reverse Venus's spell, which gave me at least a temporary advantage.

When he'd gotten a few moments of relief, I stopped sucking. I held his cock in my taut jaws, cautiously, as a spaniel is trained to hold the bird it fetched. Grant glanced down at me, then saw the challenge in my eyes.

'So you've refused to invite Crystal to Satan?' he asked, gyrating lightly to loosen my grip. 'Not a wise move to deny Dr Meeh – but then, I doubt Jimmy would come for you anyway. He's gotten many a rustler hung, and I watched him bring down some big guns when he worked with the Earps in Dodge City. But he's bull-headed about women.'

I resumed sucking him, considering this. Jimmy and I had been together in the northwest for several years, but this information illuminated the past my handsome blond barkeep had kept in the shadows – a history Grant Galloway had apparently witnessed. To encourage his further revelations, I licked at his shaft, rubbing my tongue against the broad, slick knob that wanted to go down my throat.

Grant exhaled softly. 'When I heard you were working for him, I was surprised, Rosie,' he continued, 'because Crystal could be brutal and hot-headed – and you always steered clear of that type. He never had much respect for whores, even when he kept a few upstairs in Wyatt Earp's Long Branch Saloon. Saw him shoot a floozy in cold blood once, simply because she accepted a gift from another man.'

Brutal? Hot-headed? Never could I have associated those words with Jimmy! But then, he'd given up his lucrative career as a hired gun long before I knew him – and a young man with that many notches on his barrel had to have a damn good reason for laying down his guns.

I eased my wet, rounded lips along Grant's cock with a slurping sound that made us both chuckle. His expression grew wary for a moment, as though he might leave me hanging before he finished this inform-ative chat, but his relentless need forced him to rub against my tongue again. Wrapping my hand at the base of him – which kept him from plunging the way he wanted to – I gazed pointedly up into his catlike green eyes.

'I can see why Crystal took to *you*, though,' he muttered, humping with ill-concealed restraint. 'A man can ignore that birthmark when the rest of you is so damn delicious. So willing.'

I let his remark pass, for what good was biting him if he'd shut up – and then punish me? No, I smiled coyly, as I'd learned to do with despicable men. Then I teased at his hole with the tip of my tongue, coaxing out a droplet of honey.

'Sally Bingham was a restless little redhead. Higher class than a lot of the gals who whored in Dodge,' he mused. He was starting to pant, looking hopeful of the climax that had eluded him for so long. 'Had nice, wide hips and a pair of tits big as bed pillows. Rumour had it Crystal asked to marry her, and Sally had agreed. But then he caught her wearing another man's jewellery.'

Grant stroked the hair back from my forehead, watching as I sucked him in and then slid my mouth up his quivering cock. He fingered the crystal angel, his expression foxlike.

'It was this little gew-gaw here, Rosie. Except she wore it on a pretty gold chain. You can guess who gave it to her.'

I choked, but Galloway caught my head between his hands and refused to remove himself from my mouth. His whole body trembled with impending release, yet his eyes told me it wouldn't be coming.

'Jimmy shot her in the back as she was boarding the outbound stage with Meeh,' he continued in that soft, insidious voice. 'I'm surprised he let you leave Oblivion alive, after you got my letter. But then, it just proves how cruelly Crystal leads his women on, only to make them pay for his mistakes in the end.'

Any other woman would've bitten Galloway, but I was too full of a scream to clamp down. Up from the depths of my soul came that betrayal, spilling out around the cock that kept me quiet. To think that Jimmy had known Grant – had known Devlin Meeh! – yet had allowed me to come to Satan anyway! It was the virile blond bartender I'd seen in my dreams for so many lonely nights, yet now I'd learned the rest of his story.

And the angel that had made Sally Bingham a target – and then became such a potent plaything for Venus – was marking me as Meeh's next victim. The deceitful little fiend stole Jimmy's fiancée all those years ago, and had made me the bait to lure Crystal here, so he could avenge Sally's death!

I jerked out of Grant's grasp to let my wrath echo in the cavernous white mine chamber. A woman in my profession, at the constant mercy of men, had her limits – and I'd reached mine! I kicked and clawed at Grant when he tried to stand me up, and meanwhile my cries rang like sirens. This brought dozens of slaves and overseers in white togas pouring out of the mine's passageways, to fill the centre hall with a silent yet boisterous crowd whose curiosity spoke louder than any words.

I heard the clink of keys, the creak of an opening gate, and suddenly the Titzler triplets came around from behind me. Their glee was a palpable force driving the three of them to act as one: before I knew what was happening, they got me off the floor and tossed me into the Playpen. The door made of black iron bars slammed shut with a thunderous finality.

'Fancy meeting *you* here!' Zelda crowed, her breasts bouncing as she leered between the bars. 'We figured Grant would get you to open up. Sooner, rather than later.'

'We just couldn't wait to start our new jobs –'

'– so we could be near you again, Angel-Face!' her sisters chimed in. 'You're the loveliest fuck we know.'

Nelda and Esmerelda flanked their bolder sister along the barred wall, their blonde hair swept up in engaging disarray and their faces alight with lust. Unlike the other overseers, these three had foregone the short, white togas, and instead they sported their holsters and side-arms. Zelda hooked the Playpen keys on her gun belt so they dangled above her hairless sex, which she wiggled at me from between two bars. Then she climbed up the side of the cage, balancing on a crossbar to look out over the gathered crowd.

'It's time we showed Rosie the consequences of speaking when not spoken to – of causing such an uproar here in our mines,' she announced. 'Washing her mouth out with soap would be too juvenile a punishment for a such a naughty puss, wouldn't it? After she's lapped at us all, perhaps she'll observe the proper silence of servitude!'

I couldn't believe it! Men and women thronged the sides of the narrow Playpen and began to thrust between the bars like rutting animals. At least ten erections poked through the openings, interspersed by the spread, wet pussies of women who'd clambered up to use Zelda's crossbar as a foothold. Never had I been so surrounded by bare bodies demanding gratification. A woman of a higher calling might've fainted dead away.

'Don't stand there gawking!' Grant commanded above the illicit whispers of wiggling bodies. 'Every minute these slaves miss means less productivity. And *you*, Angel-Face, will make up the day's deficit by working after the rest have gone to their cots.'

Had someone told me Meeh's mines operated on such twisted principles, I wouldn't have believed it.

Who could imagine being ordered to service so many peckers and pussies, as penance for crying out in the pain of betrayal?

Yet, as I approached the first erection – a stubby one that poked out from curl-covered nuts – I reminded myself that punishment became what one made of it. As I child, I'd driven my poor parents crazy with my pranks and then laughed when they spanked me. In this situation, from a wanton's viewpoint, I was merely facing about a hundred hungry bodies demanding pleasure like only Rosie DuBris could give them. All in a day's work – rather like a New Year's orgy I'd attended in San Francisco. And as long as my overseers didn't realise I *liked* what I was doing, I could despatch this crowd without much trouble. I'd be tired, but not dispirited. Certainly not penitent.

I went at the first man with a fire that took him by surprise – and had him turning to the nearest primed pussy within a minute. Next came a girl with a closely cropped bush that curled around the edges of her slick pink skin, as though she'd spent considerable time arranging it that way. I splayed those folds with my fingertips and thrust deep inside her with my tongue – wondering if these people's outcries would get *them* tossed into the Playpen, because this one screamed immediately. Her juice oozed around my mouth and her folds fluttered with a need she couldn't control. Then she too sought satisfaction from a more accessible partner.

Were these Playpen sessions the only time slaves could indulge in sex? Were they forced to work, eat and sleep among so many naked bodies – made all the more lurid by their black harnesses – without sating the lust such conditions inspired?

I could only wonder about such things as I moved from pussy to pole. I could only be grateful that most of these slaves, faceless to me as I carried out my sentence, chose to complete themselves by coupling with someone rather than coming all over my face. By entering a detached state, or entertaining myself with the wide variety of scents and tastes and skin textures, I made the continuous round of the cage's congregants. Keeping count might've been interesting, but even a lady like me didn't always want to know the score. Not when she was trying to get through the game and get on with whatever came next.

I badly wanted a drink of water, but the press of bodies between the iron bars prevented my asking for it. Occasionally someone speared fingers through my hair to control the motion of my head, but it was usually the low, guttural moans resonating in the chests above me that bespoke my success. I moved on to the next pecker then, the next slit quivering for my kiss, grateful that bathing was a regular thing here in the mines and that no one seemed to feel more entitled than the others.

Still, by the time I'd slurped and licked and tickled and sucked about seventy sets of genitals, I was getting shaky. Awfully damn dry, despite the dew I'd lapped from so many roses. From all around me came the sighs of the sated, the groans of those still going at it on the floor of the mine, a shiny white floor, smooth as glass: salt, pressed and polished to solidity. I sank onto that surface with a surge of relief when Grant's voice filled the large hall.

'All right, you slaves, the party's over. Back to work!' he commanded. His voice echoed with authority, needing no help from a bull horn because the cave's domed ceiling carried it everywhere. 'If you didn't get your licking, it's your own damn fault for being slow! We've seven more boxcars to fill before dinner, so mush, you huskies!'

Even here in the Klondike, his dogged humour fell short. As those remaining around the Playpen eased away from its bars unsatisfied, I caught mutterings that suggested Galloway left a lot to be desired as an overseer.

Politics weren't my concern, however. I remained on the floor, licking my parched lips, hoping Grant and those obnoxious KlonDykes were satisfied by my performance. I wouldn't give them the satisfaction of catching me at anything again, for I saw the imposed silence as a chance to think about my situation, to ponder my options for getting out of this shining white purgatory before I became as browbeaten as those walking away from me.

When the gate behind me creaked open, I prepared to walk away – but was hoisted up by the harness, which cut deeply between my breasts, and then slung across the slick floor. For the first time since I'd begun my servicing, I looked up to see who was handling me. My heart sank.

'You didn't think we'd let you go before we got *our* licks?' Zelda demanded with a laugh.

'Oh, I can't *wait* for my turn!' Nelda exclaimed with a gleeful wiggle. 'Because after watching this Angel-Face lapping and tonguing and sucking so many slaves –'

'– it's impossible not to notice how wet and scented *she* is! Let's get her while Grant's organising the others.'

In a flash they were on me, right there in the centre of the main hall. With three naked, pistol-packing blondes demanding my attentions, I didn't stand a chance for escape, and in my tired state I could only submit to their ornery trick. They had all grown leaner in their pursuit of climaxes that eluded them. Their concave stomachs, hollowed cheeks and burning blue eyes bespoke an inner frenzy that threatened to consume them. One of them – Zelda, most likely – straddled my face to take her pleasure first, flexing her reddened folds as she pressed her nether lips to mine.

'We can't stop, you know,' she mumbled, humping so her clit made the most direct contact with my tongue. 'This need drives us. We can't eat or sleep without having to handle each other.'

'I have constant dreams of fucking,' the triplet wedged between my legs went on. 'Can you imagine convulsing in your sleep? Trying hard to find a cock that lasts long enough to make you come?'

'You're our only hope, Rosie,' the third girl pleaded. I couldn't see her, but I suspected she stood facing Zelda, so she could get a tonguing while she waited for more solid contact. 'We haven't seen Venus for days, to plead for her mercy. We simply *must* get that crystal off your –'

Take it! I wanted to cry. But with Zelda's relentless rubbing, all I could do was ply the folds of her pussy with my tired tongue, swallowing what cream didn't dribble down my chin.

It wasn't all bad, being held captive by three eager partners ... their sighs and grunts spurred my own wanting, because now my privates were catching fire. The Titzler between my legs got up, but then her sister planted her mouth there and tickled the clit made sensitive and needy from so much rubbing. I shuddered, for the scents and sensations of these three – plus the dozens I'd done before them – had a heady effect. My climax began as a slow tightening below my stomach, sending little jolts of awareness all over my body, until I began to buck in that mindless frenzy that refused to be denied.

Zelda dismounted, pivoting quickly. 'Keep her coming, Esmerelda, just like we talked about.'

My eyes flew open in time to see the triplet between my feet stand up, then reach for her pistols with the practised speed of a Wild West Show performer. With matching flashes of silver, the six-shooters twirled expertly around her fingers until she stopped one and cocked it. The hammer's *click* echoed ominously in the otherwise silent room as she pointed it at me. The other gun, already a cock, she slid smoothly inside me as she squatted, her aim never wavering.

A jolt of momentary fear upped the tension throughout my body, until I was again writhing, watching Esmerelda work the dildo in and out of my pussy. She teased me with it, grinning when my honey smacked faster with each of her skilful strokes. Nelda, meanwhile, came around to hold me down at the shoulders, while Zelda eyed my crystal angel with obvious intent.

'Let me have this,' she said, reaching towards my cheek, 'and I promise you things will go easier for *all* of us, Angel. I can see that you never have to haul salt, or get thrown into the Playpen again, or –'

The first prying of her fingernails made me scream, caught up in my body's climax while afire with a searing pain in my face. Zelda too yelped and fell backwards – or, more accurately, was propelled away by some force within the crystal. She landed hard on her ass and stuck her singed fingertips into her mouth, looking frightened out of her mind.

A nasty laugh made us all freeze in place, for we hadn't heard anyone approach. My breath caught in my throat, although I badly needed to gasp for air: from where I lay, flat on the floor, Venus appeared, impossibly tall, an imposing figure arrayed in a silken gown of carnation pink that accented her ebony lines and half-masculine strength. The Titzlers scurried off me, but they didn't get far.

'Pathetic! Absolutely pathetic!' Meeh's queen of discipline declared. She scowled as though the sight of us gave her indigestion, and then shoved Zelda further away from me with the very pointed toe of her pink pump. 'Like three bleating sheep, you triplets! So busy believing Galloway, because he caught my wad, that you're prisoners of your own limited thinking.'

Venus glared imperiously at each blonde in turn, yet I had the feeling she actually wanted to laugh. Then I recalled something Devlin said once, about invisible handcuffs. But the thoughts had no chance to make connections in my befuddled brain.

'Such piss-poor excuses for overseers, you three!' she jeered. 'Get back to the mines, you humping hussies! Dr Meeh will demand an accounting of your crew's day – and *you* will make up the shortfall.'

Zelda, Nelda and Esmerelda half-crawled until they were out of reach of those dangerous pumps, and then hurried towards the mine shafts. What a difference, from when they were luring me with their hookah and holding me down, defenceless – but I wasn't laughing. No, with an Amazon-like Venus towering over me, her breasts bulging above the immodest cut of her taut bodice, I knew better than to tempt her wrath. I was in no position – or condition – to defend myself from whatever purpose she'd had in coming down to the mines.

Her smile grew wickedly thin. 'Don't go thinking I did you any favours,' she whispered.

Her words slithered like snakes in the domed enclosure, and I sensed I'd soon be feeling her fangs. I lay absolutely still, not even daring to breathe.

'My angel will stay on your face until I want her back. Until I'm through playing with you, Miss Debris.' Balancing more elegantly than I would've thought possible, she ran the toe of her shoe down the centre of me, caressing the undersides of my bare breasts before blazing a trail towards my cleft. There, she spread the wetness until I jerked, exhaling loudly.

Venus laughed. 'Shall I tell Devlin you've changed your mind? Shall I bring you pen and paper, to send for Crystal?'

I nipped my lip, determined not to scream and be tossed into the Playpen again.

'All right then, slave – you've chosen your fate. Who knows when – or if – you'll be given another chance to leave Meeh's mine?' She squared her broad shoulders, taking her leave. 'The sun *will* shine again, come spring. But I doubt you'll see it.'

18 **Paradise Lost**

As the weeks went by, I lost all track of time, for there were no clocks or calendars in the mines. The enforced silence wore me down. I worked like a herd animal among the other naked slaves, hauling wheeled carts of salt up from the belly of Meeh's mine, growing raw and sore where the leather harness chafed an X between my breasts.

At meals I sat wedged between two men, one of whom ogled my breasts as they rested on the table. The other, a younger fellow with rust-coloured hair and gorgeous green eyes, smiled when the dining room monitor wasn't watching. He had his story – sure as he had a hard-on at every meal – but he didn't dare share it.

For all I knew, I'd pleasured him during my stint in the Playpen. Sometimes I felt his fingers slithering up my thigh, checking the regrowth of my bush beneath the table. But when I began to react, he stopped. Safer that way. And safety – along with anonymity in the crowd – was something we slaves worked very hard to maintain in this nether world where all else had been taken away from us.

It was a hell of a life – no, it was merely existence in a very low form. My skin grew pallid from lack of sunlight. I walked with the others from the mine shaft to the dining hall and the dormitory like a living ghost, reflecting the whiteness of the salt walls. It was never dark, because sconces burned constantly, but the light was weirdly unreal. Even when I closed my eyes to sleep, its ghastly glow penetrated my lids and I got little rest.

Of course, the silence and the repetitive drudgery of the days gave me far too much time to think. Among others who were as sleep-deprived as I, and as unable to express any emotion or thoughts, it was best to work with eyes averted, putting my back into hauling a cart or swinging a pickaxe while my mind idled away the unmarked hours.

It had occurred to me, after Venus left with a swishing of her pink skirts, that the Titzlers were living in the invisible handcuffs Meeh had once mentioned: if the spiderlike she-man had only released her powerful cream inside Galloway, Grant alone suffered the fate of not being able to climax. The triplets, then, lived in imitation of this hex simply because they believed they couldn't come either.

I'd seen this problem several times in my line of work: if a man believed himself unable to perform, there was no way he could rise to the occasion – unless an artful lover like myself convinced him otherwise. Here in the silence of the mines, however, I had no way of pointing this out to Zelda and her thinning sisters . . . and perhaps it was a revelation best left to a better time anyway. Whenever I heard their furtive whisperings and humpings – whether with each other or with slaves in their crews – I drew a grim sense of glee from knowing what I knew. There below the surface of the earth, we took our delight wherever we could find it.

Other subjects weren't nearly as pleasant, however. Grant's story, about how Jimmy Crystal killed his fiancée when she accepted Meeh's angel, could leave me quaking with suppressed anger until I couldn't sleep, even after an exhausting day. How could my Jimmy, my lover of so many years, allow me to leave for Satan?

Over and over I replayed my last day in Oblivion,

until my mind wore the images threadbare. Jimmy had stood up to Dynamite Dick so I could read my mail upstairs, even after hearing where it came from. He'd coaxed me to stay, promising to move on to greener pastures, but made no real effort to keep me there. Indeed he'd been patient and understanding about my restlessness – and had slipped me more money to travel on!

He hadn't read the letter when I offered it to him ... perhaps because he knew what it said; knew that Grant Galloway – although I'd never spoken his name – would be wagging the finger of an alluring first love, all the way from Satan; knew that Devlin Meeh awaited me too, and had let the little priss claim me, just like he'd put the moves on Sally Bingham! What sort of a man allowed such an affront to be repeated?

Not the sort I wanted to return to.

Not a man who would answer, even if I did write him, because he figured I deserved this fate for leaving him. Out of the frying pan, into the fire. And Jimmy was too aware, too wise to the world, to get burnt again himself. Probably had another saloon by now, and another loose woman plying her trade in his upstairs room.

I tried to tell myself I didn't *care* what Crystal was doing. But denying such ideas took as much effort as shutting out those mental images of my past. I grew so distracted I made mistakes on the job – such as the time I hauled my cartload of salt chunks into the bathing cave. Instead of turning right, down the gleaming white corridor to where the boxcars got loaded, I absent-mindedly kept my gaze on the floor and walked until the damp pungency of the mineral springs – their soothing sound as they cascaded over rock formations – alerted me to my mistake.

The all-male crew taking its shift in the pools let out

a collective murmur. I stared, embarrassed, at their heads and chests above the surface of the burbling water, at a dozen pairs of eyes fixed on my naked body, criss-crossed by the black harness, which was pulled tight by the weight of my cargo.

'Look at them titties,' a fellow near the water's edge said. 'Been a long time since I had me a handful like that!'

'I'll take your load if you'll take mine!' another man ventured.

Such remarks had never rattled me, yet the very fact that they spoke aloud told me their overseer wasn't with them. I backed up, shoving the cart towards the doorway. My stint in the Playpen was still fresh in my mind, despite the weeks that had passed, and Grant would come looking for me if I dallied.

'Don't be shy, sweetheart! You don't know our names and we don't know yours – so we can't spread tales, now, can we?'

'Can't tell me that pretty little pussy's not hungry for some hot sausage –'

'Looky there, boys! She ain't even seen our cocks yet, and the honey's runnin' from her.'

'And I'm still horny from that sucking you gave me on your first day here.'

Their words reverberated in the open cavern above the springs, wearing down my resolve. I licked my lips, trying to decide. It meant trouble, if I got caught frolicking with these randy men, yet the onerous day-to-day drudgery almost made such an adventure worth the risk. I recalled Venus's threats, however, and resolved to walk away.

But I'd lingered too long. One of the men had hoisted himself from the water, his lean body dripping as his prick stiffened. It was gorgeous – thick and pink, rising up from springy, auburn curls and topped off by a purple head resembling an elongated mushroom cap. I glanced at his face and gasped. It was the man I sat beside in the dining hall, the nicer one who seemed genuinely interested in my welfare. The one who stroked my returning fur under the table.

He slipped his damp fingers into my hair and kissed me. I whimpered, giving in to the sweet sensations only a man's eager lips can impart. How many months had I lived without such a touch, so basic to every woman's romantic notions? His mouth slid warmly over mine, exploring and enticing me ... inviting me to make love instead of just fucking him.

'I'm Harry,' he whispered against my ear.

'Yes, you are,' I teased, ruffling the swirl of wet curls around his chest. 'And I'm Rosie.'

'Delightfully so. A delicate flower among us thorns.'

Such a simple exchange, yet I craved the conversation even more than the elemental dance of a male body leading mine. Harry kissed me again, and this time he reached behind me to unfasten the salt cart's heavy clasps, letting his body play lightly against mine. I sighed with the release of so much weight, and then eagerly wiggled out of the leather harness. As it dropped down my breasts and belly, I felt the other men's gazes following every tweak against my nipples, each inch of skin as the leather caressed it.

Silence, broken only by the gentle music of the springs; anticipation so ripe I could smell their desire above the earthy scent of the minerals. They looked ready to lunge up and grab me away from Harry – but then came footsteps in the corridor where I'd made my wrong turn. As one they all inhaled, foretelling our doom when their overseer would block our exit. Fear drove the sweetness of Harry's kiss from my mouth.

But he grabbed my hand and loped away from the salt cart, ducking us behind the rock formations where bars of soaps were set to dry. Further back into the cave we went, our steps light and quick, spurred on by a desire I'd almost forgotten how to feel.

'What if someone tells your overseer –'

'They won't. They'll live in hopes of this happening to *them* someday.'

Deeper into the cave we ventured, among boulders worn slick from years of the spring's flow. The rush of the waters sounded louder now, as though we were approaching the mouth of a river, and when we rounded another curve my jaw dropped. From somewhere far above us came a lovely waterfall, tumbling down a rocky cliff with enough daylight that a few plants braved out an existence alongside the water's path. Spray bathed the air with a freshness I hadn't felt since I'd left Oblivion. A fragile rainbow glimmered above it in delicate pastels.

I stood in awe, clasping Harry's hand. 'I had no idea.'

'No one else does, either. But once, when I simply couldn't stand another day of being herded to work, and then crammed into the benches to eat, and then forced to lie in a room full of naked bodies, I lagged behind.' He grinned at me, rubbing his thumb over my fingers. 'My exploration's paid off, Rosie. All I've been able to think about, since you came to the mines, was how I'd spirit you away from the others. Into our secret paradise.'

'A bold move,' I agreed, moving close enough that my extended nipples brushed his bare arm. 'But what if they come looking for us? What if we –'

'What can they do that's worse than our current fate?'

I so badly wanted to believe in his bravado. But I touched my cheek, not wanting to lead him down the primrose path. 'I'm a marked woman, Harry. If you're caught with me, the price'll be high.'

He shrugged, endearing himself to me all the more when he kissed the crystal angel. 'What else can they take from me?' he whispered. 'Zelda stripped me of my pride. God only knows what happened to the cash and belongings I brought along. Whatever happens, I'll have no regrets about getting to know you, Rosie. This is the most exciting moment of my life, and I intend to *live* it!'

What more did he need to say? Harry's hair clung damply to his neck, a shade of brown somewhat redder than mine and looking quite soft, now that it was drying. He slowly came towards me for another kiss, a meeting of two hungry minds as well as mouths eager to taste gentle affection. Although he was erect, he took his time enfolding me in his arms, savouring the brush of his bareness against mine as we tried each other on, face to face ... the first notes of an intimate duet we were about to play, accompanied by the waterfall.

'How do you suppose things *work* here?' I asked when we broke apart. 'I mean, the weather in Satan makes no sense at all. And now here's a setting similar to Eden, tucked away from the rest of this hell-hole.'

'I have no idea,' he replied, enjoying the view, our closeness, as though time would stand still simply because he'd willed it. 'I came here unaware, lured by Zelda's assurance that she'd found a place to call home. A place to have a family when we married. Should've known she and her sisters had mischief in mind.'

'Ah,' I said with a sad nod. 'Similar to my history with Grant. I was foolish enough to believe my girlhood fantasies of him could come true fourteen years later.'

Harry smiled, as pleased to solve these little mysteries as I. Was he also thinking back to my first misstep, which landed me in the Playpen – and the performance that followed? If so, he was too kind to point out that I had far more experience at taming a crowd of randy, rutting men than a lady should.

'You're way too much woman for Galloway,' he murmured, untying the ribbon that held back my hair. 'He's so engrossed in himself, I doubt he's noticed the beauty of these twin peaks ... the little dip down your middle that points the way to your secret self. The Rosie only a patient, caring lover can discover the best of.'

My throat closed and I could only stare. How many moons since I'd heard such tender sentiments? How many stars had burned out in my life, that I'd forgotten such men might exist?

Jimmy loved you this way. Or at least you believed he did.

I blinked away that rueful realisation, reminding myself that even Harry, nice as he was, had separated me from the crowd – risked placing both of us in danger – because he wanted to get between my legs. That was the way of it, no matter what sort of wishful thinking a man and a woman shared in their more innocent moments.

But I closed my eyes on those worries and kissed him with all the pent-up longing of my past months in Satan. Except for Collin and Faren, I'd met no one I could care about, even on the most basic level. I twined my arms around his neck, pressing against his chest, feeling the prod of that insistent cock against my belly as Harry, too, sought out the primal fulfilment of body and soul he'd done so long without.

We walked to the edge of the waterfall's basin and stepped into its rippling pool. The warmth of it soothed me, washed away my fears of being caught here. When we walked far enough into the centre that my breasts bobbed on the surface, Harry bent to suckle, reverently, as I stood on tiptoe to accommodate him. Lord, but he sent a fine wildfire streaking through me! My moans rode over the gentle rush of the falls and I felt the first stirrings of a climax.

As elemental as Adam, my escort led me towards the rushing waters with an awe-filled smile ... a promise of wonders to come in our secret Eden. He dove beneath the surface, and moments later reappeared on the other side of the waterfall's translucent veil, gazing in blatant invitation. I giggled and followed his lead, recalling the joy of swimming underwater as a child, sensing my pass beneath the falling water as a rite of passage into another realm. A secluded, private world only Harry and I would ever know.

His lips tasted urgent as I surfaced, my face tilted up to his. Our bodies revelled in the wetness that made us slippery, and our passions ignited. Long, strong fingers pressed into my backside, kneading me against his erection, and when my legs parted, Harry lifted me effortlessly. I held my breath, for my legs were clinging around his hips and I was mere inches from his prick – more excited about sex than I'd been in years!

He met my gaze and guided me slowly downward. I gasped at the touch of his slick, hot head against my hole, and then opened, bracing my legs so I wouldn't rush this wondrous moment. Inch by inch he eased inside me, pausing to kiss me and let his sighs mingle with mine.

'Oh, Rosie ... Rosie ... so glad it's you I'm loving,' he murmured against my wet hair. 'Let's just stay this way and enjoy it for awhile, honey. No hurry, you know. They'll never find us.'

I relaxed against his wet body, which felt enough larger than mine to support me without overwhelming me. He rocked side to side, humming low in his throat. And with the singing of the waters and the lush warmth of the air, I could pretend I'd never even heard of Satan nor fallen for Grant Galloway's ploy. I was just a woman being loved by a man.

Harry's cock grew more insistent then, pulsing and pushing up inside me. I flexed my inner muscles, squeezing the fine, silken solidity of him, breathing with him as we moved in slow, sensual beauty towards a fulfilment we didn't question. Since the first touch, we'd known the flames would consume us. It was merely a matter of letting our bodies catch fire, without thinking. It was total immersion in the warmth and wetness, the taste of our quickening kisses, the scent of our blended bodies, our sighs and the deepening gaze we shared as we got carried away by chemistry.

He clenched his jaw, pumping faster with a cock that filled me. I tilted back, letting the pressure play against my aching clit until I had to gasp for air.

'Are you going to come, love?'

'Oh, Harry, yes – don't slow down, and for God's sake don't drop me!'

His laughter rumbled against me and, as my shoulders arched so I could rub my mound hard against him, his hands spanned my back to hold me. He was gritting his teeth, thrusting straight-on, meeting my crazed body with fast, splashing slaps until I cried out as though struck by lightning.

'Squeeze me,' he grunted, pumping like a man possessed. 'Take it all, Rosie! I can't hold it any longer!'

I gripped him hard, bucking against him until I felt the surge of hot, thick jism filling me, overflowing to warm the water between our bodies. Harry dropped backwards with a triumphant shout, immersing himself and taking me down with him. We splashed like playful otters beneath the surface, letting the force of the falls pummel our still-tingling privates until we could stand no more.

When we popped up for air, both of us were laughing

and spitting spray. I felt like a brazen child skinny-dipping on the sly, naked and free and happier than I'd ever been. Harry shook the wet hair from his face and reached for me, his smile radiant.

'See?' he exclaimed. 'Didn't you just *know* we'd be wonderful together?'

'Yes indeed, that was quite a performance!' someone above us crowed.

We froze, not needing to look towards the shore to identify the owner of that sibilant, insidious voice. Harry took me protectively into his arms, and we turned to face Devlin Meeh. To accept whatever punishment he'd devise for catching us this way.

He leaned forward, grinning, his face aglow from a Mandarin-cut shirt of candy-pink satin, with matching pants. 'I'm *so* glad you two have enjoyed this little patch of paradise I created just for your pleasure,' he crooned. 'Now, of course, you must pay the price of your crime – in full view of your peers. Move along, you two. Venus doesn't wait well.'

19 **Our Dance with a Tarantula**

Meeh herded us mercilessly back to the bathing cave and then out into the white, shining corridor. Because I was dripping wet, with my hair clinging to my back, I felt even more naked than when Jarold stripped me to enter this nether world of the salt mines. But I took courage from Harry. Whenever Devlin wasn't watching, he flashed me a grin, as cocky as a young swain who'd plucked his first cherry. He wasn't the least bit ashamed or afraid!

As we waited for the elevator, however, my nerve failed me. The squeal of the pulleys called out to all the slaves and their overseers, who then congregated in the corridors to see what was happening. Our colourfully clad captor turned towards them, raising his hands like a king acknowledging his subjects.

'See you in the theatre!' he announced, his voice ringing in the domed hall. 'Galloway – you and the others shall proceed upstairs and be seated. The show will begin momentarily.'

I didn't like the sound of that. And to make matters worse, as we stood beside the elevator shaft, I heard eerie voices from out of nowhere, which sounded like the spirits of poor slaves gone before us whispering our doom. *Devvvlin Meeeeh*, they sighed. *Devvvill inn meeeee.*

I stiffened, trying not to believe what I heard. Surely this was another sign of how my confinement in the mines had affected my mental health. Devlin Meeh. *Devil in me*! the voices seemed to say.

Yet it suddenly made more sense than anything I'd heard since I arrived in Satan, where none of the universal rules rang true. What if this stocky little strawberry blond was indeed the ruler of the afterlife-gone-wrong, and –

Meeh's laughter cut into my ominous thoughts. 'You *should* look worried, my dear,' he said, caressing the angel on my cheek. 'You've been truly foolish this time. And just when I was about to bring you back home.'

Beside me, Harry scowled. 'Don't fall for those ghostly voices, Rosie,' he murmured. 'This domed hall was designed as a whispering gallery, where someone on the opposite side of the circular chamber – an overseer at the mine entry, for example – can say something against the wall's surface, and the message travels here. I saw the KlonDykes over there just moments ago.'

Of course I pivoted to catch the triplets at another trick, but the wrought-iron elevator door rolled open and Devlin pointed impatiently for us to enter. I huddled against the back wall with the curlicues of cold metal cutting into my back, hating this overweight weasel more by the moment. Once again he was dangling that carrot of freedom in front of me, and I was tired of it! How many other illusions would he fool me with to keep me under his thumb?

His boyish face split in a grin, for I suspected he could read my mind. 'You still have the option of redeeming yourself,' he said, his monocle twinkling. 'When we reach the main level, the elevator will stop and I'll give you pen and paper. You can write to Jimmy Crystal and all will be forgiven. It's that simple.'

As we lurched into our ascent, my thoughts warred within me. 'Will Harry be set free, too?' I rasped.

'Of course.' Nice as pie. Mr Benevolence, whenever

my fate hung in the balance with the scales tipped his way.

I glanced at my companion, whose pointed look confirmed my immediate suspicion: wouldn't Meeh think it delicious if Jimmy *did* come here at my request, and then found me with another man?

'No thank you,' I replied, my stomach knotting. I'd be damned if I'd drag Harry into the maelstrom this angel on my face was causing.

'My, my – where's our loyalty?' Devlin jeered. 'Not fifteen minutes ago you were joined at the hip and screaming out your delight with this man. Just the cock you've been looking for, isn't he?'

'It was I who led Rosie astray,' Harry stated. 'I'll accept full responsibility – and the punishment coming to us both.'

'Such a noble sentiment,' the little ogre said with a sarcastic sigh. When he shifted a lever on his control panel, the elevator lurched again, angling into a shaft that travelled at a diagonal. 'But Venus intends to have her fun with you, meting out her punishment. And who am I to deny her? It's a joy to watch both her and Miss DuBris in action, bringing their instincts and unique abilities into play. Imagine my delight when I pit them against each other!'

The elevator door rolled open then, and we stepped into an area of velvety darkness, where the expectant murmur of a large crowd drifted back to us. I glanced ahead when a groan of different pulleys signalled the drawing of curtains, and I recognised the black back-drop of a stage ... the shimmering silver strands of Venus's spiderweb.

'I recall how you enjoyed watching the Titzlers and Galloway being punished for your abduction.' Meeh's voice pierced the darkness. 'So imagine now how thrilled the girls and your old flame will be to watch *you* spinning on that web, my dear! I can only guess what Venus might have in mind for the woman who wears her crystal talisman.'

I swallowed hard, taking no comfort from the warm hand Harry clasped around mine.

'Last chance, Angel,' Devlin whispered, reaching into the darkness beside him to strike a match. He lit a lantern atop a small table, and took a fountain pen and writing paper from its centre drawer. 'You can remain in safety, backstage, and I'll send the slaves back to the mines. All you have to do is ask Jimmy to come for a visit. I bet he misses that pussy you've trained with so many tricks! Here – write your ticket home, Rosie.'

My pulse pounded so loudly I could hear nothing else. I saw visions of my life passing by in perpetual shame in Satan, for having the audacity to assume I could rise above my first mistake of coming here. Why was I being so belligerent – arrogant enough to endanger poor Harry, as well – when with a few simple words, I could get our lives out of hock?

I grabbed for the pen, but Meeh jerked it away. 'April fool!' he cried out, laughing maliciously. 'And you two make a perfect pair of them, fucking in the sunlight, as though you'd not get caught!'

He shoved us out to the stage, but I was so stunned I paid little attention to the harnessed spectators who filled row upon row of the theatre. April fool, had he said? Could I possibly have lost two entire months in the mines? I turned to Harry, who'd stumbled out close behind me – and who, at the sight of our colossal audience, took me protectively into his arms. Applause and cat-calls rang around the arena, so we used the opportunity for a few precious moments of private talk.

'How long have you been in the mines?' I whispered urgently.

His brow furrowed in thought. 'Possibly a year. I've lost track of –'

'Do you want out? Maybe it's the lack of sunlight, but I'm losing my mind, Harry! If I agree to what Meeh wants, perhaps I can get us –'

'Don't believe everything he says,' my gentle escort insisted. 'Don't sacrifice a chance for escape by taking his bait on impulse. He'll go back on his word –'

'Silence!' a powerful voice cried out.

The raucous crowd came to order, for Venus was stepping into view from the opposite side of the stage. Her glare panned the theatre before lingering on the two of us huddling together.

Was it cold in here? Or did I shiver with fright at the sight of this imposing virago? Clad in a garment of sleek black fur that covered her body like skin, with her ebony hair in three stiff plaits that stood out like spikes, Venus was a tarantula walking upright, approaching us with a predatory air that was at once sinister and mesmerising. The crowd held its collective breath, aware that this hermaphrodite was minus a leg of the spider she resembled – but only fools would discount her power. This creature didn't *need* anything more to inflict her venom: that prick was now sticking out like a stinger. Ready to fill me, and Harry, with a desire that might drive us to our deaths.

'On with the show!' Meeh crowed, coming from behind the curtain with his arms held high for the audience's approval. As the applause began again, he bowed, quite the flamboyant showman in his shiny pink attire. Then he pivoted, pointing a pudgy finger at us.

'As punishment for evading your overseers, and engaging in private pleasure while you should've been working – and for breaking the silence,' he announced in a grand manner, 'you, Rosie and Harry, shall now do your coupling here on the stage, where we can all enjoy it!'

Cheers and whistles made my face go hot. The crystal angel in my cheek throbbed as though it were burning through to the bone.

'However,' Meeh continued, his monocle twinkling in the spotlight, 'Venus will be directing your escapades – and participating, if she cares to – to ensure we get the full benefit of your banging. A whore and a sheep rancher should make for a fine spectacle! The one is an expert at bringing out animal passions, while the other dearly loved his livestock!'

The mocking laughter at Harry's expense made my blood boil. Yet when he caught me in a gaze that held only compassion – not a sign of scorn for my previous profession – I realised this kind fellow had lost far more than I by coming to Satan.

'You left your ranch to be with Zelda?' I whispered.

'I loved her,' he said with a sad shrug. 'And you were –'

'A *fool*,' I cut in quickly, 'for believing that Grant – or anyone else – could see me as a woman worthy of regard, much less love or trust.'

'Not so, Rosie. When I get us out of here –'

'Separate them,' Venus called to the guards. 'Enough of their intimate whispering. Let the wild fucking begin!'

The roar from the crowd must've been what the Christians heard before being sacrificed to Roman lions ... such bloodlust, from those deprived of any other entertainment! A burly guard grabbed me away from Harry and steered me backwards, towards the velvety black backdrop with its glimmering web. Faster than my eye could follow, Venus tossed her silver threads weighted with those tiny balls. My right wrist and right ankle tingled from being so rapidly wrapped to the Spider Queen's snare.

Harry, not yet subdued by a guard, rushed towards me – and was caught in a similar position, facing me, with a wrist and ankle bound. A quiet whirring noise came from behind us and the web began its slow rotation, tugging our bodies until we stood on tiptoe.

'Hook your free hand and foot around a strand,' my cohort whispered as his body landed against mine. 'We'll sag in tandem that way.'

'And the sooner we give them what they want, the sooner they'll be done with us.'

Harry scowled. 'Give them what they want, hell! No one leaves the mines alive, Rose. We must *defy* Venus and Meeh to stay sane, until we can escape.'

His bold murmurs stirred me from a dangerous complacency. Harry was right: caving in was the path of least resistance, which all the fools in those theatre seats had taken – how long ago?

'I'm for taking what *we* want, sweetheart,' he continued with a light lick along my ear. 'Have you ever made love while floating upside down?'

I recalled watching the Titzlers on this wheel – how Nelda became ill and her sisters belligerent, as Grant crawled unsteadily between them – and how Venus had made them all her prey. But I shook my head, and then became enraptured by the mischievous twinkle in Harry's eye. Because he hung suspended in front of me, I could ignore the audience, could focus on his steadfast gaze, on eyes the calming deep green of a forest.

I couldn't ignore the friction of our slowly rising bodies, however – especially the swelling of the cock caught between us. 'Will it be like riding a Ferris wheel? I saw one at a carnival once, but I didn't get to try it.'

'Oh, we'll be much more thrilling than that,' he assured me, rubbing my abdomen in suggestive circles. 'Wrap your free leg around me. Let me ease inside you, and then hang on for the ride of your life!'

His warm breath falling on my face ... the scent of his strength, mingled with the manly reassurance of his low voice ... Harry was potently persuasive, and when I dared myself to follow his suggestions – convinced myself that I'd met someone I could trust – the sensations were awe-inspiring! I was at my lover's mercy, hanging literally by a thread as he kissed me into submission, into forgetting that a tarantula watched us from below. Instead, I clung to Harry, opening myself to his words and his wonderful cock, just as we reached the uppermost position of the web.

He slipped inside me with a soft grunt, filling me with his solid shaft. My muscles clenched around him and suddenly, in my mind, we were in that waterfall paradise again. I let out a sigh and sought his lips with mine.

'Fuck her harder, Harry. Must I show you how?' Venus taunted.

He rocked me upward with his thrust, which distracted me from the panic of turning head-first towards the floor. My pulse raced in my veins, spurring my hips into action beneath him – and when my body realised that Harry's weight would steady mine, and that he had a firm enough hold to keep us both from falling into a loose dangle, I began to enjoy the drop-stomach feel of flying – and fucking – upside down!

'Oh my God,' I breathed, even though the blood was draining into my head. 'This is crazy! I want to giggle and wiggle and –'

And when I did, Harry laughed too, gently swinging our bodies back into the direction I'd pushed us from. The filaments of the web were dipping with us, allowing our feet to fall forward only for a certain distance before snapping us back, like elastic. Our playful exchange distracted us from actual lovemaking, yet it made a powerful aphrodisiac, that swaying.

'Oh for Chrissakes,' Meeh muttered below us. 'Have your way with them, Venus. They're missing the whole point of their punishment.'

The web sagged with the added weight of the spider-like creature who'd slithered on, but I held tight to Harry. 'Ignore her,' I whispered. 'She hates that.'

'I have eyes only for you, Rosie,' he replied. He was getting caught up in that frenzy that precedes a climax, with dilated pupils and breathing that accelerated to a pant. 'But I hope you'll understand if I pull out at an inopportune time. A diversionary tactic – not a reflection on you, my sweet.'

What on earth did he mean by that? My body was following his in that elemental dance of the sexes, aided by the excitement – the excruciating joy – of floating through the air. I could hear Meeh muttering something else, ordering Venus into faster action because the audience was sounding restless, no doubt. But all I cared about was the man who shoved his shaft in and out of me as we drifted topside-downward with our hearts in our throats.

'I'm going to take my turn now,' came the sinuous whisper of the hermaphrodite in black. 'I've got enough gush to drown your posy, Rosie – and then Harry's going to wonder what hit him. He'll remember how good it felt to be fucking you, and he'll spend the rest of his useless life trying to climax. Too bad it has to be this way. Too bad you've both been . . . too bad.'

The sag of the web, just above us as we tilted to travel parallel to the floor, suggested Venus was about to sideswipe us. But Harry thrust harder, to keep us bobbing and weaving our way towards an orgasm.

'Hold tight,' he murmured against my ear.

I clung to him, concentrating on the vibrations inside my pussy. Somehow, the knife-edged danger of Venus the Spider Queen – the brush of her furred arm – drove me into more of a frenzy, and my inner muscles clenched his cock, hard. Possessively. Because I refused to give him up.

'My turn,' the creature above us insisted, stroking the sides of our joined bodies with her insidious fingers.

'You'll have to wait,' Harry panted, thrusting more vigorously inside me. 'I know how badly you want me, Venus. I've seen you sizing me up for when you could corner me ... planning to smother me with those big tits and stick your cock up my ass. But Rosie comes first.'

'It's Rosie I want, fool,' Venus jeered. She was rubbing against us now, using the rhythm of our swinging to bring us into contact with breasts held fast beneath her tight black suit ... nipples so hard they grazed my skin as though she were writing her name along the arm that held Harry tight ... a fur-covered cock so insistent it pried between our thighs.

I glanced at her and wished I hadn't: her midnight eyes glowed with poison, in a face dark with fury and the desire to consume me.

'Bitch!' I hissed at her. 'If Meeh wants me to suffer, tell *him* to climb up here. That little prick surely must miss me. Especially when he sees a real man like Harry making me squirm!'

Our audience chuckled, yet I heard the furtive brush of bare bodies, the whisper of skin upon skin, as they reached for their neighbours. Devlin's face assumed the colour of his cerise suit as he stepped closer to the rotating web.

'You've cooked your goose now, Angel,' he taunted. 'Plenty of other pussy to be had –'

'Then go out and get some!' Harry grunted. 'And take your pet tarantula with you!'

Tight laughter erupted in the theatre, and as we angled slowly upward, out of Meeh's reach, I could see the veins standing out in Devlin's neck. Venus, however, was positioning herself behind Harry's flexing backside. And from where I lay, beneath the agile lover who was about to bring me off, I saw her black spikes of hair and tight, textured arms and realised the wicked arachnid could just as easily fill one of our assholes.

But my partner knew that too – and when he felt her pointer poking for its target, he reached between us to grab it. Venus yelped and, in her split-second loss of concentration, Harry slipped out of me to swing his leg in a hard arc behind him, throwing his weight into the attack. This launched our intruder backwards against the wildly swaying web, scrabbling for a hold, while Harry wrapped his legs back around her and held on to that monster cock. He rode Venus like a cowboy busting a bronc, his bound hand grabbing the web above his head as he thrust his butt into her stomach, gripping her bristling dick with his free hand.

From where I clung to the slithering strands of silver, I could only guess what Venus would do to him when she regained her senses. She was bouncing wildly, fettered by a foot-long braid that had snagged in the web, enraged that Harry had snatched her advantage.

'I'm going to come,' he panted, rubbing himself against her furred pelvis, 'and you're going to come with me, Venus. I can feel you straining ... feel the heat in your meat because I'm riding you, making you lose control.'

'No!' the writhing spider protested. 'I'm going to –'

'You're too far gone to *know* what you're doing,' Harry gasped. 'You're going to shoot like a cannon, Venus! You want to come up my ass so badly you're shaking with it. And I'm going to let you. Scoot us higher, so you can watch!'

With a desperate upward thrust, the ebony creature shifted them high enough that Harry's trapped wrist came even with his hip. Their heads were now at the top of the circling web, which gave him much better leverage. Venus, however, had gained equal advantage because her sense of control had been restored. Her eyes narrowed. Closing in for the kill, she began to curl around her prey from both ends at once.

I gazed in horrified fascination, along with the entire theatre full of people humping in their seats. Harry, clinging with his muscled calves, angled himself upward as though to open his back door for her – flashing his tight backside so Venus could see precisely what she was about to get herself into. Like trapeze acrobats fallen into the net they struggled, for the spidery hermaphrodite was taller than the panting, puffing little insect tormenting her.

Just as Venus clasped his shoulder to shove him on to her cock – to sate herself and fill him with her liquid hex – Harry began to squirt. His come splashed her black abdomen, and then he aimed it at her cock. When his cream ran down her towering shaft, he closed his hand around her to rub it in, still pumping like a fire hose himself. Venus convulsed with an unearthly cry.

Thick juice shot up like a fountain and, in a flash of inspiration, Harry repositioned that big hairy prick. The next shot caught Devlin Meeh in the face, and when he shrieked in surprise, he got a mouthful. Venus's final shudder splattered buttery come all over the front of his Mandarin jacket.

'Guards!' he sputtered. 'What the hell are you waiting for?'

But pandemonium was running amok: not only were the burly men on stage engaged in various stages of release, but the ecstatic moans and pleas of the naked slaves drowned out their master's commands. It was Venus who quickly unfastened Harry's and my bindings, and used them to tie us together with our hands behind our backs. She and Meeh then marched us offstage like errant children – towards that wrought-iron elevator and back to those damn salt mines.

At least Devlin got a dose of his own medicine, I mused, my grin telling Harry how tickled I was – for we knew better than to talk. Meeh was still wiping his sticky face with a handkerchief the colour of a ripe lime, and wiping out his mouth, and obviously wanting a bath. Venus stared unflinchingly at the two of us, pressed against those hard iron designs in the walls, trying to resume her aura of authority despite the way her armour now sported a proverbial chink.

I wasn't surprised when Venus unlocked the gate to the Playpen, with an evil grin. But as Devlin steered me towards its door, he gripped my arm. 'I'm not finished with you, missy,' he hissed. 'You'll be on permanent display here, at the mercy of Venus and anyone else who approaches the Playpen, until I give you another chance to write to Jimmy. Nothing to eat but bread. One bowl of water a day. Absolute silence.'

I rolled my eyes, yet I knew he held my future in his fat little hands. 'Why do you want Crystal?' I demanded. 'Why don't you just go after him yourself?'

Devlin's chubby face took on a feral tightness that frightened me: it suggested the absence of judgment; indeed, the absence of reason or decency. 'I have a score to settle, and I want you to witness it,' he said in a coiled voice. 'I'm having Crystal come to Satan because I *can*. I need no other reason for what I do, Rose. Don't ask me again.'

As his grimace made his monocle wink, I saw another shimmering image of Jimmy Crystal – this time his full face, with his coffee-coloured eyes focused on mine. I swear to God he was mouthing, *I love you, Rosie . . . I love you, Rosie – God, how I miss you!*

'Bastard!' I breathed, for I had no doubt Devlin Meeh

was somehow projecting these images on to his lens, driving me to fulfil his devious plan. I slapped him so hard the *smack* echoed in the domed, white entryway to the mines – followed by the shrill tinkling of glass when that damn monocle hit the floor.

He shoved me into the Playpen and slammed the gate. As he and Venus strode towards the mine shafts, steering Harry roughly between them, I wondered what they had in mind for him.

Would I ever see my friend's bright smile again?

20 **Rumblings from Above**

Spending the days naked in a cage gnawed at my soul. Like a nasty rat, doubt nibbled away the confidence Harry had inspired in those fine few hours we'd spent together. It now felt degrading when the other slaves came to stick their dicks between the Playpen's bars, or to spread pussies that leered wetly, expecting me to lick their cream and be grateful for the taste of it.

Since the Playpen was so small – only four paces long, and I could grip the bars on both sides – there was no escaping my tormentors. My spin on Venus's web with Harry had inspired those who'd watched us flying united: now the larger fellows reached inside to lift me, lowering me on to their prodding cocks as I grasped their shoulders to keep from falling backwards. The shorter ones would tug me, seated, so my legs went around two bars and they could kneel and prey. Or they'd demand I present myself like a bitch in heat, so they could take turns at me from behind, in whichever hole suited them.

I searched their faces, hoping to see Harry's grin above one of those jutting cocks. But as the weeks passed, I lost hope of ever knowing his gentle touch, his encouraging words, again.

Why were these people so smug in their silence? I'd done nothing to them – nor had my misbehaviour with Harry made their state of servitude any worse. I could only guess that when a curious finger touched the angel on my face – and then drew back, as though from an electrical shock – they assumed I was magic like Meeh, except my magic had gone bad because I'd defied him. And I'd helped make a fool of Venus, the crystal's previous owner.

Sometimes they studied me through the bars, staring at my nakedness – even watching as I used the chamber pot in the corner. I also became a spectacle as I drank my water on all fours, like a dog, because the crockery bowl was too large to lift. Sometimes they humped each other and then made me lick them clean – or they came all over my face. Then the next one would demand I rinse off in my water bowl, so he could have a fresh go of it.

Mostly, however, they went about their work in the mine shafts, or their eating and sleeping in the communal rooms, leaving me alone in the Playpen, in the centre of that cavernous entry hall. I felt small and forlorn. Useless. Each day stretched like an endless night of bad dreams, even though it never got dark.

True to Meeh's orders, I was given bread scraps left from the others' meals and my water crock got refilled each day – or what I guessed was a day. Down in the mines, lit by sconces that made the salt walls glisten in continuous, shiny white, I was as much a prisoner of my wandering thoughts as I was of the timeless, restless monotony of my narrow cell. Each time Venus came down – mostly to taunt me with her threatening ebony presence – I wondered what would trigger her next feeding frenzy. That I would be her chosen morsel was a given; a glint in those midnight eyes when she gazed at my angel told me she'd strike in her own good time.

In my hours alone, I also mused about how Devlin might be feeling by now. Had he succumbed to the madness from swallowing Venus's come? More likely he was immune, because he himself had cast the spell over the nasty hermaphrodite's juice. The longer I stayed in Satan, the more I realised that things I'd considered coincidence probably were not: they were part of this infernal little world that turned on Meeh's tilted axis, to suit his whim. After all, he needed no other reason for making things go his way!

What preyed on me most, however, was that last image I'd seen in Devlin's lens – where Jimmy said he loved me. How many times had I *wished* to hear those words? I tried to tell myself it was one of Meeh's tricks, to scare me into writing that letter. But how could he possibly make such pictures appear, as though projected from his mind on to his monocle?

Or were the pictures there at all? Perhaps, in my despair of ever lifting my face to the sun again, or of knowing a normal life, my mind entertained itself by showing Jimmy Crystal in various scenarios designed to inspire my pity, or fear, or remorse: my soul's revenge for how I'd left him on a whim.

I firmly believed that when the barkeep gave me money for passage, he knew what awaited me in Satan. Yet, considering the treatment I'd received here from other men who supposedly adored me, my sense of being betrayed had softened. In Meeh's monocle, I'd seen Crystal display many different moods over these past months. It hadn't escaped me that his condition – like mine – was deteriorating each time I saw him.

I glanced down at my hollowed body, licking my parched lips. My limbs had lost their sleek strength and my ribs were visible. My breasts hung limply; curls now covered my mound again, but even there I'd become noticeably thinner. I'd stopped pacing my cage, not only to save valuable body fuel but because I had less strength.

Even if I wrote that letter – and even if Jimmy

showed up – I doubted he'd want me now. I was becoming a sad shadow of the spunky sporting woman he'd kept in his upstairs room.

This was a part of Meeh's plan, of course, to make me too weak to fight next time Venus took me on. And there wasn't a damn thing I could do about it.

In my despair one day, I didn't notice the squeal of the elevator pulleys ... was absently wondering what had become of Grant Galloway and the KlonDykes, whom I hadn't seen for weeks. I was curled on my side, on the hard salt floor of the Playpen, resting before the next crew of randy slaves came to harass me with their hard-ons ... wishing this endless *waiting* – for whatever Meeh had in mind – would come to an end. I sensed I'd soon slip into a state of mental oblivion, which might not be such a bad thing ...

'Angel, can you hear me? Dear God, you look positively wretched!'

I heard the familiar voice and drifted higher in my dreamlike state. But I felt no need to turn towards whoever had addressed me. Why bother, if she didn't like the sight of me?

'Rosie, wake up! I haven't much time before they find I'm gone.'

The urgency in that childlike whisper compelled me to lift my head. And when I saw those shiny black shoes, the white-stockinged legs – and caught sight of a naked pink puss beneath that dark uniform – I came more awake than I'd been for days.

'Faren!'

It came out as a rasp, so I rolled to my water bowl to wet my throat. Of all the positions this brazen little maid had seen me in, it hurt like hell when she watched me lap my water like a homeless mutt. 'What's happened that – I thought you'd forgotten me after ...'

'No, love, ever since Collin and I saw your face in

Meeh's carriage window, we've been waiting for the right time. And it's now!' Faren gripped the bars and squatted, so she could peer at me on the same level. 'Things have really gone to hell in Satan these past few days –'

I rolled my eyes at this understatement, yet my heart was thudding hard. This freckle-faced redhead's ringlets bobbed as she talked, and from where I lay on the floor I was looking at her parted pink petals, centred between two white thighs ... a place that smelled of her lemon grass bath salts and the scent that was uniquely Faren.

'– and we've been overrun by prospectors, come to the Klondike for a gold rush,' the little maid continued. 'Thousands of them! Mostly men, forced to camp all winter at Lake Bennett when it –'

'Froze over,' I murmured, recalling Captain Manley in his jaunty red jacket, and how he'd saved us from that fate. I inched a finger towards that enticing sex, suddenly craving the taste of her ... licking my lips at the sight of her gathering dew.

'Collin's tried to tell them the gold's all spoken for – the claims all taken. But they refuse to believe him! He's the mayor now, you know, since Galloway can no longer manage the post –'

Now *that* made me wake up! I had assumed Grant's absences from the mines meant he was checking in at the Brazen Lady and taking care of city business.

'– and Devlin is beside himself, trying to restore order. The saloons and whorehouses are packed with men demanding –'

'All manner of satisfaction, after a long winter of waiting to find their fortunes.' I slipped my middle finger inside her, up to the first knuckle, and then wiggled it.

'Yes! Oh, yes,' she whimpered, spreading herself wide between the bars. 'Oh God, Angel – *please*, please lick me off – and then we have to get you out of here. It's been *horrid* at Devlin's without you, but he's had Jarold watching me like a hawk.'

It was all I needed to hear. The past months of wondering whether she'd taken up with Collin and forgotten me disappeared as I angled my mouth towards her pretty pink lips. Running my tongue lightly around her, I breathed deeply, drawing strength from a desire I hadn't felt in weeks. Her sighs fuelled my own fire, and as I prodded her with my pointed tongue I felt her hand slip between my legs.

She was quivering with need and her clit pressed against me to beg for attention. I sucked it gently between my teeth, thinking of the times I'd lapped chocolate from these lips, throbbing with hope and a burgeoning determination – the will to seek my own release – both from the fingers now sliding inside me and from the situation I'd languished in for too long. If all hell had broken loose above ground, things were about to change for us slaves as well. And, by God, I intended to be the first one out!

Her fingertip was diddling my clit, driving me wild, so I plunged my tongue inside her. Faren gasped, gushing a little honey for me, squirming with the girlish delight I'd missed so badly. Hope flitted like a butterfly in my stomach – or were those the flickerings of an acute desire I hadn't felt since I'd met Harry?

Within moments she was shuddering, her petals a deep carmine as the cream seeped between them. Gasping, thrusting against my tongue to beg for release, Faren began to pant loudly. 'Please, Angel ... yes, lick me there ... harder now – harder – ohh – ohh – OHH ...'

With a sharp intake of breath, she thrashed against my face. I lapped furiously, as eager to taste her as she was to be laved. Recovering quickly, she glanced around the unoccupied entry chamber. 'Stand up and spread for me,' she commanded in a whisper.

As she knelt, my foot went to her shoulder through the bars, and then she was licking, lapping, rubbing me with the brunt of her upper lip while her tongue teased me into a frenzy. I stepped wider, my head drifting back, flexing against the tongue that darted to all the sensitive places it knew I loved. Too soon I was shaking with a white-knuckled grip on my cage, but how long could we tarry? I closed my eyes and let the spiralling sensations run amok, filling me with a madness that could only be satisfied by penetration.

'Fuck me with your tongue,' I wheezed, lifting my pussy lips with two fingers to give her better access.

Faren obliged, shoving against my wetness and spreading it with her eager mouth. When her hard tongue shot inside me, I cried out in spite of myself. I had to hang on, to keep from collapsing from an irrepressible orgasm like I'd forgotten I could have. And then we just smiled at each other, panting. Wiping our faces.

It was then I noticed something different about this little woman whom time and development had forgotten: she was sticking out, above the waistband of her white, ruffled pinafore!

'Where'd you get those tits?' I whispered, giggling so hard the tears dribbled down my cheeks.

'Took you long enough to notice!' she fired back. Reaching beneath her pinafore, Faren pulled out one cloth sack, and then another, and pressed them into my hands.

'It's chocolate, Angel. I had wild imaginings of you smearing it all over me, but there's no time for that right now,' she whispered. 'Just thought it might come in handy. I get the feeling all the seams'll soon bust loose here in Satan, you know.'

I trusted her instincts, thanking her profusely as I stashed the cream-coloured bags beneath the wide rim of my water bowl. They weren't invisible, but they attracted less attention from there.

'Do you have a hair pin? Or better yet, Venus's key?' I asked, looking towards the mine corridors. It wouldn't do for the slaves or their overseers to witness my escape.

'Venus's key? Oh, of course I do!' the maid teased as she walked around the Playpen. Then she stared quizzically at the gate, where the large padlock fastened it to the barred frame of the cage. 'Angel – Rosie – I – I don't know how to ...'

When my redheaded friend lifted the bulky lock from its place, my jaw dropped. It wasn't even closed.

My water got poured between the black bars, usually by an overseer. Only Venus emptied my chamber pot, so only the tarantula – wearing marvellous gowns of many colours to mock my naked state – had handled the padlock, which I couldn't see from inside the Playpen. Had I been so befuddled – so resigned to my fate – that I hadn't noticed the lack of a *click* when she closed the gate after each visit?

How long had I been held prisoner in an unlocked cell?

'I feel incredibly stupid,' I wheezed. 'Never thought to try the lock. Never figured –'

The creaking of cartwheels alerted me to the end of the work shift, and suddenly Faren's safety – and anonymity – were more important than my own witless victimisation. 'Replace the lock and get on that elevator,' I urged, pointing towards its open door. 'I'll be fine now, thanks to you. Tell Collin I miss him!'

'Oh, I'll tell him much more than that,' the maid called quietly over her shoulder.

She'd just trotted into the wrought-iron contraption that would carry her back to Meeh's other world – back to where I now vowed with a vengeance to return –

when a crew of slaves entered the cavernous entryway. The pulleys' squeals alerted them to something they'd missed, however. So, as they surrounded my cell, fondling themselves to attention, they gazed at me with questions in their eyes. Questions as pointed as the cocks that now sprang up beneath their black leather harness straps.

But I remained on the floor, sitting along the pen's centre length to gaze at them with a stoic serenity. Knowledge was power. And the devious Devlin Meeh and his wicked mistress had taught me an invaluable lesson – a lesson about handcuffs we had all created in our minds.

'Forget it,' I said, casting a derogatory glance at their dicks. 'I refuse to service you any more. I know something you don't – just got my ticket *out* of this hellhole! But I'm not sharing it with you, because you've known all along my cage wasn't locked. *Haven't* you?'

Their hands went still. Their furtive glances confirmed it.

'I suppose I've been sitting here, a prisoner, ever since Harry and I put Venus in her place,' I went on, my voice rising with my emotions. 'And you probably think your little secret's funny! That's why you've had such smug, superiour looks on your faces, isn't it? The joke's on *me!*'

I stood then, glaring at each one in turn. 'But you know what?' I challenged. 'You're just as much a victim of your stupidity as I am! Had you shown me the padlock was undone, I could've slipped away and made plans for your escape – out of sheer gratitude – during all these endless days you've been working Meeh's mines and I've been sitting here. But no! Like a herd of mindless pack animals, you've just kept hauling salt and then coming out here to rub yourselves in my face.'

'Silence!' came the voice of an overseer. 'Silence, or I'll call the guards.'

He was a dark, hairy fellow I'd seen down here ever since I'd been banished from Meeh's bed, but I had no intention of following his rules – or anyone else's! Instead, I gazed intently at the slaves surrounding me.

'Are you going to die here in silence? Are you going to spend what's left of your lives labouring for a prissy little prick who wears pink pants?' I asked in a low voice. 'How'd you end up down here anyway? Did you break one of Devlin's asinine rules? Or did you refuse, like I did, to lure your family and friends to this farce he calls a paradise? Are you going to sacrifice yourselves – your honour – by allowing him to play God when he's really the devil?'

They shifted, glancing nervously towards the approaching overseer.

'So *what* if you don't produce his quota of salt each day?' I continued, coaxing them into a plan that had sprung to mind when Faren showed me the loose lock. 'And why are you afraid to *talk*, for Chrissakes? This means you don't even know your overseer's *name*, yet he controls your life!'

I pressed my fists into my hips, inspiring them with the sight of my taut, quivering body. 'If *everyone* talks and laughs, how can they possibly punish us all? Who can control this many strong, able-bodied men and women, once we decide to live by our *own* fucking rules instead of Devlin Meeh's?'

'Enough, Miss DuBris!' that overseer in the toga barked. Glancing around the huge room, where other slaves were now pouring in to see what this commotion was, he gestured towards one of the corridors. 'You, Lexter! Fetch Venus, quickly! Tell her Angel's out of control!'

He forced his way through the outer crowd surrounding my cage, but the ones hugging the bars formed a solid human wall to prevent his coming any closer. Heartening, but Lord, they were slow!

'You're in for it now,' one of the slaves dared murmur. 'Venus wants that crystal back, so she'll shoot you fulla that –'

'You're telling me this roomful of men can't put that mixed-up bitch in her place?' I prodded. 'Hell's bells – Venus doesn't know if she's a pointer or a setter! She's got you all so pussy-whipped, quaking at everything she says or does –'

'As *you* should be, Miss Debris,' came a noxious hiss from behind me.

The room sucked air and everyone turned to where the queen in question stood glaring at us. She wore a tight vest of a fabric so blindingly white I had to look away – but not before I'd noticed how her ebony breasts strained at the laces so her nipples poked out like pointed bullets. With her hair pulled back into a severe topknot, her expression looked deadly – but not as lethal as that hard, dark weapon jutting out of a hole in the white fabric stretched between her muscular legs. Boots completed her ensemble – tight white boots with high pointy heels that could do some real damage.

She was dressed for war. She intended to win, once and for all. But I refused to just lie down and spread my legs, for I'd put myself in that position for too many years now! I might as well risk getting pumped full of her noxious come, for what did I have to lose? If I didn't make it out of the mines, I'd spend the rest of my life miserable and unsatisfied anyway.

And if I prevailed, I had friends above ground – where things were apparently running riot – who'd help me escape from Satan.

I crossed my arms, curling my lip at her. Rosie DuBris might be shorter, and skinnier, and weaker – without an icicle's chance in hell of surviving this showdown, really. But she wasn't dead yet!

'Get in here, Venus!' I cried. 'Find out how a *real* woman fights!'

21 **Unexpected Guests**

Her laughter rang out in the room's high canopy as she strode towards the Playpen. 'This pussy's going to claw you to shreds, little mouse!' she jeered. 'If you think for one minute that angel on your face will protect you – just because Meeh said it would – you're a first-rate fool.'

Had Venus seen through my ruse? Or had she just handed me another key? Now that she loomed outside my cage – was hoisting herself up by the crossbars and over the *top* of the damn thing! – I had no idea how to outsmart her. I turned to the slaves murmuring among themselves, watching this impending catfight with eager eyes.

'See there?' I challenged them. 'Another example of the lies we've all fallen for! Another set of handcuffs we've forged for ourselves. Help me break these chains! We'll all get out of here together!'

A roar went up from the crowd and it gladdened my heart. But the creature who'd climbed into the narrow, confining pen with me kept sneering. 'Give up, while you're still in a condition Devlin can adore,' she spoke below the noise. 'He's on his way down here, to take you home, Angel. Why spoil the chance to wear his jewellery and furs, and spend the rest of your days in play?'

'Take this angel off my face,' I taunted, pointing to the crystal. 'For somebody who wants it so badly, you haven't tried very hard.'

From out of nowhere she struck, her slap resounding

above the crowd. But it was my burning breast I grabbed, rather than my face. The angel in my cheek throbbed – no protection at all. A distraction, in fact. And I wondered if I'd been a fool to invite this fight. Around us, the other slaves cheered loudly on my behalf, but no one lifted the lock to rescue me. They were carousing among themselves, while overseers in rippling togas tried to quiet them.

Venus came at me, and too soon – too late – I felt cold iron bars biting into my back. 'If you want to get rid of that hideous crystal, take it off,' she taunted. 'You were a marked woman before Meeh planted it there anyway. Marked for failure!'

With that, the bitch kicked high and landed the hard toe of her boot between my legs.

'A punt to the cunt,' someone called out. 'Oh, this is getting good!'

'Punt *me*,' one of the women cried, and pandemonium broke loose. There in that round, cavernous hall, the slaves' voices created a cacophony that rose to a deafening level. They hadn't heeded a word I'd said! I was truly alone, caught in a cage that didn't feel much larger than a coffin with tall bars.

Venus was snickering, standing at arm's length, as I quivered against the end of the Playpen. 'You've taken all the sport from it, inviting me here this way,' she said with a devious grin. 'Not that you'd have any better chance of winning if I let you out.'

For a fleeting moment, my hopes rose and I pictured myself scrambling over the shoulders of those who rioted around me. But Venus was right: no one in that unruly mob was paying enough attention to help me.

When a crowd of naked people got excited, only one thing could come of it, and they no longer felt inspired to free themselves from a tyranny that felt like normal life. They were going at it, the fastest men grabbing at the few women while the others filled whatever openings they could find. The entry hall was a blur of bare bodies in black harnesses, grunting and humping. The overseers had either shucked their togas to join in or disappeared into the mine shafts.

Venus loomed closer, slowly extending her hand, palm upward with the middle finger sticking out. I watched helplessly, pressing harder against the bars as she circled one nipple, then the other, with her fingernail. Ripples of fear mixed with pain and desire shot through me. In all my months here in Satan, I'd not felt this virago's caress – although her mixed attributes and overwhelming presence had held me in awe.

She let her fingertip trail down my hollowed-out stomach, her obsidian eyes glowing. Like a panther she looked, all hard and sleek and invincible; more alluring than I wanted to admit, with those breasts heaving against her white vest lacings while her cock – surely the most formidable thing in the room – throbbed visibly, as though sniffing out my sex. Had I put aside who she was and who she worked for, I could've succumbed to the hunger of a puss long unfilled by anything that even remotely satisfied it.

And that thought was my undoing. I gasped when her long, coffee-coloured finger got shoved up my pussy, and Venus ground the butt of her hand against my mound.

'I'm going to make you come until your knees buckle,' she crooned, all the while pushing that finger like a piston inside me. 'I'm going to have you convulsing, out of control and begging me to fuck you full-on with this cock you've been admiring. Then you'll be mine, Angel.'

I groaned, humping helplessly against a hand that knew precisely where to press – hard, against the spot made sore by her boot. It shocked me, how quickly the momentum had shifted, yet what could I do? I was caught between a wall and a hard-on.

'You see, I couldn't care less about that stupid crystal. That was another of Devlin's fairy tales,' the devious queen continued. She moved closer, sensual and slow, pulsing with that relentless finger. 'It's *you* I want, Rosie. Let the man in me claim you with this cock – more than Meeh can ever offer you. And I promise that, come the new empire that's dawning above us at this moment, you and I will *rule*, Angel.'

Was I too distracted by her finger to remain rational? Or was she making me an offer I could never have anticipated, merely to rub Meeh's nose in it?

I inhaled sharply when the first spirallings started inside me; tried desperately to separate myself from the intense pleasure she delivered, to consider the motivation behind this ... bribe. Could Venus really overthrow the man who created Satan? And would I be better off if she did?

'Take my cock in your hand,' she whispered, her face only inches from mine. 'Stroke it the way you did Harry's – Christ, but the two of you could *move* together! And I'll move you too, Miss Slippery Slit. You're so ready, you're going to gush all over my hand. *Aren't* you?'

I held my breath, closing my eyes so I wouldn't see the bulging breasts in front of my face. If I could have just a few moments to collect my thoughts –

'I can feel you vibrating, deep inside,' Venus whispered. She ran her tongue along the outside of my ear, and I could feel the heat of her white vest ... her dark, taut body wanting mine. 'I'm going to lift you now, so your feet will be on the crossbars as you lean against the wall ... so I can see the honey gush from you when you can't hold back any longer. Then I'm going to fuck you, Angel.'

I let out a whimper of protest as I felt myself being slid up the iron rails. I'd never been had by a man this strong ... fearing this vixen, yet unable to combat the orgasm that was building with a volcanic pressure, making my pussy clench around the finger that stroked it. My feet left the floor, then found the crossbars on either side of my cage – out of the need to maintain some shred of balance, some sense of bearing and control. This left me gaping open, my legs spread to their fullest extent while my hands grasped the bars above my head.

Venus supported me with one arm, leaning into me as she kept pumping with that wicked finger. Suddenly she turned it like a corkscrew inside me, catching my clit with her thumb, and my scream echoed above the din of those humping around us. My hips thrust against her and I came in a rush, spewing juice against the hand that kept pumping me.

Then she shifted me forward, for the trip down to her cock. It was prodding me from below, wet with pre-come, but she was letting me ride out my own wild climax.

'Beg me,' Venus muttered. 'Tell me how deep you want me to shove this big dick, Angel. Ask me to fuck you until this cock explodes. Then you'll be mine, and Meeh can go screw himself. What will we care?'

Could the serpent in the tree of Eden have spoken more persuasively? I was still thrumming from my first enjoyable climax since I'd met Harry – past the point of *caring* whether Venus was leading me on with another lie. That incredible erection was poking up between our bodies, getting into position for my open, wet hole. Didn't matter that it was a dildo. All I had to do was say the word, and ecstasy – and perhaps a whole new role in Satan – would be mine.

'I ... please, Venus, I –'

'Don't you *dare* go an inch further!' a familiar voice called from across the mine's entry hall. 'Dammit, Venus, you *know* how I've wanted to watch you two pussies get into it! Wait for *me*. I want to see every thrust and hear every slap of your bodies.'

I groaned, still reeling from being on the verge. The elevator had delivered Devlin Meeh, but the floor was so covered with coupling slaves, the little imp couldn't walk across it. He shone like a gaudy sun, in a frock coat and trousers of brilliant yellow brocade. His smile was just as bright. My gut told me I'd played right into his hands, for it seemed the rules of this godforsaken place had been changed on me again. He didn't appear the least bit upset that Venus was laying claim to me. In fact, he was cheering her on!

'Keep your mouth shut,' my captor intoned. 'What Devlin doesn't know can't help him.'

Wise advice. I was good at keeping Venus's secrets.

Then shots rang out! The revellers on the floor scurried apart to duck for cover, while Venus and I instinctively huddled closer, fearing hits from ricocheted bullets if not those intended for us. What sort of idiot opened fire in an enclosed dome? I strained to see through the veil of smoke; could tell that Meeh was still standing, grinning at his grand entrance. The acrid pungency of gunpowder stung our noses, and when the man in yellow stepped from the elevator he gestured to someone behind him.

'Come along, girls. We've things to see and people to do.'

Out stepped Zelda, twirling her six-gun on her finger before spinning it down past her hip into its holster. Her sisters joined her, proudly displaying the same finesse with their pistols, and all three blondes beamed at the orgy they'd interrupted. They sported new gun belts of sparkling scarlet satin, slung low over their hips with holsters tied to their lush thighs. A diagonal slash of colour had replaced their leather vests: matching satin sashes with rows of carbine shells! The new costumes showed off their bouncing, rouged nipples and bare pussies to great advantage and, as they strutted behind Meeh, the heels of their red boots clicked with authority across the hard salt floor.

'Oh, Jesus,' Venus muttered. 'If there's anything more witless than a Titzler, it's a Titzler armed with ammunition bigger than her brain. I hope to God he gave them blanks.'

I seized this rare moment of my opponent's distraction to clarify something, before Meeh stole the spotlight again. 'Were the KlonDykes really hexed? Or did they just think so?'

Venus's lip twitched, while her gaze remained on the girls. 'Nymphomania has its place, Angel.'

She shifted, so I gripped the cell bars. I could still feel the behemoth erection poised to penetrate me, and couldn't miss the way Zelda, Nelda and Esmerelda were assessing my situation, couldn't miss their exuberance, either, or that unmistakable glow of restored health – not to mention the triple grins that matched Devlin Meeh's. The foursome came to stand beside the Playpen, glancing briefly around the entry hall at the silent, naked slaves who wondered if they were safe yet.

'Jarold!' Devlin called towards the mine entry. 'Fetch me Galloway! Tell him the girls have come to see him.' The diminutive man turned to me then, brushing aside a boyish shock of strawberry-blond hair ... gazing with obvious desire at the dark prick positioned a hair's breadth beneath my pussy.

'Grant's been demoted to kitchen duty,' he explained, obviously pleased with himself for thinking of it. 'I thought if I removed him from the constant temptation of the girls – gave him a menial task he could handle –

perhaps his life would become productive again. He's been peeling turnips and potatoes these past four weeks. Obviously, the KlonDykes have been with me. Don't they look fabulous?'

I was mentally calculating what month and day it must be by now – but I couldn't miss his implication. Zelda, Nelda and Esmerelda straightened to their full height, thrusting their ripe breasts around the scarlet sashes. Amazing how quickly allegiances could change. But then, it was Meeh's town, wasn't it?

'I must say, Angel, that I'm a bit disappointed,' Devlin whined. 'I expected more fight from you – more resistance to this she-male's advances. Why, you're sitting in the palm of her hand, just waiting for her to take you. Not even a token protest!'

He reached up with a proprietary air to adjust his monocle – except it wasn't there. Was this out of habit? Or was he posturing, reminding me of the sin that had earned my confinement? I wondered if Devlin needed that lens to see, or if it had been a prop all along ... another way to keep his subordinates guessing about what was reality and what was a lie.

Venus's glittering eyes narrowed, pulling me from my thoughts. 'Beg me,' she whispered. 'Choose who you'll serve, Miss DuBris.'

The entire room went quiet. The only noise was the tattoo of the KlonDykes' heels as each of them moved to a different side of the Playpen for an unimpeded view. My throat went so dry it clicked when I swallowed, which made my tall, dark assailant snicker.

'It's a matter of who's going to fuck whom – and who's going to get fucked,' Meeh prompted softly. The little twit had the nerve to sound cheated by the way things looked, which made me bristle with resentment. I was *tired* of this man's manipulations. Tired of his endless games and insinuations!

Venus's mulberry nipples taunted me from between the white lacings of her vest as she gazed at me, waiting. On impulse, I grabbed those slender tethers and yanked *hard*, at the same time shoving her away with my feet. 'Fight me for it!' I rasped.

She shrieked, stepping backwards to maintain her balance – while letting me drop. Somehow I landed on my feet, enjoying the way her breasts bounced free of the vest, like huge balloons full of chocolate pudding. An inspiration in itself ...

'Please, *please* make me struggle and suffer,' I pleaded – and then I charged forward, ducking between her legs. I brought my head up hard against her balls, and somehow made it to the opposite end of the Play-pen as Venus pitched forward.

The cheers and whistles were deafening. Slaves who'd scrambled for cover were now moving in for a better view, chanting, 'An-GEL! An-GEL!' until I thought my ears might split. Meeh gripped the bars, his round face alight with glee.

But none of this encouragement changed the fact that it was I, Rosie DuBris, in that cage with Venus. Alone. And without a clue about what to do next.

Luckily, my opponent appeared caught up in the game rather than peeved by it. After all, it was more sport for her this way, as she'd wanted.

'Nice try, but it'll be your last one,' she said with a smirk. 'You've only made me want you more, Angel. I won't be denied. You can either beg me to shove it up your cunt – and be spared the agony that Grant and the Titzlers have endured – or I can just take it and make you squirm forever, for a climax you'll never reach.'

At one time I would've fallen for that threat – yet another contradiction – but the triplets were looking mighty fine in their showy red holsters and sashes. Completely healed from their infirmity.

'I'll take my chances. You'll have to come after it.'

'Yes! Now we're on to something.' Devlin Meeh's pudgy hands were wrapped around the black bars he was peering between, squeezing tightly enough that his ruby ring flashed me the signal that had previously mesmerised me with its crimson power.

But I ignored it. That's what Devlin despised most – being ignored.

'What's the matter, Venus?' I mocked more loudly. 'Pussy got your tongue? *My* pussy would love that! Maybe you'd better lick my cream before I give your cock its reward.'

To further inspire her, I slipped my fingers between my legs and brought out some of my wetness, rubbing my fingertips and thumb together to entice her. 'Here kitty, kitty . . . come to Angel now. Nice kitty . . .'

Damned if she didn't get down on all fours! Her fully-fleshed ass protruded in one direction and her breasts bobbed between her arms as she crawled towards me, a demure smile overriding her usual wicked grin. The bright white vest flickered with light each time she moved, an alluring contrast to her matte, coffee-coloured skin. When she sidled up beside me and began to purr against my thigh, I lifted the other leg to the lowest crossbar, opening myself to whatever attentions she might give. It was a treat to see Venus in this position – taking orders rather than giving them – and the first touch of her tongue had me moaning.

My head lolled back between two bars and I gripped each side of the cage for support. The cocoa kitten had slipped between my legs to insinuate her tongue into me, to tease me with delicate lappings. Driving me insane with wildfire sensations, she was . . . running her tongue between my folds and teasing my open sex with it . . . lifting my mound with gentle fingers to drink more deeply of the dew.

Venus sat back on her heels, an enticing sight as she caressed my leg between her firm, brown breasts. This rocking motion imitated the way she'd look while fucking me, and I imagined the big prick I couldn't see from here ... how it must be jabbing at the air and eager for solid contact ... eager to slide deep inside my hot, wet pussy. I closed my eyes, a prisoner of anticipation.

Was that the creaking of pulleys I heard, or my own desperate breath? I could only thrust and flex, knowing I'd once again relinquished control to my opponent. But I was too far gone – too near to falling over the edge of a mind-boggling climax – to care about such details. The vixen had cast her spell and was now licking her way around my throbbing clit, driving me towards a release I craved like nothing else in my life.

I convulsed and caught myself, wanting to make the pleasure last. I was vaguely aware that several observers followed every thrust, every lap of that long tongue ... every quiver that coursed through my body as though I were connected to an electrical current, helpless in the throes of its power. Was that the scent of a hundred horny slaves, or my own inflamed sex I smelled?

The Titzlers had shifted so they were all three on one side of the Playpen – close enough to fondle each other and let out inspiring sighs. I also heard a murmur rippling through the crowd, and imagined those slaves were reaching between each other's legs too – caught up in this erotic spectacle and unable to control their own urges.

Venus slipped her fingers where her mouth had been and licked her way over my mound and slowly up my belly, spreading my legs as she straightened hers. As my body got shifted higher up the bars, I envisioned that hard, dark cock she was ready to ram into me ... imagined its silken wetness as it tested my hole, and then its brutal girth as it filled me from here to kingdom come.

'It's my turn,' she confirmed with a moist whisper against my ear. 'And I've earned it. Haven't I, Angel?'

'Yes. Oh, yesss, Venus,' I rasped, my hips bucking of their own accord. 'Please take me – now! I can't stand it anymore. I have to – I have to –'

'My God!' a crisp British voice rang out. 'Would you look at the *prick* on that bitch!'

Spoken with undeniable authority, the words brought everyone in the room to attention. Venus curled her lip at another interruption, yet when she turned to see who belonged to that alluring accent – and who'd obviously meant the compliment for *her* – her cinnamon lips formed an O. A low whistle came out.

And it was no wonder, for Captain Broderick Manley cut a stunning figure in his scarlet Mountie jacket and trim black trousers, his handlebar moustache twitching with his grin. He stepped between the naked slaves as though he didn't notice them – as though he had eyes only for those of us inside the Playpen.

'Ace!' I cried. But when I caught sight of the man walking behind him, I could only stare, unable to breathe another word.

'You *know* this gentleman?' Venus murmured, glued to his every move. 'He'd better be more than a pretty face, if he thinks he's going to waylay my plans for *you*, Angel.'

I couldn't reply. But then, Ace Manley had never needed anyone else to speak for him.

'*So* glad to find you alive and well, Rosie,' he murmured, his gaze riveted on the exotic creature whose assets were hanging out of her tight white vest. 'And would you look at *these*? Why, those are the finest tits I've ever seen! If you don't mind my saying so, you have everything a man could possibly want. All in one atrociously gorgeous package.'

As he spoke, Captain Manley reached between the bars to caress the dusky breast nearest him, easing his hand beneath Venus's arm to cup it and test its weight. She shuddered, watching him with an incredulous expression, drinking in his broad shoulders and the way his crimson coat clung to his muscled body. When he returned her gaze, his brown eyes burning into hers, his palm followed the dip of her ribcage oh, so slowly, until he was gripping the dick that had first aroused his attention.

Did he know what he was holding? How far would she let him go?

They sucked air as one, and had my feet not been planted on those crossbars I would've hit the floor. Venus's nostrils narrowed and then flared, and she pivoted slightly on her boot heels to allow him freer access to that prodigious pecker.

'I don't know who you are,' she finally managed to say, 'but you'd better have a damn good reason for handling me this way, mister!'

'Captain Broderick Manley of the North West Mounted Police, at your service,' he crooned, 'and I am so honoured to finally meet the fabled Venus the Penis! I've heard so much about you.'

He held her gaze, his grin tightening with his grip. 'I bet this cock I'm fondling started the Klondike gold rush, and I'm making damn sure I get first crack at it. If you're half the lover I've heard you are, I think you'll see the advantage of coming along with me ... to someplace more private. The others in the room are simply not ready for the show we'd put on, don't you agree?'

Venus inhaled, considering it; rocking with the rhythm of his fist. 'Am I under arrest?'

'Do you want to be?'

My captor blinked, fighting a smile. 'What makes you think you can just sashay in here and haul me away from –'

'My cock's even bigger and thicker than yours, sweet creature. But you'll have to come out of that cage so I can prove it.'

'And you're taking me with you,' I whispered, playing upon the advantage Ace was handing me. 'After all, it was my turn this – this *braggart* interrupted! If you think you can just drop *me* for –'

In a heartbeat, Venus gathered me against herself. With a defiant glance at Devlin and the Titzlers, who'd watched this exchange with wary fascination, she flung open the Playpen's gate – forcing the little man in yellow to jump aside. Out she marched, cradling me like a baby as the crowd backed away to let her pass, until she reached the opposite side where the Mountie awaited us. I kept waiting for Meeh to retaliate – to bring this charmed moment to an abrupt halt – but he seemed as stupefied by the hermaphrodite's actions as everyone else.

Yet when she let me slip to the floor, her breasts heaving with anticipation as she extended her hand to Manley, I could believe this was no joke. She was setting me free! Falling for the siren song of the handsome redcoat who knew precisely what she hungered to hear.

'Venus, I can't believe you'd fall for this man's obvious –'

But Devlin's protest stopped dead in its tracks when the smitten queen turned, from halfway across the room, to aim a threatening finger at him. 'Believe *this*,' she said, her hiss resounding like an agitated snake's. 'Before the sun sets, little man, you'll be answering to *me*!'

This left everyone in the room staring speculatively after the pair boarding the elevator, and then back to the elf in yellow, left gaping in their wake.

Everyone except me. I stood trembling before the one who'd accompanied Manley, feeling very naked and vulnerable as I drank in the blond hair that had gone uncut for months, and the moustache that had grown downward to join a thick, curling beard. His face was sunken and the eyes – those eyes that at times had scalded me like coffee yet could soften to brown velvet when he leaned in for a kiss – were fastened upon the crystal embedded in my cheek.

I wanted to laugh, but could only cry. He looked ragged and haggard, the most disreputable beggar ever to enter the gates of Satan. Yet at that moment, I found him the best-looking thing I'd ever seen.

'Jimmy,' I whispered, my hand flitting to his bony shoulder. 'Jimmy, is it really you?'

22 **Breaking Away**

'You left me! Without saying goodbye!'

I wished he'd ripped my heart out, rather than slapping me with the agony in that haunted face and voice. Most in this room wouldn't recognise Jimmy Crystal, or realise that he'd once earned his living – and his legend – as a hired gun who'd helped tame the West, but they all sat forward. Here was another drama unfolding, hot on the heels of Venus's departure with a sweet-talking Mountie!

Yet for Jimmy, who winced at my thinness as he gripped my upper arms, and for me, equally appalled at his condition, the world shrank to the inches between our eyes. His gaze flickered to the crystal angel. He stiffened, as though hardening himself against any pity. As though deciding whether I was worth his time and an explanation. Had there been any clocks in the mine, they would've stopped – like my heart did, when his silence stretched until the slaves around us shifted and coughed expectantly.

'When I realised you'd slipped away in the night, I boarded the next stage. But I was a day behind you, Rosie,' he finally went on, gaining strength from the expression of his pain. 'Got to the docks in Portland in time to see your ship leave. Booked passage on the next boat, and worried about you getting as sea-sick as I was – and then wondered how you'd manoeuvred your supplies on board, and hauled that ton of stuff over the Chilkoot Trail . . .'

As his voice faded, I wished for a crack to open up in

the floor and swallow me. His words had me reliving the rigours of the trek, feeling horribly guilty for abandoning a man who'd worried a lot more about me than I had about him. I tried to call up the rancour I'd felt for Jimmy – the sense of betrayal after Grant told me why Devlin wanted Crystal to join me. 'But – but Jimmy, you sent me on my way! Slipped me more money to –'

'I didn't want to hold you back! Or keep you from a dream that might come true,' he insisted, his shaggy beard quivering. 'But I never intended for you to go *alone*! As I trudged along that dangerous trail, I could only hope you hadn't died from exhaustion – or been buried in an avalanche. Thank God Captain Manley assured me you'd made it to the Mountie outpost –'

He had to catch his breath to go on. Never had I seen the stout-hearted Jimmy Crystal act as though he might fall to pieces. And while I felt secretly thrilled that he cared this deeply about me, I was mortified as well: I'd been so keen on rekindling an old flame, I hadn't considered how I'd burn the man I left behind.

'Yes, I owe Ace for his hospitality, and his skill at surviving some treacherous conditions last winter . . . as well as a few moments ago.' I smiled, although it was a weak effort. 'He'd heard of you, Jimmy. Respected you enough to look after me, and get me safely on my way before Lake Bennett –'

'Froze over,' Crystal groaned. He was warming to his subject, digging his fingers into my flesh. 'Do you know what I went through, stuck there all winter, Rosie? Knowing you'd found a good-looking young *partner* to make the trip with?'

His gaze pierced mine, demanding answers I couldn't give. He didn't realise he was shaking me, and I didn't shrug out of his grasp, for I deserved to share his torment. I'd never agreed to marry him, but invisible ties bound us, all the same.

'I got so damn restless, I might've *killed* people if I hadn't been pounding boats together for the float to Dawson,' he continued in a low, driving voice. 'Night and day – even a couple of times when I nearly died of exposure – I saw your face, Rosie. It kept me going, all those thousands of miles. Because I had to find you. Had to know you made it all right.'

I nipped my lip, near to tears. Had those images in Meeh's monocle been sent there when Jimmy was at his lowest? By some power of this desperate man's mind?

I could only speculate about that, didn't want to check Devlin's reaction to these revelations, and lose my intense connection with the bartender who'd left his whole world behind to find me.

'I'm so sorry, Jimmy,' I breathed. 'I never gave a thought to –'

'And why would you?' He pried his hands from my shoulders, disgusted with himself now. 'You'd told me we should move to greener pastures a dozen times, and I was too hard-headed to – should've married you *years* ago, so you'd know how I –'

Jimmy stopped to swallow, his Adam's apple bobbing in a throat that had hollowed on his gruelling trip. 'You figured I didn't give a damn about the future – about *our* future. You had every right to leave, Rosie-girl. Don't mind me, carrying on this way.'

Was it my vivid imagination, or had the entire room just drawn a deep, soulful breath? I could feel the Titzlers gazing from my face to his, awaiting my response to such a heartfelt outpouring as they'd probably not experienced themselves. From the corner of my eye I saw a yellow movement, and then Devlin Meeh was standing beside us, demanding our attention with his pointed gaze.

'A touching tale, Mr Crystal. But you and I have a

score to settle.' The little fiend reached into his pocket, and positioned a monocle at his right eye.

Jimmy scowled, shifting so he stood between me and the man who came only as high as his chest. 'Well, well. Devlin Meeh,' he muttered. 'I should've known a bastard like you would be running a place named Satan. Should've known the ... *crystal* you stole from Sally would show up again.'

'But of course you knew! You read about me in Rosie's letter –' Meeh ducked his head around Jimmy's thin body, so he could meet my eye with a nasty laugh '– and he let you come here anyway! If you believe Crystal's clap-trap about caring for you –'

'No,' Jimmy cut in sharply. 'Rosie offered me the letter, but I didn't look at it. She told me an old flame invited her to the Klondike, and that was that.'

'Then you're *both* so naive and gullible –'

'Wait just a fucking minute!' came a shout from across the room. 'This is my fight too!'

Heads turned and gasps rang out when Grant Galloway appeared by the mine entrance. He struggled towards us, flanked by Jarold and the guard named Lexter, both of whom held him on short leashes attached to his black leather harness.

Craning her neck beside me, Zelda grimaced. 'My lord, but Grant looks horrible!'

'Like a mad dog left on a tether and not fed,' Nelda chimed in beneath the jeers of the slaves.

'I sure hope he doesn't want to fuck us with that thing.' The three of them locked elbows, as though this would ward off any disease that might be spread as Galloway approached.

That *thing* looked red and raw and swollen, as noxious as the expression on Galloway's face. I had indeed been naive and gullible, to come here on a gut response to the letter he – and probably Devlin – penned months ago, but this situation would snowball fast if I didn't take matters into my own hands.

'Why, Grant!' Meeh mocked from across the crowd. 'I thought you might enjoy peeling something besides potatoes today. Look who's finally arrived.'

While he was blustering like the Arctic wind, trying to silence the rowdy crowd, I eased in front of the Playpen's gate. Signalling for the Titzlers, I gingerly lifted off the padlock.

'You girls look wonderful,' I whispered, hoping to plant some seed in their fertile imaginations. 'Stunning outfits too.'

Three smiles beamed back at me, and three sets of breasts thrust out around those bullet-stuffed sashes. Zelda winked. 'Love your cunt, Angel. Some girls just look better with a bush.'

Keeping my expression conspiratorial, I checked to see that Meeh was still following Grant's approach. Now that the slave population had taken a taste of freedom, they were impossible to shut up – for they, like the KlonDykes, had discovered power they didn't realise they'd had all along.

'You see those two bags under my water bowl?' I continued in a hushed voice. 'They're full of chocolate!'

Their eyebrows rose as they located this lure.

'Something warm and sweet might tame a potentially nasty situation,' I continued, praying they played along, 'so why not soften some of it up? Might be the distraction that keeps Grant from coming at us. And you know how Meeh can't resist *anything* chocolate.'

With a sly grin, Esmerelda slipped into the Playpen on her mission, taking the padlock while I swung the gate all the way open. Her sisters positioned themselves in front of the cage, so their lush bodies would block Devlin's view when he turned around. Jimmy slipped an arm around me, steering me forward as though we, too, were terribly interested in Grant's big entrance – so Meeh couldn't watch us and monitor the KlonDykes at the same time.

'I love you, Rosie,' he mouthed – just as I'd seen before I'd slapped the monocle from Meeh's face.

Beside us, Devlin cackled. 'Too late for that, Crystal! You had your chance. Angel knows she's got a finer life as *my* mistress!'

'You call this a life?' Jimmy snapped, holding me close against his wiry body. 'What kind of a man doesn't even feed his woman? Or give her some clothes, for Chrissakes?'

'What kind of a man shoots his woman in cold blood?'

The room grew deathly quiet. The crowd had another juicy tidbit to nibble, so they turned away from Grant as he struggled forward against his leashes.

Meeh's monocle flashed when he focused on me. 'I bet Crystal's never told you about Sally Bingham – *has* he?' he challenged. 'Did you know he loved her enough that he planned to marry her too? And then shot her in the back? Even the lowest thief isn't that cowardly!'

Jimmy's arm tightened around my waist as I felt my fury rise. In Grant's rendition, Devlin had figured in that long-ago shooting, but he seemed to be forgetting that. The little devil in yellow stepped closer for my reply, but then spouted off before I could.

'And since Jimmy didn't come armed and ready to fight for *you*, he can't be too concerned about your welfare, now can he?'

Crystal's other hand snaked out and grabbed those yellow lapels, hauling Meeh to his tiptoes. 'Let's leave Rosie out of this, shall we?' he said in a vicious whisper. 'She's the best judge of human nature I know, so she's already got you figured out. The *real* question is, what kind of a man would duck the bullet I intended for him? To use an innocent woman as his shield?'

I shivered at this thought, and heard three sharp breaths drawn behind me. A suspicious murmur slithered through the crowd, while Meeh tried to shrug out of Crystal's grasp.

'That's a lie and you know it,' he countered. 'You shot Sally for running out on you – for taking up with me! You just couldn't stand it that –'

'That's not the way I saw it, Devlin.'

Grant Galloway and his two guards now stood beside us, as ominous as the knot on a hangman's noose. The former mayor of Satan had a rabid insanity burning in his pale green eyes, and his body bespoke the hours of abuse he'd endured ... probably by his own hand, and because he'd believed himself infected by Venus's hex. But he levelled his gaze at Devlin and spoke clearly, for the benefit of everyone in the room.

'As I recall, Dr Meeh, you'd lured Sally Bingham into running off with you – just for the fun of spiting Crystal – with the same sorts of promises and lies you dangled in front of Rosie and all the rest of us! And since Crystal was never known to miss a shot, you dived into that stagecoach like a scared rabbit. Left Sally to fend for herself!'

'I did no such – you'll pay for saying that, Galloway!' Meeh twisted in Jimmy's fist, his face flushed as he confronted me. 'Who do you believe, Angel? Haven't I carried out every promise I made you? Haven't I –'

Who do you believe?

At that pivotal moment – with all eyes riveted on my bare body, as Jimmy held us a mere arm's length apart – Meeh's question defined my entire time in Satan. It became painfully clear that Devlin and Grant had played upon my ambitions – had perhaps started the entire Klondike gold rush to win me away from a legendary gunslinger with a woman's blood on his hands. And Grant had reached the end of his patience, too, it seemed. Although I didn't trust his motives, even now.

Yet Jimmy claimed I was a fine judge of human nature.

A fool, that's what I was. A woman who'd fallen for her own youthful fantasies rather than listening to common sense – or to the man who'd asked her to stay. My throat closed in agony. I hung my head.

'Who do you choose, Angel?' Devlin demanded. He raised his hand to flash that big ruby at me, but I swatted it away.

'Get behind me, Satan!' I rasped, even as my body was wracked by shudders of fear. Or was there really magic in that man's ring? 'I'm tired of your threats and your sneaky little tricks!'

'That's right, Angel,' somebody from the crowd piped up. 'He's done you nothing but wrong.'

'He's treated us *all* like dirt,' another cry rang out, and some in the restless crowd began to stand up.

'But *we* love you, Devlin!' Zelda exclaimed, rushing to his side.

'You've taken wonderful care of us! Made us well again,' Nelda bleated above the rising rumble of the crowd. 'Grant and Angel are just ungrateful –'

'Oh, my God! There's chocolate gushing from my pussy!'

For a fraction of a second, all heads snapped towards the Playpen, where Esmerelda was slipping a blunt column of chocolate into herself, with a quick in-and-out that already had her quivering. A stream of brown oozed down her thighs, between her red satin holsters.

Zelda and Nelda deftly unsnapped Grant's leashes, and his howl set the rest of the crowd off like a pack of foxhounds.

Jimmy dropped Meeh and quickly steered me away from the Playpen. As the slaves surged forward, muttering about mistreatment, the man in the monocle dashed into the cell as though his life depended upon it, pulling the gate shut behind him. But when he searched frantically for the padlock that would secure his safety, Esmerelda clicked it around her gun belt.

'Come and get it, big boy,' she teased, loving her sudden rise to the limelight.

Devlin lunged – but Galloway got into the cage, and then the slaves surged around it, several layers deep, to prevent their escape.

'Get him, Grant!' someone cried.

'Show him how it feels to get fucked by someone he trusted!'

The last thing I saw as Jimmy and I struggled through the harnessed bodies towards the elevator was how Zelda and Nelda had grabbed Devlin's hands when he went for their sister, and then pulled his arms between the bars. One was removing his ruby while the other popped his monocle from his face.

'Time to move on,' Jimmy remarked. 'Little bastard's too slippery to stay in their clutches long. Got a line for every occasion.'

'And one of them'll fall for it,' I murmured as we reached the elevator doors. 'Wasn't that an awful suit he was wearing? Yellow really isn't his colour.'

'Oh? Far as I can see, Meeh's been yellow all along. Just wealthy enough to pay his way out of his mistakes – until now.'

The grin he flashed me beneath that bushy beard brought back summer afternoons of leisurely love-making; tugging on the elevator's cables made his leaner body a reminder of the hardships he'd endured to see that I was safe.

I felt suddenly shy and undeserving of whatever he still felt for me. 'I can't believe you came all this way to – after I took off like a bat out of –'

'So believe this.'

He kissed me full-on, his lips driven by the desperation of a dangerous moment – for we still hadn't escaped. There was no whirring of gears or creaking of pulleys coming from the elevator and, when we'd sated our momentary need for each other, Jimmy looked up the shaft.

'The car's stuck up there. And it's thumping,' he muttered. 'Dammit, Manley, unlock the brake! There's going to be a riot!'

Indeed, the slaves were chanting and calling out encouragements to Grant. Yellow trousers got tossed to one end of the pen, and a wild cheer went up: 'Fuck him! Fuck him! Fuck him for me!' rang out, echoing loudly in the domed hall.

Frantically I glanced around, feeling the vibrations of the car as it lowered in the shaft beside us. It was still thumping and shuddering, in a telltale rhythm that had me snickering despite the shortness of our situation's fuse.

'Open up!' Crystal commanded, pounding the door with his fist. 'There's no other way out – and they just finished drilling Meeh a new downspout. Hurry up, dammit!'

The final cheer rose with applause, and then the droves of naked slaves turned our way with one purpose in mind. Slowly the door rolled open, and before Crystal could push it any faster, someone raced up behind us and slipped inside. A squawk of protest – voices we certainly recognised – greeted the intruder, but Jimmy and I stepped in right behind him.

'Harry!' I cried, returning his hug.

He glanced back, to where Ace was bent forward between Venus's knees, while she stood gripping his hips, glaring at us. 'So good to see everyone – especially you, Miss Rose!' Harry said. 'After our interlude in the waterfall, Meeh chained me in the dormitory toilet. Made me eat and sleep in there, and clean the damn place every day.'

'Thought I smelled a another piece of shit from the privy,' Crystal muttered. 'First it was Collin Cooper, and then Captain Manley, and now –'

'Jimmy, please.' I slipped out of Harry's embrace, bumping against the couple in the rear as the elevator lurched up the shaft. 'I couldn't have survived the trip without help from friends, and you know it.'

'But they're all –'

'Strong and persuasive and extremely good looking?' Venus panted. Even with her breasts bulging out above the white fitted vest and Manley's pants around her ankles, she commanded the car with her exotic presence. 'I can use every one of them – and you, Jimmy – as I take the reins of Satan. You'll get eye-popping pay and prime living arrangements, for keeping some semblance of order as those prospectors pass through to the gold fields.'

She closed her eyes for another deep thrust down Manley's hole, and then focused on me. 'And my offer to you still stands, Angel. Lord knows, all those randy miners will listen to a lady with your abilities.'

I'd never expected to hear praise in this creature's voice, but I wasn't falling for it. Neither did Jimmy. 'Begging your pardon, ma'am, er –'

Crystal glanced at the chocolate-coloured cock and the big bosoms bouncing above Ace's arse, blinking in disbelief. 'Now that I know Devlin Meeh's running this town, I want to just get the hell out and take Rosie home, where she belongs.'

Home. What a fine ring that word had to it!

'But there's a great deal of money to be made. Enough to pay for your trip home a hundred times over, once the rush ends,' the dusky queen coaxed. She was easing herself into Manley's backside again, looking positively blissful as she ran her fingers around his firm cheeks.

'Collin says there's no gold,' I ventured quietly. 'The claims were all staked before we got here last fall.'

'These men refuse to believe that, after months on the trail and having their dreams deferred,' Venus quickly explained. 'That's why I'm offering you the *best* of everything. And you know how good that can be, without Meeh running things, Angel. Otherwise, what do you have to look forward to but the gruelling trek back? Empty-handed, no less.'

The car bumped to a halt and the five of us stared at each other in the tiny, confining space. When Jimmy shoved the lever and the door didn't open, I wondered if Venus's magic – or wrath – would win the day, after all.

'Thanks, but no,' I insisted. 'Satan's yours for the taking.'

Venus's dark eyes narrowed, but I suspected Ace had increased his squeeze on her – yet another timely distraction the gallant Mountie was providing. 'You realise Devlin can come after you. He's clairvoyant – that's how he knew where to send Grant's letter. That angel on your cheek marks you wherever you –'

'I don't believe you.'

The force of those words stunned me, for I'd never dared say them to anyone's face. Venus appeared shocked by my defiance, but I didn't care! After believing Grant's love letter and having him betray me, and then falling for Dr Meeh's lofty promises, only to end up naked and undernourished, I finally realised there were people in the world I couldn't trust. People waiting to prey upon poor nobodies who dared to dream of a better life they couldn't bring about by themselves.

The crystal angel throbbed as Venus scowled at it, but I set aside the pain. 'Open the door, Jimmy. They can't keep us where we don't want to stay.'

'Yes, ma'am!' he said, and this time it rolled open, to reveal the short stairway that led to the old stable. 'Ace, you coming?'

The Mountie flashed us a wink from his position between Venus's knees, and then slid himself up the length of that prodigious dildo. 'Again and again,' he breathed. 'Every time this gorgeous creature lets me!'

Jimmy led me out of the elevator with Harry close behind us. As we stepped through the trapdoor's opening, into the hay-strewn area behind the farrier's forge, I breathed deeply – and looked around for anyone situated to ambush us. After spending weeks in the white shine of Meeh's mine, the darkness here tested my eyes and sorely disappointed me. Were we still victims of that sunless time of year? Or was it night?

A rustling in the hay bales behind us made Jimmy pull me against his body as he searched the stable's dim interior. 'Who's there?' he demanded.

'It's Faren – oh, Angel, you made it! You made it!'

I was suddenly caught up in the maid's bearhug, and as my eyes adjusted I saw the urgency on her pale face. 'Where's your Mountie friend? Isn't he coming out?'

'Manley will follow us in good time. He's keeping Venus distracted for now,' Jimmy whispered. 'Did you bring some clothes?'

'Yes, here,' she said as she thrust some folded garments into my hands. 'Collin's waiting by the back road with the horses and supplies. Be careful, though! It's a madhouse out there, now that another bunch of miners has arrived.'

I slipped gratefully into the trousers and shirt she'd handed me, which felt almost foreign after so many weeks of living naked. Not far away, I heard Harry dressing too. Something about this whispered conversation bothered me ... rang with the finality of a knell, when I realised plans had already been made without me.

Then I squinted into the darkness, barely able to make out Faren's pale face. 'You're coming along, aren't you?'

Her eyes widened, whiter from the reflection of her starched pinafore. 'Me? Why would I want to leave Satan?'

'You just answered yourself! *Meeh*'s the best reason of all to come with us.'

'Oh, I couldn't –'

'Why not?' My demand rang around the rafters of the creaky old stable, but as silent seconds – precious seconds – passed, my heart heard the answer.

'I've lived with Devlin more years than you can count, Angel,' she finally murmured. 'Once I set foot outside Satan's gate, I'd cease to be Faren Poole as you know her. I would be –'

'Old?' I breathed. As my fingers fumbled with the buttons on my shirt, I didn't want to believe what I was hearing.

She nodded, stepping back as though not to contaminate me with whatever dark forces dwelt within her ... or just some very firm beliefs. 'Meeh and Venus exist in a special realm, my dear friend. Leave now, before they catch you for keeps. That crystal on your cheek really will leave you vulnerable to their powers, so scoot! No awkward goodbyes between friends who will recall one another fondly – forever!'

A lump rose to my throat, but I knew better than to endanger my escape – or Jimmy's and Harry's. The three of us hurried into the star-studded night, accompanied by the rowdy laughter and tinkling piano tunes that overflowed the saloons from the main part of town. In about five minutes we found Collin awaiting us with saddled horses, their dark silhouettes lumpy with bed-rolls and bags of supplies.

Off we rode, into a wickedly thick mist that swallowed us the moment we passed through Satan's gates. I glanced back, fearful that whatever lurked in the Klondike's wilderness might be far worse than the things that went on under the fiendish glow of those ruby street lamps.

But I had to believe we'd make it.

23 I Get it All, in the End

'Did you really think I'd let you go free, Angel?' Meeh mocked.

When Venus backed me against the end of the Playpen, the man in the baby blue suit caught my arms behind me, between the bars. The *snick* of the cold metal handcuffs told me it was no joke: they both intended to go at me, to remind me that I'd be under their power – their protection, they called it – forever. Zelda, Nelda and Esmerelda looked on, their faces alight with this new game as they peered at my thrust-out breasts.

Silly me, to think Jimmy, Ace, Harry and Collin could outrun or outwit the man who created Satan!

'You came back for this chocolate cock, didn't you?' Venus asked as she stopped in front of me. She now wore a red satin ammunition sash and gun belt like the KlonDykes, but I knew her pistols weren't loaded with blanks. 'You couldn't get it out of your mind, how I'd come within a hair's breadth of fucking you senseless, and we never connected. I hope you're ready. Once we've made each other gush, there'll be no stopping us! We're going to *run* this town!'

Every rational fibre of my being fought the need to go through with it – to let Venus ram that hard, vibrating cock into me and shoot me full of her come, while Meeh snickered in victory and the Titzlers fingered each other. Why, that would be throwing my life away! But with the slaves cheering me on, and hot honey seeping between my folds, I was losing control over anything rational ... excited enough about my opportunities here that I'd never consider leaving Satan again. No matter *how* many good-looking men came to take me home.

The alluring creature before me stroked that amazing erection until its glossy, brown length quivered. I licked my lips, longing to taste it – curious about how that leather would feel against my tongue. My pussy throbbed, and I couldn't keep my hips from thrusting forward in invitation. *Please, please fuck me!* my body was saying, and I was whimpering helplessly, wanting so badly to be filled by the hardest, darkest, largest cock I'd ever seen. A woman like me deserved the best now and then, and it was surely my turn!

The first touch of that blunt tip against me made me grimace in anticipation. My head fell back and I hooked my legs around her waist, suspended now between her lush, solid body and the bars I'd been pinned against. I angled up to take the full length of her, crying out with the sheer size of it – the hot, frenzied vibrations that would soon consume me.

Venus smiled, grasping my arse in her two strong hands. Together we pumped, rocking faster, until she ground herself against my clit to drive me absolutely insane. I arched, crying out until my screams filled the high domed ceiling with my ecstasy ... my hellbent insanity ... my –

'Rosie-girl, it's all right, honey. You're safe now. With me.'

– eyes squeezed shut and I continued to pound myself against her hard hips, hearing the slap of her breasts against her chest. I couldn't stop coming! I kept –

'Shh! You'll have every man in this hotel knocking on our door.'

Hotel? That's what they called the salt mines now? Although my body kept quivering, my mind tried to wrap itself around this new information ... to identify that voice.

Behind me, Meeh chuckled. 'Think about Jimmy Crystal all you want, Angel-Face, but he won't be coming after you. It's all in your mind – all a matter of what you believe. And you might as well face the facts. You're here with Venus and me, and you belong to us now!'

'No! I don't want – but please don't stop fucking –'

'Is that what this is about?' that other voice said. It was low and calm, and it belonged to the hand that slowly ran up my side. Belonged to the warm, welcoming body I seemed to be resting against.

But where were the bars? Why had Venus stopped –?

I convulsed one final time and my eyes flew open. I saw an unfamiliar room, dimly lit by a distant street light ... a wash stand with a pitcher and bowl, and a highboy, and this bed I was in with ... my heart pounded hard inside my chest. Who was holding me against himself? Cuddling me to keep me from crying out. Trying not to prod me too hard with the cock that had shot up between us.

I exhaled, trying to make sense of things. 'Was that another dream?'

'I think so, sweetheart. We're in a hotel in Dawson City,' he added to clarify my thoughts. 'They really had you going, didn't they?'

My body relaxed against him. A sense of extreme relief flooded my soul. 'This time Venus was taking me, while Meeh had me handcuffed against the Playpen walls.'

'Must've been quite a sight.' He nuzzled my ear with his kiss, chuckling. 'If it's handcuffing you want, Rosie-girl, we'll see about getting some. Anything to make you happy.'

'Anything?'

'Sky's the limit. Ask and you shall receive.'

I chuckled, facing him as we snuggled beneath the covers. 'I want a hot bath ... a big breakfast ... and some wonderful loving. Not necessarily in that order.'

Jimmy moaned against me. His lips started to work, caressing my neck until I tilted back, inviting him to the sensitive base of my throat. Still excited from my previous dream, I entered into this one fully awake and aroused, thankful this man had spent the last several months trying to find me. His mouth found my nipples and he laved them with the sweet friction of his tongue, until I was squirming against him, wanting him desperately.

Then he kissed lower, following the ridge of my inner rib with his tongue. I sucked in my breath, knowing where he was headed – for Jimmy, more than anyone, knew precisely what made me insane. When the tip of his tongue teased my clit, I yelped with the almost-ecstasy of it, rocking to coax him inside me. He was on his knees, his head between my legs, so I reached over to stroke that long, lovely cock he was prodding the air with.

'Oh, Jimmy ... oh, Jimmy ... Jimmy,' I sighed, riding the inner spirals that were rising in earnest. 'I want you inside me. Roll me over and ride me from behind.'

'Your wish is my command.' When he tickled me with his bristly beard, I recalled cutting his hair last night and trimming until his face sported only a pair of devilish lines drawn down from his moustache, around a closely-clipped chin.

I was on my stomach quickly, arching up to receive him. From that angle, he went into my pussy tight and hard, sliding far enough inside to tease my sweet spot – slowly going in and out so I could feel every pulsing inch, and his ridged head, and the balls he rubbed against me. I tightened, squeezing him, wanting to make it last but knowing I couldn't.

Wadding the pillow beneath my face, I pressed my legs tight together, which forced me to wiggle from both ends while I pinched Jimmy in the middle.

'Rosie, jeez – I – can't hold it back!' he rasped. With a grunt, he pumped in earnest, filling me with warm jism that seeped out with each thrust. His moans went on and on, breathless, as he rode the wave of the climax that had started deep inside me. When he collapsed, his warm weight surrounded me with a deep sweetness I hoped would never end. Too long I'd gone without this man – without *this* man, who knew I wanted much, much more than his solid cock.

When Jimmy slid off to the side of me, to pull me into his arms, I scowled. Something hard was scratching the flat of my chest, something –

'Oh, my,' I murmured, holding it up in the dimness.

Jimmy plucked it from between my fingertips, grinning. 'I liked this little angel on your face, Rose, but –'

'No! Meeh used it to brand me – to mark me as his mistress. His ... whore.' For never had I felt more like a prostitute than when I'd bent to Devlin's devious wishes and believed he had control over my every move. Access to my every thought.

'– that's because this little sparkler was originally mine,' he insisted in a whisper. 'I had it cut this way to take advantage of its unusual shape in the raw, when I got it from a South African mine. It tickles me that for all his worldly ways, Devlin didn't know a diamond – or a real gem of a woman – when he saw one.'

'You've been to South Africa?' I breathed. But mostly I felt normal again, without that stone in my cheek. Not like a sideshow freak to be gawked at and whispered about. Not like a pampered prisoner who'd fallen for one story after another. Just ordinary. And restored.

'There's lots you don't know about me, Rosie, and we'll talk about anything you want, including my past,' he said softly. 'Seems only fair, since I want you to share my future as well.'

A tingling shimmied through me. He'd suggested this before, but I'd never really listened. Never realised what a fine idea it might be, having this man as my own. Maybe Crystal wasn't as predictable as I'd thought, when I left him for Grant Galloway.

'Too bad Sally Bingham wanted the diamond – she wore it on a necklace – more than she wanted me. Never intended for her to get killed over it though.' He sank into the mattress, turning my chin with his finger so I couldn't look anywhere but his eyes ... those deep, secretive eyes the colour of dark chocolate. 'I hung up my guns that day. You believe that, don't you – that Meeh ducked, so Sally took his bullet?'

'He'd do that – and then he and Grant would both lie about the whole situation,' I muttered. 'And you'd never, never shoot a woman, Jimmy.' The first ray of morning light was coming in under the window shade and I delighted in spraying the wall with rainbows when I wiggled the diamond.

'It would look nice as a ring, wouldn't it?' he hinted, lightly rubbing the top of my left hand. 'Like a rose, with two leaves.'

When had Jimmy shown such imagination? I sighed, nestling against him, loving the fact that I was no longer Angel-Face. I was Rosie. Just Rosie again.

'I'll go down the hall and run your bath water,' he suggested, shrugging out from under the covers, 'and I'll bring us up some breakfast when I get back. Going to join Harry and Collin – they want to scout things out around town. I didn't do much of that when I passed through last week. Had other things on my mind.'

I still reeled at the implications of this whole adventure: I had been following a dream, what I'd hoped was a new life with an old flame. But Jimmy had followed *me*. Rosie DuBris. Even after I left him for another man.

He kissed me, and dressed, and went down the hall. I heard the squawking of hot water in the pipes ... soft voices of other guests ... smelled coffee and sausages from the kitchen downstairs, as I lay naked in the warm spot that Jimmy had made in the bed. Such everyday sensations, but this morning they seemed especially sweet.

Since I had no robe, I hastily wrapped myself in a sheet. I stepped into the steamy bathroom with every intention of lolling in that tubful of hot water, but on impulse I shut off the faucets and went out on to the balcony that overlooked the hotel's entry and the main street of Dawson City.

The spring wind chilled me through the flimsy sheet but I didn't care. It was daylight! The sun beamed down at me. For the first time in more months than I cared to count, I raised my face to it, soaking in the sweet feel of freedom.

I marvelled at how this town had sprung to life since I'd first seen it – how rows of buildings with smart, wooden facades had replaced those shanties so hastily raised on the banks of the Yukon. The bellow of a boat's horn and the clopping of horses' hooves sounded like civilisation; the pounding of nails on a framed-in building rang out with opportunity. When I saw a rider in a red jacket, astride a bay stallion with a black mane and tail, my pulse pounded.

'Captain Manley!' I sang out, ignoring people's stares as I waved to him. 'You've made it out of Satan!'

'Rosie, darling!' His English accent and handlebar moustache rendered him absolutely irresistible as he stopped below my balcony. 'I had to wear Venus down to a nub to get away, but duty calls! Did I tell you I've taken command here in Dawson? It's rumoured that the real gold's to be found in Nome, and we're expecting scores of prospectors. *Someone* has to maintain order!'

'You're the right man for the job,' I replied, feeling a sudden tug on my heartstrings. A tingling in my gut and below, as well. But there was something I just had to know. 'And was Venus's ... *nub* all you'd hoped it would be, Captain?'

Proper gentleman that he was, Manley flashed me a grin and then winked. 'We all have our secrets, Rose. Some of them are just bigger – and better kept – than others.'

I chuckled, gazing at his jaunty crimson coat and the way he filled it out. If this stalwart Mountie was calling Dawson home ... if Crystal and Collin and Harry wanted to look around town more than they wanted to hit the trail back to the States today ...

The appearance of these three men, greeting the red-jacketed Captain on the street, made me glow all over. How could I look at them and not recall some of the finest times of my life? My years with blond Jimmy Crystal, whose grin was now framed by that brazen beard ... my long trek north with Collin, whose blue eyes had seen me through many a mishap ... that afternoon of delight with Harry in paradise – well worth the trouble this redheaded rogue got us into! That they were all here, talking together – because of *me*! – made my head spin with possibilities.

Jimmy glanced up, grinning as the wind whipped at my sheet. 'Watch out, boys. That look on her face can mean only one thing,' he teased. 'She sees a clutch of studs like us, and Rosie just can't help herself. She starts making plans for bigger and better things.'

'And where could I possibly find bigger – or better – *things* than yours?' I teased, leaning on the rail to give them a glimpse of my bare breasts. 'Matter of fact, I do have plans – because all these miners passing through are bound to need our supplies and services! I'm betting Collin could more than make peace with his daddy by establishing a branch of his family's mercantile here. And Jimmy could open a new saloon – or hire out as a lawman. And Harry – well, after ranching and then surviving the salt mines of Satan, Harry can handle anything!'

They rolled their eyes at each other, having had these ideas already.

'And what about you, Rose?' Collin prompted. 'An enterprising woman like yourself surely won't sit idle.'

'No, I'm going to make more money than any of you!' I fingered my nipples into enticing peaks, to hold my dear friends in suspense a few moments longer. 'I'm going to open Rosie's Chocolate Shop – specialising in pies, of course. But right now I'm going to take my bath, and ponder other possible confections I might sell. Tarts, perhaps. Any of you boys have any hard and fast feelings on this subject?'

I could see the cogs turning in those male minds: *hard and fast ... should we look around town, or go upstairs? Is she Jimmy's woman, or does she want us all? Will the five of us fit in that bathroom?*

Manley spotted a hitching post and swung his leg over his horse. 'Something tells me the law's going to get called in to keep the peace. I'd best be in position.'

'Clean living appeals to me. How about you, Cooper?' Harry said as he headed for the stairs.

Collin chuckled, falling into step behind him. 'Listening to Rosie's plans got me where I am today. Why stop now?'

This left Jimmy gazing up at me, his blond hair blowing softly beneath the brim of his hat. My heart stopped. Had I overstepped my bounds? Ruined my chances for happiness with the man who wanted to give me a ring?

'I love you, Jimmy Crystal,' I said. And I meant it with all my heart.

The smile on his rugged face rivalled the sun. 'I've always known that, Rosie. I wouldn't have come all the way to the Klondike for anything less.'

Visit the Black Lace website at
www.blacklace-books.co.uk

FIND OUT THE LATEST INFORMATION AND TAKE ADVANTAGE OF OUR FANTASTIC FREE BOOK OFFER! ALSO VISIT THE SITE FOR . . .

- All Black Lace titles currently available and how to order online
- Great new offers
- Writers' guidelines
- Author interviews
- An erotica newsletter
- Features
- Cool links

BLACK LACE – THE LEADING IMPRINT OF WOMEN'S SEXY FICTION

TAKING YOUR EROTIC READING PLEASURE TO NEW HORIZONS

LOOK OUT FOR THE ALL-NEW BLACK LACE BOOKS – AVAILABLE NOW!

All books priced £6.99 in the UK. Please note publication dates apply to the UK only. For other territories, please contact your retailer.

I KNOW YOU, JOANNA
Ruth Fox
ISBN 0 352 33727 3

Joanna writes stories for a top-shelf magazine. When her dominant and attractive boss Adam wants her to meet and 'play' with the readers she finds out just how many strange sexual deviations there are. However many kinky playmates she encounters, nothing prepares her for what Adam has in mind. Complicating her progress, also, are the insistent anonymous invitations from someone who professes to know her innermost fantasies. **Based on the real experiences of scene players, this is shockingly adult material!**

THE INTIMATE EYE
Georgia Angelis
ISBN 0 352 33004 X

In eighteenth-century Gloucestershire, Lady Catherine Balfour is struggling to quell the passions that are surfacing in her at the sight of so many handsome labourers working her land. Then, aspiring artist Joshua Fox arrives to paint a portrait of the Balfour family. Fox is about to turn her world upside down. This man, whom she assumes is a mincing fop, is about to seduce every woman in the village – Catherine included. But she has a rival: her wilful daughter Sophie is determined to claim Fox as her own. **This earthy story of rustic passion is a Black Lace special reprint of one of our bestselling historical titles.**

Coming in October

SNOW BLONDE
Astrid Fox
ISBN O 352 33732 X

Lilli Sandström is an archaeologist in her mid-thirties; cool blond fisherman Arvak Berg is her good-looking lover. But Lilli has had enough of their tempestuous relationship for the time being so she retreats to the northern forests of her childhood. There, in the beauty of the wilderness, she explores and is seduced by a fellow archaeologist, a pair of bizarre twins, woodcutter Henrik and the glacial but bewitching Malin. And when she comes across old rune carvings she also begins to discover evidence of an old, familiar story. *Snow Blonde* **is also an unusual, sexy and romantic novel of fierce northern delights.**

QUEEN OF THE ROAD
Lois Phoenix
ISBN O 352 33131 1

Private detective Toni Marconi has one golden rule: always mix business with pleasure. Provided, that is, she can be in charge. When she sets out on the trail of a missing heiress her friends worry she may have bitten off more than she can chew. Toni's leads take her to a nightclub on the edge of the Arizona desert where she meets characters with even stranger sexual appetites than her own. And then there is 'Red' – the enigmatic biker who holds a volatile sexual attraction for her. One thing's for sure, Toni will not give in until she's satisfied, whatever the consequences. **Macho bikers and horny cops get sleazy with a sassy heroine who likes to be in charge.**

THE HOUSE IN NEW ORLEANS
Fleur Reynolds
ISBN O 352 32951 3

When Ottilie Duvier inherits the family home in the fashionable Garden district of New Orleans, it's the ideal opportunity to set her life on a different course and flee from her demanding aristocratic English boyfriend. However, Ottilie arrives in New Orleans to find that her inheritance has been leased to one Helmut von Straffen – a decadent German count, known for his notorious Mardi Gras parties. Determined to claim what is rightfully hers, Ottilie challenges von Straffen – but ends up being lured into strange games in steamy locations. **Sultry passions explode in New Orleans' underworld of debauchery.**

Coming in November

NOBLE VICES
Monica Belle
ISBN O 352 33738 9

Annabelle doesn't want to work. She wants to spend her time riding, attending exotic dinner parties and indulging herself in even more exotic sex, at her father's expense. Unfortunately, Daddy has other ideas, and when she writes off his new Jaguar, it is the final straw. Sent to work in the City, Annabelle quickly finds that it is not easy to fit in, especially when what she thinks of as harmless, playful sex turns out to leave most of her new acquaintances in shock. **Naughty, fresh and kinky, this is a very funny tale of a spoilt rich English girl's fall from grace.**

A MULTITUDE OF SINS
Kit Mason
ISBN 0 352 33737 0

This is a collection of short stories from a fresh and talented new writer. Ms Mason explores settings and periods that haven't previously been covered in Black Lace fiction, and her exquisite attention to detail makes for an unusual and highly arousing collection. Female Japanese pearl divers tangle erotically with tentacled creatures of the deep; an Eastern European puppeteer sexually manipulates everyone around her; the English seaside town of Brighton in the 1950s hides a thrilling network of forbidden lusts. **Kit Mason brings a wonderfully imaginative dimension to her writing and this collection of her erotic short stories will dazzle and delight.**

HANDMAIDEN OF PALMYRA
Fleur Reynolds
ISBN 0 352 32919 X

Palmyra, 3rd century AD: a lush oasis in the heart of the Syrian desert. The inquisitive, beautiful and fiercely independent Samoya takes her place as apprentice priestess in the temple of Antioch. Decadent bachelor Prince Alif has other ideas. He wants a wife, and sends his equally lascivious sister to bring Samoya to the Bacchanalian wedding feast he is preparing. Samoya embarks on a journey that will alter the course of her life. Before reaching her destination, she is to encounter Marcus, the battle-hardened centurion who will unearth the core of her desires. **Lust in the dust and forbidden fruit in Ms Reynolds' most unusual title for the Black Lace series.**

Black Lace Booklist

Information is correct at time of printing. To avoid disappointment check availability before ordering. Go to www.blacklace-books.co.uk. All books are priced £6.99 unless another price is given.

BLACK LACE BOOKS WITH A CONTEMPORARY SETTING

☐ THE TOP OF HER GAME Emma Holly	ISBN 0 352 33337 5	£5.99
☐ IN THE FLESH Emma Holly	ISBN 0 352 34498 3	£5.99
☐ A PRIVATE VIEW Crystalle Valentino	ISBN 0 352 33308 1	£5.99
☐ SHAMELESS Stella Black	ISBN 0 352 34485 1	£5.99
☐ INTENSE BLUE Lyn Wood	ISBN 0 352 34496 7	£5.99
☐ THE NAKED TRUTH Natasha Rostova	ISBN 0 352 34497 5	£5.99
☐ ANIMAL PASSIONS Martine Marquand	ISBN 0 352 34499 1	£5.99
☐ A SPORTING CHANCE Susie Raymond	ISBN 0 352 33501 7	£5.99
☐ TAKING LIBERTIES Susie Raymond	ISBN 0 352 33357 X	£5.99
☐ A SCANDALOUS AFFAIR Holly Graham	ISBN 0 352 33523 8	£5.99
☐ THE NAKED FLAME Crystalle Valentino	ISBN 0 352 33528 9	£5.99
☐ ON THE EDGE Laura Hamilton	ISBN 0 352 33534 3	£5.99
☐ LURED BY LUST Tania Picarda	ISBN 0 352 33533 5	£5.99
☐ THE HOTTEST PLACE Tabitha Flyte	ISBN 0 352 33536 X	£5.99
☐ THE NINETY DAYS OF GENEVIEVE Lucinda Carrington	ISBN 0 352 33070 8	£5.99
☐ EARTHY DELIGHTS Tesni Morgan	ISBN 0 352 33548 3	£5.99
☐ MAN HUNT Cathleen Ross	ISBN 0 352 33583 1	
☐ MÉNAGE Emma Holly	ISBN 0 352 33231 X	
☐ DREAMING SPIRES Juliet Hastings	ISBN 0 352 33584 X	
☐ THE TRANSFORMATION Natasha Rostova	ISBN 0 352 33311 1	
☐ STELLA DOES HOLLYWOOD Stella Black	ISBN 0 352 33588 2	
☐ SIN.NET Helena Ravenscroft	ISBN 0 352 33598 X	
☐ HOTBED Portia Da Costa	ISBN 0 352 33614 5	
☐ TWO WEEKS IN TANGIER Annabel Lee	ISBN 0 352 33599 8	
☐ HIGHLAND FLING Jane Justine	ISBN 0 352 33616 1	
☐ PLAYING HARD Tina Troy	ISBN 0 352 33617 X	

To find out the latest information about Black Lace titles, check out the website: www.blacklace-books.co.uk or send for a booklist with complete synopses by writing to:

Black Lace Booklist, Virgin Books Ltd
Thames Wharf Studios
Rainville Road
London W6 9HA

Please include an SAE of decent size. Please note only British stamps are valid.

Our privacy policy
We will not disclose information you supply us to any other parties. We will not disclose any information which identifies you personally to any person without your express consent.

From time to time we may send out information about Black Lace books and special offers. Please tick here if you do <u>not</u> wish to receive Black Lace information. ❑

Please send me the books I have ticked above.

Name ....

Address ....

....

....

....

Post Code ....

Send to: Cash Sales, Black Lace Books, Thames Wharf Studios, Rainville Road, London W6 9HA.

US customers: for prices and details of how to order books for delivery by mail, call 1-800-343-4499.

Please enclose a cheque or postal order, made payable to Virgin Books Ltd, to the value of the books you have ordered plus postage and packing costs as follows:

UK and BFPO – £1.00 for the first book, 50p for each subsequent book.

Overseas (including Republic of Ireland) – £2.00 for the first book, £1.00 for each subsequent book.

If you would prefer to pay by VISA, ACCESS/MASTERCARD, DINERS CLUB, AMEX or SWITCH, please write your card number and expiry date here:

....

Signature ....

Please allow up to 28 days for delivery.